The Delivery

by

Jonas Saul

PUBLISHED BY:
Imagine Press Inc.
Ebook ISBN: 978-1-927404-54-6
Paperback ISBN: 978-1-998047-70-3
Hardcover ISBN: 978-1-998047-71-0

The Delivery
Copyright © 2020 by Jonas Saul

The Sarah Roberts Series

Dark Visions (One)
The Warning (Two)
The Crypt (Three)
The Hostage (Four)
The Victim (Five)
The Enigma (Six)
The Vigilante (Seven)
The Rogue (Eight)
Killing Sarah (Nine)
The Antagonist (Ten)
The Redeemed (Eleven)
The Haunted (Twelve)
The Unlucky (Thirteen)
The Abandoned (Fourteen)
The Cartel (Fifteen)
Losing Sarah (Sixteen)
The Pact (Seventeen)
The Terror (Eighteen)
The Chase (Nineteen)
The Betrayal (Twenty)
Sarah's Return (Twenty-One)
The Hunt (Twenty-Two)
The Delivery (Twenty-Three)
The Trap (Twenty-Four)
The Ultimatum (Twenty-Five)
The Depraved (Twenty-Six)
The Condemned (Twenty-Seven)
Payback (Twenty-Eight)
The Unknown (Twenty-Nine)
Wrath (Thirty)
The Damned (Thirty-One)

The Game (Thirty-Two)
The Decoy (Thirty-Three)
The Disappearance (Thirty-Four)
The Whole Truth (Thirty-Five)
Alex (Thirty-Six)
Parkman (Thirty-Seven)
Darwin (Thirty-Eight)
Aaron (Thirty-Nine)
Remains To Be Seen (Forty)

The Jake Wood Novels

The Immortal Gene (Book One)
The Immortal Target (Book Two)

Standalone Novels

'Til Death Do Us Part
The Drowning
The Woman in the Woods
The Threat
The Specter
The Mafia Trilogy
A Murder in Time
Frequency of the Dead

Co-Authored Novels

Collision Course (Written with Gary Ponzo)
There Will Be Blood (Written with Rania Stone)
The Soulless (Written with Rania Stone)

Short Story Collections

Twisted Fate (Tales of Horror)
Twists of Fate (Tales of Hope)

5

Chapter 1

Edward Sweeney enjoyed the rush before the blood came and welcomed it. He flicked the top of the lighter open, spun the tiny wheel, brought it to flame, then closed the lighter. Repeating this process over and over calmed him. Edward wasn't a smoker, but he often carried the lighter for his nerves, and nights like this took nerve.

Parked in the darkened shadows of tall trees, he checked the time. It was slightly after midnight. His target, Jason Grant, would exit the premises soon. After watching the man for over a week, scoping out the lay of the land, Ed knew a lot about his target. Research was important for Ed. Without it, mistakes could happen. He'd learned that lesson early and wouldn't make a mistake again.

The gate moved.

Ed watched it slide into the wall on the left, disappearing

behind a chunk of fieldstone and shrubs. Headlights edged closer to the exit, and a car moved past the gate. The black Mercedes paused at the road, waiting for the gate to close.

The Mercedes's windows were tinted, so Ed couldn't guarantee it was Jason Grant driving, but no one else lived at the address, and the man was single. Jason had killed his own parents—butchered them with a knife, then set their cottage on fire and burned them inside to erase all evidence of his presence. Tonight, Jason would pay for that crime.

Ed waited until the Mercedes started west along King Vaughan Road before easing out of his hiding spot in the dark, lights still off as he steered onto the road. At this hour, no one was in the area. King Vaughan was a busy road through the day, with large trucks heading toward Highway 400 and dozens of vehicles traveling to and from several golf courses in the area, but after midnight, it was quiet.

Ed waited a moment on the shoulder, watching Jason Grant's taillights as they drew smaller in the distance. They rose, angled slightly, then descended as Jason crested a hill in the distance.

His mirrors were dark. Edward Sweeney turned on his vehicle's lights and eased off the shoulder of the road to follow Jason, getting his van up to a hundred quickly. There was still time to catch up because Jason wouldn't turn left until Nobleton, taking him south to Queen Street and over to Torbram, where his current girlfriend worked.

Six nights over the past seven, Ed had followed Mr. Grant to the massage parlor. He'd watched him enter the building, then return to his Mercedes over an hour later, his clothes ruffled, his smile wider.

And all that time, Edward's anger increased.

How could he move on so easily? It was like the death of his parents meant nothing. Sure, it'd been two years in court, and sure, he'd been absolved of all wrongdoing in the eyes of the law, but he did it. They had him at the scene, placed there by witnesses, yet Grant's lawyers worked tirelessly to prove those witnesses were unreliable and that Mr. Grant was, in fact, at home, alone, at the time of the cottage fire.

All that didn't matter to Edward Sweeney because Jason Grant stabbed his parents and burned their bodies. Smoke damage was detected in his mother's lungs, so she was alive when he started the fire. And if society's court system wasn't going to exact consequences, it was left to its members to fulfill that task.

After several small inclines, Jason Grant's taillights came into view several hundred yards ahead. Ed eased off the accelerator, let his van slow to the speed limit, and then hit the steering wheel button for his phone.

"Call Dale," he said out loud when the van prompted him.

A moment later, Dale's phone rang in the speakers.

"Dale here."

"You in place?"

"Yeah. Ready to go."

"Okay, we're just approaching Nobleton now."

"That gives me at least an hour."

"It does. Perhaps more. I'll call back when we're on the return trip."

"Got it. I'll be ready."

"Remind me again how you'll get around his alarm

system."

"It's done."

"What?" Ed frowned. "Done? As in, you've already circumvented it?"

"Yeah. I watched him leave. I'm already inside. Everything's fine. Now I'll wait for you guys to return."

"Well, fuck, that's great."

"Just don't lose him. Make sure you give me a heads up."

"I will. Find what you can."

"Okay, gotta go. It's a big house to search. Give me a fifteen-minute warning."

"Keep your phone handy." Ed clicked off and slowed as he entered Nobleton.

Jason had already turned, his car no longer visible. Ed clicked his signal downward to turn left, eased to a stop at the light, and waited.

Dale would go through Jason's house. Hopefully, he'd find whatever he needed in the time he had.

The light changed, and Ed moved into the intersection, turning wide. On the far side of the intersection, his headlights spanned across a car at the all-night gas station, filling up.

A black Mercedes.

Ed glimpsed Jason Grant as he drove by, standing close to his vehicle with a hose at the side of the car.

Their eyes locked a moment.

Then he was by the gas station, his heart racing.

Did Jason see him? Could he recognize him from his time in court?

"Shit," Ed shouted, then slammed the steering wheel.

He'd gotten careless. Of course, Jason had to gas up. And Ed had sat at the traffic light long enough for Jason to see him from the gas station—it was practically at the corner. If Ed had been paying better attention, he would've seen the Mercedes when he sat at the light.

Too late now. All he could do was wait to resume the tail.

He slowed to look for a hiding spot. After a hundred yards, he found a dirt road on the right. With one last look in his mirror, he swerved off Highway 27 and onto the dirt road, then killed the lights. He parked nose-in to watch the mirrors, waiting for the Mercedes to pass his position.

Being cautious wasn't something he had to school himself on. He wouldn't have made it this far, this long, without being alert and aware. Mistakes do happen, but he'd survive this one. Even if Jason saw his face, he would be unlikely to recognize him. Not after this long. At least, Ed hoped not.

Ed flicked open the lighter, lit it, and closed it. He did it again and again, waiting.

But no headlights lit up the road behind him.

"Where the fuck are you?" Ed whispered to the empty car.

He'd give him another minute, maybe two, then he'd have to drive back and check on him.

After five more clicks of the lighter, headlights brightened in his mirrors.

"Finally," he mumbled. He'd broken out in a sweat, his underarms wet now.

The sound of the vehicle increased as it neared. He wiped his brow. Without wanting to present a silhouette for the driver, he lowered in his seat until his head was below the headrest. Then he adjusted his side mirror to see the road.

Something was off, though.

The engine was too loud.

It couldn't be the Mercedes unless he'd had one of those external mufflers added to make a racket.

A jacked-up pickup truck roared by his position, headed south toward Brampton and Toronto beyond.

The road darkened in the mirrors behind him.

He'd fucked up. He'd let Jason Grant slip away.

Edward pushed himself back up in his seat, readjusting his mirrors.

There was no light on the road behind him.

No Jason Grant, no Mercedes.

Ed turned on his van, backed out to the road, and scanned the length of it.

No car traveled in either direction now.

The road was empty.

"Shit," he shouted, easing onto the road and spinning the wheel to aim back toward the intersection where the all-night gas station was.

The tires squealed once, and then he was moving quickly.

At the gas station, the pumps were empty.

There was no sign of the Mercedes.

Jason had given him the slip.

Ed swung a right and started back toward Jason's house while hitting the call button.

He had to warn Dale. Jason could have already been there, entering through the gate while Dale roamed the house freely.

"Call Dale," he said, trying to remain calm.

The phone rang.

And rang.

Dale didn't pick up on the other end.

Edward shouted, his head tilted back, mouth aimed upward, then mashed the accelerator to the floor and gunned it for Jason Grant's house, dialing Dale's cell phone again.

Chapter 2

SARAH ROBERTS STARED AT the ceiling of the spare room, fists clenched, unable to sleep. How could she sleep when her life was falling apart? Although, that wasn't entirely true. It wasn't falling apart. She'd only lost her boyfriend. Others would say her life was falling apart when the mafia or a cartel was hunting her, but not Sarah. All of that could be dealt with. Losing Aaron was a fight she had no idea how to win.

And maybe that was the problem.

They were at an impasse.

She felt helpless, which turned to restlessness, which irritated her because she was visiting her parents to take some time off. To reflect on what had happened and how they would deal with the future.

Yet her sister, Vivian, had said Sarah was supposed to

receive some sort of delivery. Why would she offer a prophecy of something as mundane as a delivery?

Sarah rolled over and stared at her cell phone on the side table. Only Parkman had called to check in on her. Alex, Benjamin, and Daniel had asked about her. But Aaron was strangely absent from the dojo. Apparently, he was still nursing his wounds at the apartment, taking time to return.

Parkman said Aaron told them to give him another week, that he was too beat up to teach at the dojo anyway, so he'd rest.

Even though she'd taken no active role in what happened to Aaron, she felt wholly responsible, which hurt even more. His nose was broken, and his face was a mess. Doctors were saying other than the broken nose—which would heal slightly crooked—the prognosis was looking good. Aaron would mend completely and be a hundred percent again.

She wondered if Aaron was going through what she was going through. Parkman mentioned Aaron had been grieving the state of their relationship and that he would break out of it soon. He'd call her. Everything would work out. Just give him time.

There would probably be new rules when they did talk again. Rules restricting his involvement with Vivian. There'd have to be. Although, Sarah had no idea how that would work.

She rolled onto her other side and stared at the wall. She'd been at her parents' house in Santa Rosa, California, for several nights now, losing more sleep as each night crept by. They'd been amazing to her, taking care of everything. Her mother had even taken her shopping yesterday. Sarah had grabbed a large coffee, nursing it as they strolled through the huge mall, her mind elsewhere.

Maybe she'd get up and pour a whiskey. One shot, perhaps two, and she'd be able to sleep.

Without wanting to wake her parents, she eased off the bed, slipped into a robe that hung from the back of the bedroom door even though she wore sweatpants, and crept out into the hallway. Nightlights had been plugged into the sockets, so there was plenty of light to tiptoe along the hall, past their bedroom, and into the kitchen.

She found the whiskey bottle in the liquor cupboard to the right of the fridge. With barely a noise, she poured two fingers and stepped down into the sunken living room to drop onto the couch.

If she were alone, she'd turn on the TV, drink several glasses of whiskey, and fall asleep on the couch while watching some Netflix show, but turning on the TV would wake her parents or her mother at least. Then she'd come out and ask what was wrong, and the conversation would head down a path Sarah wasn't willing to go.

She placed the glass to her lips, then stopped.

A shadow crossed the frosted pane of glass near the front door.

What the fuck?

Were they that close to the road that someone walking by would cast a shadow that long?

There was a vineyard at the back of the house. And the nearest neighbor wasn't too close at all. People rarely strolled past the front of the house, especially at this time of night.

She pushed off the couch, thankful she hadn't turned on

any lights and set her whiskey glass down. The shadow hadn't crossed the window again. Was someone standing at or near their front door?

Whoever it was couldn't tell she was sitting in the living room. They had to assume everyone in the house was asleep as it was close to one in the morning, and the lights had been out since slightly after eleven.

She waited another moment, then stepped quietly to the side window. Her back to the wall, she moved the thick red curtains just enough to view the side of the house that led up to the road.

The entire area was empty and quiet.

Another glance at the front door and the tall, thin, frosted glass to the right revealed no moving shadows.

Her heart had sped up, but this wasn't freaking her out yet. It could be nothing. If it were something big, Vivian would've told her.

Wouldn't she?

Could it all have been imagined? Or was someone standing just outside their front door? If they were attempting to break in, she would've heard them fucking with the lock already, so that couldn't be it.

Was this the delivery Vivian had been talking about? No, it couldn't be. Who delivered packages in the middle of the night? She'd heard of late deliveries, but that would be ridiculous.

Never one to be deterred by fear, she moved to the front door and used the peephole to look outside.

The front porch was empty.

"Well then, what did I see?" she whispered, wondering if

the lack of sleep had been playing tricks on her eyes.

After one more check outside, she unlocked the door. Someone could be standing to the side, just out of view. She'd feel better with a weapon, but it probably wasn't needed. No one knew she was visiting her parents but a few friends. If someone was outside, it was probably just some tweaker looking for a fix. And even if someone was going to try to break in, they were taking their sweet ass time.

The door opened quietly, and Sarah stepped back to avoid anything someone might swing at her.

A single brown box sat on the welcome mat.

She checked the street, scanning the bushes that lined the street for movement but saw nothing. Someone had dropped off this box no more than four minutes ago.

She edged closer to peer around the side of the door, but the entire front of the house was empty. Whoever dropped it off was gone or watching from the shadows across the street.

The box was a standard size. Something a basketball or soccer ball could be shipped in. She estimated it was about the height of three shoeboxes piled on one another and slightly wider.

Vivian, what am I dealing with? No bomb, right?

There was no answer, although she wasn't expecting one. Vivian was in Sarah's life on Vivian's terms. She came and went when Vivian decided. If a bomb were in the box at Sarah's feet, then perhaps Vivian would show up to warn her.

It had taken a decade, but Sarah was finally settling into the relationship she had with her sister. A level of acceptance had enveloped them, and it was warming. There wasn't much pleading or begging for Vivian to show up when Sarah felt she needed her the most. Because Vivian already knew Sarah didn't actually need her. That was Sarah in search of a crutch, a helping hand.

Her sister would be there, or she wouldn't be. End of story. That was that.

In the meantime, Sarah would deal with whatever was before her and live her life.

Which meant she needed to see what was in the box. To sate her curiosity or not to sate it wasn't even a question.

After one more slow survey of the immediate area, she inspected the box. Her nerves were already settling as she ran a hand over the top of the cardboard. There was no label on the box. Only her name etched into the surface—Sarah.

That was it. One word.

So, someone knew she was here and wanted to send her something.

A message? An explosive?

Should she take it into the house?

Vivian?

Even though they understood, it would be nice to hear if she's okay with taking it inside the house. She couldn't leave it on the stoop, and she wasn't going to sit there staring at it all night, front door open.

Decision made—she'd take it inside and open it.

Vivian would be there if that were a dumb idea. And by dumb, she meant deadly.

A quick test of the box's weight told her it was no more than five pounds.

She lifted it to chest height, glanced out at the road, then stepped inside and placed it on the wooden chair by the shoes. Once the front door was shut and locked, Sarah grabbed a knife from the kitchen and returned to the box.

Before opening it, she stared through the peephole in the door again.

The road out front was still empty.

Why would someone deliver a box without a shipping label at one in the morning?

Perhaps the better question pertained to the object inside the box that facilitated such a delivery at such an hour.

Could Aaron have sent her something?

Even though she was about to open it, she wondered who could've sent it. She only arrived a few days ago, and other than Parkman and the guys at the dojo, no one knew where she was. Unless she accounted for the random customs agent she handed her passport to when entering the States before her flight from Toronto.

She applied the knife to the top of the box and paused.

That left two possibilities. The box was from Aaron or Parkman, and they had it delivered covertly on purpose.

Or someone was following her, tracking her whereabouts. One was weird, and the other was creepy because it certainly couldn't be random. She'd never lived in this house, only visited it. The address had never been associated with her name.

The knife slid inside the lip of the top flap and sliced through the tape with ease. She applied the knife to the other side. Then, once the top was cut, she set the knife on a pair of running shoes beside the chair.

Her mind racing as to what could possibly be inside, she eased the flap up and pulled it back.

A white circular container sat atop what looked like a small platform at the bottom of the box. The white container sported a clasp near the top.

Before Sarah undid the clasp, she wanted to inspect the sides first. With the knife back in her hand, she carefully sliced along the box's four corners, eased the sides downward until they were horizontal, and then set the knife back on the shoes beside her.

Now, the white ball was totally exposed. She got up and walked around it, checking it from all angles.

After a moment, she moved to the peephole in the door again and checked outside.

Empty.

"Vivian?" she whispered, spinning back around to stare at the white orb. "What's inside?"

The feeling she always got when Vivian hovered close wasn't there. Her sister was nowhere to be found.

That alone couldn't guarantee the contents of the orb weren't lethal, but she took some comfort in all the times she was about to be shot or killed—her sister had shown up in time.

Decision made. She would unclasp the top and see what was inside. It was that, or she'd gather the entire contraption, walk it back outside and across the road, and leave it there until the morning.

The whiskey on the coffee table beckoned. Sarah moved there first, took a large sip, then moved back to the white orb. Careful not to disturb the contents, she applied her fingers to the clasp, lifted upward, and then eased the orb apart. It opened as if an egg cracked perfectly in half.

Inside was some kind of bowl, the top covered in a black velvet cloth.

She inhaled, unsure why she had been holding her breath.

What did the shipper intend her to see? Whatever it was, it had the faint smell of metallic copper.

Was the bowl filled with blood?

Only one way to find out.

She grabbed the knife, and with the sharp tip, she lifted the edge of the cloth, then jerked her hand once to dislodge the cloth completely. It had provided a seal on the bowl, like one attached to the top of a yogurt container.

The cloth dropped over the edge of the bowl to reveal a dark liquid with something floating inside.

At least it wasn't a bomb. She had doubted that would be the case, but the thought lingered at the back of her head anyway.

The smell grew more intense now that she had unsealed the bowl. With no desire to touch the liquid without a better view of what floated inside, she leaned over and flicked on the front foyer light overhead.

The bowl was filled with blood.

She could tell it was blood in the harsh white light, coupled with the smell. This made her want to back away, but she had grown accustomed to the sight of blood.

Something floated in the blood, just below the surface.

With the tip of the knife, Sarah leaned in closer and poked at the item obscured by the crimson liquid.

It floated to the top.

She gasped, placing her free hand over her mouth.

A man's penis, savagely cut from the body, floated to the

surface. Based on the rate of decay, this penis was still attached to the man less than twelve hours ago. She was sure of it because of how *alive* it still looked.

Was this the delivery Vivian had been telling her about?

Why the hell would someone want to ship her a cock in a bowl of blood? A message of some kind?

Whose penis was it, and why was it no longer attached?

Could it be … Aaron's?

She leaned closer to inspect it more seriously.

No, it wasn't Aaron's. She knew what his looked like, and this certainly wasn't it.

She plunged the knife deeper to see if anything else was in the soup bowl of blood and cock.

Something moved from under the little stand the bowl was attached to.

Knife still hilt deep in the blood, Sarah leaned down and glanced under the bowl.

Her heart literally skipped a beat when she saw it looking back at her.

Reactions don't allow for thought. When Sarah reacted to seeing the tarantula edging toward her from under the bowl, she let out a short scream, jerked away from the white orb, and knocked it over because the knife was still touching the bottom.

By the time Sarah was four feet from the box, the bowl was upside down, the blood soaking into the corner of her mother's carpet where it met the tile floor near the front foyer. The large spider crawled away from her, but that didn't matter.

The worst thing about seeing a spider—especially one as

large as this one—was losing it.

She couldn't take her eyes off it as she collected herself from the floor and grabbed her father's large work boot. In two steps, she slammed the boot on the spider. Then again. And again.

When it stopped moving, she took a breath and slumped to the carpet to assess the damage.

"Sarah?"

She screamed and spun around.

Her mother stood at the opening to the hallway.

"I'm sorry," she whispered. "Didn't mean to startle you."

Sarah placed a hand on her chest as she panted. "I just … didn't expect anyone to be awake."

Amelia moved into the living room, pushing hair out of her face. "I heard you out here. I thought I heard the door."

"That arrived."

Amelia stopped a few feet from the boot, staring at the open box. "Arrived? As in delivered?"

Sarah nodded.

"At this hour?"

She kept nodding.

"What was in it?"

"The tarantula under Dad's boot and a bowl of blood with a dismembered penis."

She shot Sarah a harsh glance. "A penis?"

"Fucked, I know."

"Whose?"

Sarah shrugged. "I'm sure we'll find out soon."

"Your sister say anything?"

Sarah shook her head. "Nothing. She's been silent

tonight."

They stared at each other for a moment. Then, her mother started back toward the kitchen.

"I'll grab a few cleaning supplies. Let's clean this up, have a shot of whiskey together, then get some sleep. Figure it all out tomorrow."

That's where Sarah got it all—from her mother. A bowl of blood with a penis was delivered at one in the morning, and her mother was ready to just clean it up and have a drink like someone spilled their dinner on the floor.

She got up, shivered once as she stepped over the mashed spider, and joined her mother in the kitchen. They worked for fifteen minutes without a word and cleaned most of it. Amelia handled the spider while wearing yellow kitchen gloves. Sarah dealt with the penis and got to work on the carpet.

The remnants of the box were placed by the door, and they sat on the couch with two glasses and the bottle of Crown Royal.

"Any idea what that's all about?" Amelia asked.

"None," Sarah said, staring at the box.

"That penis looked real."

"It was real. It was attached to its owner within the previous twelve hours or so. At least that's my best guess."

"And Vivian said nothing about this?"

"She said I'd be getting a delivery, but that was it."

"Well, like always, it'll all come clear soon enough."

"Imagine so." Sarah drank from her glass. "What puzzles me is no one knows I'm here but my few friends in Toronto."

"And it was addressed to you?"

"No shipping label. Just my name scratched into the top of the box."

They sat in silence for a moment.

"What are you going to do?" Amelia asked.

Sarah thought about it for several seconds, then said, "I'm going to check in with Parkman in the morning. Also, I'll call the dojo to speak with one of the guys to find out if they've seen anything weird. Then maybe I'll get back on the road."

"You're leaving?" Amelia leaned forward to glance back at Sarah. "You just got here a few days ago. I was hoping you'd stay for several more weeks yet."

"I've brought this here. Remember the last time my world met yours? It wasn't pleasant." Sarah shook her head. "I will figure this out and find time to return. We'll visit again, Mom. Longer next time. But I can't have this," she gestured at the box by the door, "hanging over my head."

Amelia leaned back into the couch. "I understand. I hope you figure it out soon, then."

Sarah drank the rest of the whiskey in her glass and set it on the coffee table.

The sound of an engine slowed, then seemed to stop out front. The engine died, followed by a car door being slammed shut, then another.

"Expecting anyone?" Sarah asked.

"Funny." Her mother shook her head. "Not at this hour."

Sarah got to her feet and reached the door's peephole before the unknown visitors knocked.

"Two police officers," she said, a pit forming in her stomach. "What now?"

Knowing there was no way to avoid whatever was coming, she unlocked the door and swung it open.

"Evening officers." She smiled. "Bit late for house calls, isn't it?"

"We're looking for Sarah Roberts."

Chapter 3

AT JASON GRANT'S FRONT gate, Ed didn't hesitate. When he saw it sitting open, he drove onto Jason's property, up the driveway, and stopped behind the black Mercedes.

Why would the man drive to Nobleton to fill his gas tank at one in the morning? Something must have happened. Somehow, he knew he was being followed and changed his mind. But if so, why was the gate still open? Whoever was following him would come right in after him—

Someone tapped the window beside his head, making Ed jump in his seat. A small, startled shout escaped his lips when his wrist smacked the bottom of the steering wheel.

"Get out of the car," Jason said, a gun equipped with a sound suppressor already attached to it in his hand. He waved it several times to coax Ed out.

Ed examined his options and didn't like any of them.

Where was Dale? Already dead?

They'd fucked this one up badly. Yet, something about it allowed him to feel like he would be okay. Jason Grant was a murderer, a piece of shit human being who got lucky. Ed counted on getting lucky and staying alive, and Dale was his ace card.

He clicked the door open and eased his legs out first. Then, when he pushed up off the seat, he ensured his elbow pressed into the horn. He acted startled, hit it again, then got to his feet and stood inside the open door. It had been a risk, but if Dale wasn't answering his phone and he was still alive, maybe he'd hear the horn.

The gate to the road was already shutting.

"Why are you following me?" Jason asked. "Who hired you?"

Quite a few answers rolled around in his head, some true, most not. He decided on the truth.

"Our legal system is too weak with people like you."

Jason frowned and tilted his head slightly as if trying to figure it all out.

"You're following me because I have a good defense team?" Jason laughed. "What, you gonna punch me now? Try and hurt me?"

"I hadn't decided what I was going to do yet." That was mostly a lie. He knew what he would do, just not exactly how he would do it.

"You're that rent-a-cop in court, right?" Jason lowered his weapon. "You called for everyone to rise and be seated when that asshole judge came and left."

Ed nodded. "I'm the court security officer, sworn in as a

special constable."

Jason stepped back and eyed Sweeney up and down. "So, you're not even a full-fledged cop?"

"No." The conversation remained calm. This gave Dale a chance to come outside.

"Then who hired you to play private detective?"

"No one."

Jason shook his head, the right half of his mouth up in a sneer. "Are you saying you took it upon yourself to follow me all on your own?"

Ed stared at the man a moment, then nodded.

"Okay." Jason seemed to be suppressing a laugh. "Tell me why, then."

"Observation purposes." A half-truth.

"Observation? What the fuck are you talking about?"

"Look." Ed stole a glance at the gun. "You fascinated me. I thought you were guilty for sure. Then they got those witnesses to lie to create an alibi, and here we are, talking at your house."

Jason waved the gun back and forth. "No, that's not good enough. There's something you're not telling me. Nobody *observes* someone because they were found not guilty in court." He brought the weapon to his mouth and tapped it against his lips several times, studying Ed's face. "Were you thinking of hurting me, Mr. Security Guard?"

The man asked him that last bit while staring into Ed's eyes. Even as his mouth opened to lie, his eyes held the truth, and Ed feared Jason would see that.

"Of course not," Ed said, focusing on making his tone one of conviction.

"Why don't I believe you?"

"Look, the truth is, you fascinate me. I wanted to see what your life was like, how you live day to day after losing both your parents in that fire."

"I live just fine. They were horrible people who stole my childhood. And now they're gone. The world's a better place, Mr. Security." Jason aimed his weapon at Ed's forehead from three feet away. "Tell me again why you were following me, but this time, I'd rather hear the truth."

Something moved by the bush about ten feet behind Jason Grant. Ed focused on not adjusting his eyes. The urge to track the movements and turn toward them almost made him look. Instead, he stared into Jason's eyes and focused on staying alive.

"Okay, okay," he whispered, lowering his head. "You got me."

"C'mon, out with it. Spill the beans."

"I was following you to see if you'd kill again."

"Kill again?" Jason howled, then added, "That's rich. A court of law finds me not guilty, but the court security guard finds me guilty." He shook his head. "You were there, man. You heard the evidence. I didn't do it."

"Well, I disagree," Ed said. "That alibi was fake, and we both know it."

The movement behind Jason was closer.

"Oh, really now. What makes you the expert?" Jason gave off an angry vibe like he was losing his patience. Before he worked himself up and did whatever he was planning, Ed prayed Dale made his move.

"Look, what I think doesn't matter, does it?" Ed paused,

counting in his head, waiting to speak again. He opened his mouth at the count of five, but Jason jerked around to look behind him.

"What was that?" Jason asked as he spun back around to point the gun at Ed, moving within a foot of him, gravel crunching underfoot. "I said," he was shouting now, "what was that?"

Ed shrugged. "What was what?" His voice cracked, but that wasn't fake. He couldn't hide it as he was legitimately afraid Jason would fire his weapon out of nervousness.

"Did you bring someone with you?" Jason asked, moving even closer, the sound suppressor an inch from Ed's cheek.

This was his chance, perhaps his only chance. Jason was spooked, and Dale hadn't shown himself yet. Even though the gun was still aimed at him, Jason studied the bushes lining the walkway leading to his house.

Before Jason turned around to face him, Ed moved sideways, out of the weapon's aim, then reared back and kicked Jason in the groin. As soon as he connected, Ed dropped out of the way of any possible gun threat.

It was just in time, too.

Jason fired as he recoiled into a ball and slowly lowered to the ground, moaning. He fought to raise the weapon and aim at Ed while his other hand covered his genitals, but Ed was already lunging for the gun. He grabbed it and dove for the ground, smacking hard, knocking the wind from his lungs. At least he could dislodge the weapon from Jason's grasp, though.

Ed kicked the gun away and scrambled to his feet just as Dale stepped out of the bushes.

"What the fuck were you doing?" Ed asked him. "He had a gun on me."

Jason groaned on the ground as he writhed in pain.

"What was I doing? I was hiding *because* he had a gun on you. That wasn't part of our deal."

"Our deal?"

"Yeah, you do all the violent shit. I just help you. I'm an ends to a means."

"An ends to a means? Fuck, dude," Ed pointed at Jason on the ground, "you almost caused *my* end!"

The thought that Jason had actually pulled the trigger angered him. He strode over and kicked Jason in the balls again, connecting from behind because the man was curled up in a fetal ball.

"Help me get him inside."

Dale strode around to Jason's head. "I got the arms. You take his legs."

"Fuck, shit," Ed mumbled under his breath.

Even though Jason struggled, he was weakened by the pain in his crotch. They were able to get him to the side door of the garage. Dale had left it unlocked and ajar, so Ed bumped it open. Once inside, he released Jason's ankles. Due to his two hundred pounds, the man dropped fast, which yanked his arms out of Dale's grasp.

"You could've warned me," Dale whined.

Jason grunted and curled into a ball again.

"We're here now," Edward said. "It's over. Tell me what you found."

"Nothing. There was no time. When I heard the gate opening, I killed the volume on my phone and made my way to the garage to see who was coming."

"Which is why you didn't answer me when I called you?"

Dale nodded. "I watched him park and leave the gate open. Minutes later, you pulled in, and you know the rest."

"Okay, wait here a moment. I need my supplies from the trunk and his gun. When I return, you continue your search while I speak with Jason. Then you take off before I do what I have to do."

"What—do you have to do?" Jason asked from his curled-up position on the garage floor, his voice squeaky.

"Shut up. None of your business." He glanced at Dale, then back to Jason. "Yet."

"Okay, let's do this." Dale gestured at the door. "I want out of here. So hurry."

Ed ran outside, collected Jason's gun, and slipped it into his belt. Having never had a weapon stashed there felt awkward, but it was better than using a pocket in his pants.

He opened his trunk, grabbed his gym bag, and returned to the open garage door.

The gravel crunched with each step, his anticipation rising as he neared the side of the house. Would he get a confession out of Jason Grant? Would the man be willing to say on tape that he killed his parents? That was always the challenge. To get the confession went a long way in the court of Edward Sweeney.

"Hey, Dale," he said, stepping inside the garage. "Do you think our friend here, Mr. Grant, will—"

He stopped moving, the gym bag falling from his hand. It made a solid thunk on the concrete floor of the garage.

Dale Williams was on his back. His lifeless eyes were wide open, staring at the ceiling of the garage. A pool of blood from a gaping head wound made an oval shape to the right of his head. A blood-stained brick lay three feet from the man's dented cranium.

Jason Grant was gone.

Chapter 4

SARAH EYED BOTH OFFICERS, then glanced past them at their cruiser. They looked legit enough, but one could never be sure.

"You want to come up to our door at this hour. I hope you brought some form of ID."

The officers exchanged a glance, and then both retrieved wallets and opened them.

"I'm Officer Sherman," the taller man said.

"And I'm Officer Bower."

Bower had a Magnum PI mustache, and Sherman had the workings of a beard. Both men appeared to want to keep this serious and professional.

Sarah just wanted them to leave so she could have one more shot of whiskey and get to bed. After the cock and spider show, she was tired now.

"What could possibly bring you out at this hour?" Amelia asked from behind Sarah.

"Yeah," Sarah said, the whiskey loosening her tongue, not that she needed that anyway.

Bower opened a notebook and flipped to a page while Sherman stared past Sarah into the house.

What could he be looking for?

"Mom, I'm going to talk to these officers on the front porch," she said, easing the door closed to block Sherman's view. "I'll be back inside in a moment."

The door clicked shut. "Unless, of course, you gents have a warrant to search my parents' home."

"Sarah." Bower jumped right in, his pen ready. "Can you state your full name?"

She did, and he wrote it down.

"Date of birth?"

"Why, what's it matter?"

"Date of birth, please."

"I've given you my name. You've come to my parents' house at nearly two in the morning, and you want my DOB? No, fuck off back to your car unless you give me a reason for this visit."

They glanced at each other again, and Sherman crossed his arms.

"Where were you yesterday afternoon?"

"You two have got some nerve," she whispered.

Sherman frowned.

Sarah continued. "Aren't these sorts of conversations held during daylight?" She raised a hand. "Wait, don't answer that. I think you get my point. Check the time, know that *we* are being inconvenienced, then chill out a bit, and we'll get along fine."

"Okay," Sherman said. "Could you please tell us where you were yesterday afternoon?"

He'd tightened his jaw, even clenched his teeth together, but the tone was better, so she let it go.

Sarah glanced to the side to think about what he was asking. "My mother and I went out." She met Sherman's gaze. "We stopped at a mall, did some shopping, had lunch, then came home."

"What mall?" Bower asked, his pen moving quickly. "Where was lunch?"

"Why is any of this important? We didn't break any traffic laws. We paid for all of our purchases. We even tipped the guy for lunch when we didn't have to."

Another cruiser approached quickly, then kicked up dust when it stopped, its lights flashing on the roof.

"Maybe you guys want to tell me what this is all about," Sarah said.

Two more officers hopped out and started their way.

"The reason we're here," Sherman said, "is confidential. We only want to rule out that you were a part of what we are investigating, and answering our questions will do that."

"What are you investigating?"

"Sarah," Bower said. "Just answer a few more questions, and we'll leave it at that."

Sarah nodded as the other two officers, this time a female and a male, stopped behind Sherman. They all nodded at each other while the female cop slipped gloves on.

"Sarah," Bower said. "What mall? Where was lunch?"

Something big must've happened because everyone knew she was now at her parents' house in Santa Rosa. And most likely, it had to do with that appendage she'd just received. She needed to get these cops off her front porch, and she needed a shower. Could there be blood under her fingernails? She clasped her hands behind her back and leaned on the closed door.

"We went to Costco and Target and even grabbed a coffee at Starbucks. I'm sure you all know where I'm talking about."

Bower nodded, his pen scribbling in his hand. The other three officers just stared at her.

"Where to next?" Bower asked.

Sarah shrugged. "No idea. Home, I guess. Yeah, we came home."

The female cop moved closer, blue gloves on her hands. Were they preparing to arrest her? If so, for what?

Vivian? Anything?

"Okay, I think I got it." Bower nodded, then looked up. "You went shopping, got a coffee, then came home."

"Right. Exactly. Now, will you tell me what this is all about?"

Bower raised a finger for her to wait. "Where was lunch? Earlier you said shopping and lunch. Now you're saying Costco, Target, coffee, then home." He glanced up. "I thought there was lunch, too."

The look in Sherman's eyes told her everything. They all thought she was lying. They knew something—perhaps a lot of somethings—and felt they held the better cards, the upper hand. But innocence beat their play every time. She'd done nothing wrong yesterday. Although whoever sent her that box was probably involved with whatever they were investigating.

Should she offer full disclosure and tell them about the box?

"My mother and I were considering KFC because it was right across the street from Costco, but I was able to talk her into Subway. So we went there."

Bower scribbled while Sherman backed away and clutched at the new officer's arm to lead him farther away as well. Only Bower and the female cop crowded her on the front step now.

"So, Subway," Bower whispered as he wrote something. He glanced at the female, then back to Sarah. "Anything happen there that you recall? Anything out of the ordinary?"

That was strange. How could they know? She glanced past Bower at Sherman and the other cop whispering to each other from about twenty feet away, giving Sarah furtive glances every few moments.

"You're not going to tell me what this is about, are you?"

"Sarah," the woman cop said, stepping closer. "Once we determine your whereabouts yesterday, you won't see us again. Telling you confidential information about an active case won't change where you were. Just answer Officer Bower's questions, and we'll get out of your hair."

"Okay, regarding anything out of the ordinary, a man recognized me."

"The clerk?"

Sarah shook her head. "No, a customer. He said some shit about what he'd seen in the papers regarding what happened when I was in Texas."

"What happened in Texas?" Bower asked.

"All those human procurement companies took a hit because I caught one *creating* bodies to procure. Now, many of them are being shut down and inspected."

"Created bodies?" the female asked. "Is that a nice way to say murder?"

"Yes, as in they targeted certain individuals based on race and ethnicity. Although, I don't see how this has anything to do with me shopping and having lunch yesterday." It had everything to do with that dick in a box. Then that Justin Timberlake song popped into her brain, and she had to fight to keep the smile off her face.

"So, this character recognized you. How did you handle it?"

"I didn't. The customer grabbed my drink and ran from the store. If I handled it, you'd be here for an entirely different reason."

"A different reason? Why's that?"

She looked from one cop to the other. "I was joking. A little humor."

The female cop shook her head. "Yeah, not a good time."

"And that's why you tipped the clerk?" Bower paused to run a finger along his notepad. "As you said here, you tipped the guy for lunch when you didn't have to." He quoted her word for word.

"I never tip at a takeout. But we left our change and said thank you because the clerk replaced my drink at no charge."

"Have you stayed here the entire time you've been in Santa Rosa?" the female cop asked.

"I never got your name."

"Officer Shultz."

"Yes, I've stayed with my parents since I arrived, Officer Shultz."

Sherman and the other cop were walking back over now.

"To be clear, you were never at the Western Best Hotel across the street from the Subway at any time?" Bowers asked.

The Western Best Hotel? Across the street from Subway?

"No, as I just said, I have stayed here every night."

"And can someone other than your mother or father verify that?" Sherman asked.

"Why wouldn't their word count?"

He shrugged. "Because Sarah, what parent wouldn't lie for their child?"

"Okay, your time here is done." She waved at them. "Fuck off back to your fancy cruisers. Unless you're arresting me for something I didn't do, come back another time."

"What's that under your nails?" Shultz asked.

Sarah glanced at her nails. It looked like dirt, but it was a small amount of crusted blood from the delivery mishap. No way they could know it was blood in the dim light.

"Been digging in the dirt in the past hour or so?" Sherman asked.

Sarah reached behind her and grasped the doorknob. "Time to go, guys. Come back another day when you have something to tell me."

"Sarah?" Shultz said, moving inside her personal space. "What did you spill tonight?"

That stopped her dead in her tracks. Did these cops deliver that box earlier? She hadn't even considered that possibility. Officers of the law have done all kinds of things to set her up, hurt her, and some have even tried to kill her.

"I spilled red wine," she said, less than six inches from Shultz. It was the last thing she would say without pushing the cop back if she didn't ease off. At least then, she would be detained for something real without this harassment.

Shultz did pull back, which was a good sign. Bower stepped off the front steps, and Sherman kept his distance.

"That must explain the dark spots on the bottom of your track pants, then," Sherman said, pointing downward.

Sarah took in the blood that had splattered her lower leg after the bowl fell over. Answering the door with blood on her hands—literally—might not have been the best idea.

"Hey, Sherman," Sarah said. "When you come back, I'll have the receipts to prove where I was and at what stores."

"We'll need those," he said as he started toward the road. "Because we will be coming back, Sarah. Witnesses placed you at the scene, and I think you're not telling us the whole truth."

"Wait a second," she shouted. That kind of comment pissed her off. "Witnesses placed me at what scene?"

All four cops stopped and faced her. She looked at each one in turn until Sherman spoke.

"Tell us the truth, Sarah. Because when we come back, we won't be so nice."

"The truth about what? That my mom and I went shopping? We had lunch, dealt with a crazy person, and came home. I had a nap before dinner because I hadn't been sleeping well. Then, after dinner, we all watched TV until they went to bed, and here I am, drinking whiskey to get tired. That's why I heard your cruiser pull up."

"Whiskey, is it?" Sherman shook his head. "Thought that was red wine you spilled." He nodded at her lower pant leg. "Sorry, Sarah, but your story sucks and it doesn't add up." He started walking backward to his car. "Not to mention you admit to being near or at the Western Best Hotel."

"What's that got to do with anything? I didn't have a room."

"We'll be back in the morning."

"Fuck you," she said, unable to hold it back. "Bring whatever you want. I've got nothing to hide." As immature as it was, she flipped Sherman the finger.

Something snapped and clicked beside her.

When she spun to the left, Bower took her picture with a cell phone.

"Just wanted to capture the moment," he said and started for his vehicle.

"You can go fuck yourself, too," she mumbled to herself and turned to enter the house.

"What was that all about?" her mother asked.

"I have no idea, but I think it has to do with the delivered box."

"Why did he take your picture?"

"Because I was giving Sherman the finger."

"No, Sarah." Amelia shook her head. "You were on the porch. That cop with the camera was on the grass. At his eye level, he was aiming it at your pants."

She glanced down again. "They saw the blood from the

knocked-over bowl. They know I'll change and wash my clothes. Whatever they're investigating, they wanted something to refer to later in court."

"That, or they're gathering evidence for a search warrant."

"Shit." She slapped a hand into her other hand. "I'm still going to check in with Parkman in the morning. Then I will get back on the road. I'll fly back to Toronto tomorrow."

"You're leaving that soon?"

"Mom, people know I'm here. It's too dangerous for me to stay. I'm leaving this house in the morning. And instead of staying in a motel here, I'll fly back to where Parkman is." She thought about Aaron and realized she probably shouldn't be going back to Toronto. "Or maybe I'll go to Los Angeles for a few days. Get lost in the crowds on Hollywood Boulevard."

"You shouldn't let those cops scare you into leaving."

"I'm not afraid of those cops." She stared at her mother. "I did nothing wrong. It's whoever sent that box. That's what I'm worried about. By leaving your house, I remove the shit from your life. That's all I'm doing."

"Okay, Sarah." Amelia leaned in and hugged her. "Let's have another drink, then sleep."

"That's what I was thinking."

Sarah sat down while staring at the ruined box by the door. The carpet had a wet stain where they'd scrubbed it earlier.

She wondered what would've happened if she hadn't been awake and the cops showed up while that box was still on the porch.

Or maybe that was the plan.

She'd have to get to the bottom of whatever was going on, and by the looks of things, she wouldn't be getting much help from her sister.

And it all started with the Western Best Hotel by the Subway.

A place she should probably visit in the morning as soon as she was packed.

Vivian, what the hell is going on?

No answer came.

Chapter 5

EDWARD SWEENEY BACKED UP to the wall beside the garage door, the gun in his hand, aimed stupidly outward at no one. He knew little about firearms except for the one they issued him at work. Other than in training, he rarely ever fired one.

But Jason Grant wouldn't know that.

He would call the cops now. Ed had to leave before they got there. How would he explain his presence, though?

Wait, wasn't it too late for all that?

If he left, the police would show up at his door asking why he was at Jason Grant's house in the first place. And why they broke in and followed Mr. Grant.

No, Ed had to stay and sort this out.

But how?

Jason would have a cell phone on him.

Unless …

Ed rolled against the wall, then jumped through the door, heading back outside. He bolted for the Mercedes, staying low. Hopefully, Jason only had one gun. Otherwise, he would be taking shots at Ed.

The door to the Mercedes was still unlocked. Crouched down, he yanked it open and crawled inside.

Just as he suspected, Jason Grant's cell phone was in the cup holder. Ed stashed it in his back pocket, then examined the weapon more closely.

Jason had already fired once. Did that mean the safety was off? Did all guns come with a safety?

Leaning on the open door's armrest, he aimed the gun at the bushes and slowly pulled the trigger.

The weapon jerked in his hand, and a small burst of air accompanied a violent slashing sound in the brush. It was like someone slapped the leaves.

"Damn, that's too easy."

Ed wondered how many more bullets the weapon held. Ten, twelve, maybe twenty?

He would be fine if it held two or three more.

Unless Jason was already waiting for him inside the house with another gun.

Ed pushed off the car door and ran for the bushes. It was his life or Jason's now. If he tried to leave, either Jason would surprise him one day, or the cops would, and Sweeney refused to live in fear. He didn't deserve to after what had happened to his wife and daughter. This was righteous, what he was doing.

There was a moment when he wondered why Dale's death wasn't affecting him. Maybe it would be tomorrow or the day after, but he didn't have time to think about it right now.

He had to focus on staying alive.

The garage door beckoned, but wouldn't Jason expect that? His stomach was tied in a knot, and his hands shook, but he couldn't stop now. He ran around the front of the house, mostly shrouded in dark, and made it to the far side. Dale planned to enter through the back door that offered access to the kitchen. Ed was counting on that door still being unlocked and Jason not knowing Dale had used it.

A dark curtain covered the window above him. He ducked below it and scurried to the steps that led to the kitchen door.

Just as he suspected, the door sat ajar about one inch.

A quick scan of the shrubs and trees that lined the back of the property showed no movement. Jason Grant was inside his house, which he knew well, waiting for Ed to enter.

Jason had all the advantages. Ed could run for the bushes and leave. He could hop the fence and be gone. Catch a taxi and make it home within the hour. The gate was closed, so he'd have to leave his car. And when the police came, he could swear he wasn't there. Dale had stolen his car and drove here to break in. Could that work? Or was he just trying to avoid entering the house and getting shot?

Jason Grant was a criminal, a murderer. He'd killed three people now.

That alone got Ed up and on his feet. To avoid making an easy target of himself, he pushed the door open just enough, slipped inside, and dropped to his knees as quietly as possible. The gun held out in front of him.

It was dark, but not dark enough that he couldn't see the empty kitchen. For the size of the house, the kitchen was a bit small. A rectangular island in the center of the floor held the sink. Two small barstools were placed on the outside of the island. Ed spied a large knife rack and stared at it momentarily to ensure they were all present. He was happy to see none were missing.

Above the chopping block, several small hooks hung from the roof. Maybe they once held frying pans.

While examining the kitchen interior, he listened for movement but detected nothing.

Jason was lying in wait.

Which sucked so bad and freaked Ed out completely. He could be anywhere, around any corner, just waiting with another gun ready to blow his brains out.

Yet he had no choice. He had to find him and find a way to overpower him.

Leaving was out of the question now. He'd come too far. And if he died here, then he'd be with his wife and daughter. Perhaps death meant freedom.

Even though his legs refused to move, he stood to his full height and started across the kitchen floor, keeping the weapon in his sweaty hand at the ready. His finger was inside the trigger guard, already applying a slight amount of pressure. The second Jason showed himself, the weapon in his hand would already be firing.

Ed made it to the other side of the kitchen and edged out slowly to peer down a long hallway. It had to lead to the bedrooms.

He breathed in and out, then held it.

The corridor was empty to the left. He leaned out farther and glanced down the dark hallway to the right.

A flash of movement made him jump.

The weapon fired into the ceiling, scaring the shit out of him, even before whatever had moved crashed into his left arm.

He screamed out in pain and dropped to the floor.

The pain was unbearable. A white-hot, searing fire seemed to rage in his left wrist area.

The kitchen light flickered on.

Jason stood over him, a cast iron frying pan in his hand.

Ed brought his right hand around to aim the weapon, but in the confusion, he must have dropped it after firing it.

Jason was already retrieving it off the floor.

"What the fuck were you thinking?" Jason screamed at him, his face a mask of sweat. "Are you guys so fucking stupid that you would break into my house?"

Ed heard him but wasn't really listening. A bulge was forming on his left arm just above the wrist.

"I think you broke my arm," he managed to say.

"That's not all I'm going to break, you fucking asshole." Jason did something to the gun, then tossed the frying pan aside and aimed the weapon at him.

Ed had leaned up on his good arm, brought his legs under him, and now rested on his knees. The ache in his arm was still quite intense, but it felt manageable now. At least he could think. Although, he wasn't sure how that was going to help him. Jason had the gun aimed at his forehead.

The weapon clicked, and he lowered it. "No, not in my kitchen. Too much mess to clean up later. The bathroom will work better."

"So you did kill your parents," Ed said, the pain making his voice falter and crack.

"Is that what this was all about? You and your friend playing amateur sleuth, Hardy Boys assholes, looking to do a big investigation all on your own? What, you thought you'd get a confession, and that would be that?"

"Just fess up. If you're going to …" he clenched his jaw at a wave of pain, then inhaled deeply, "… kill me anyway."

"Of course, I killed my parents," Jason shouted. "They deserved it for what they did to me."

"Tell me," Ed grunted. "What did they do?"

"Fuck you. Ain't gonna tell you shit. You don't deserve to know anything." He moved over to the island and set the gun down.

It was obvious to him Ed wasn't much of a threat anymore.

"What I have to figure out is how to get rid of the bodies. I won't burn *my* house down, too."

Sure, but he'd kill his parents and burn their house down. This man had to pay for what he did, and the court system fucked that up.

Ed glanced at the counter. The gun was too far away. He'd never make it.

Jason opened a pantry door and rummaged through items inside it, pulling out a bottle of blue liquid. The gun was less than two feet from Jason. One eye stayed on Ed as he edged toward the counter on his knees. He needed to get to his feet.

"Stop moving," Jason yelled at him. "I'll fucking shoot you."

"I'm dead anyway," Ed said.

"Oh, you're dead. Just not in my kitchen."

"And that's why I'm getting to my feet. You want to carry me?"

Jason grabbed the gun and walked around the island. "Let's go. Out of the kitchen."

Ed leaned over the counter, waiting to be nudged by Jason. The pain in his wrist had subsided to something more manageable now. It seemed to be numbing. His head was clearing, and he focused on survival.

"Start walking. To the garage."

"Fuck you," Ed whispered.

"I don't think so. Start walking, or I'll change my mind about cleaning up my kitchen."

Jason was directly behind him, which was exactly where he wanted him.

There'd only be one chance to get this right.

He whispered a few words to his dead wife. She ought to know if he would see her in a moment.

Without another pause, he lunged for the knife block. The butcher knife slid out of the block without resistance, and he was able to cover most of the movement with his upper body shifting toward the fridge as Jason was directly behind him.

A quick spin on his heels brought him around to face the tip of the gun's silencer pointed at the tip of his nose.

In the end, it was the knife that saved his life. Jason's eyes were drawn downward to see what Ed had in his hand. When his eyes registered the large knife, and he applied pressure to the trigger, Ed was moving away from the gun's aim and lunging into Jason.

The gun spat out a bullet beside his ear as the tip of the knife entered Jason's skin at the stomach area, a millimeter over the edge of his jeans.

In his anger, Ed thrust so hard he buried the knife to the hilt, and still he pushed on it. Jason's face contorted in rage and surprise as Ed shoved him into the island, dislodging the gun from his grasp. It clattered to the floor at the same moment Ed yanked the knife free and jabbed at Jason again.

The man dropped to the ground beside the island, blood spurting from the wound, a grunt escaping him. Ed was on top of him, jabbing with the blade, slashing and stabbing where he could.

In his wild flailing to get Ed off him, Jason smacked Ed's injured wrist, causing a new flare-up of pain.

Ed screamed and dropped on top of Jason, the butcher knife forgotten for a moment as the pain blurred his vision. He breathed in and out as fast as he could to avoid passing out. The pain was so intense he didn't know how he'd drive himself out of there.

Ed rolled onto the kitchen floor a moment later as Jason crawled out from under him. It was the clang of the butcher knife that snapped him out of his pain-filled hypnosis.

In a final attempt to stop Jason's flight from this fight, Ed snatched up the knife and dove sideways at him.

The blade cut into the back of Jason's ankle, slicing deep. The man shouted an inhuman cry and dropped to the floor beside the opening of the hallway.

It was over.

Jason was bleeding out through the fingers of the hand

that covered the wound in his abdomen.

"Call an ambulance," Jason managed to say.

"Fuck you," Ed seethed.

He'd let this one get way out of hand. That would never happen again. In the future, he would plan and execute his *Death Wish* attacks better.

He had no idea where he found the strength to push himself to his knees. Then he could get to his feet, where he paused, leaning against the island. He needed a moment to collect his breath. After that, the real work would start.

He had time, though. He'd be okay if the packages were delivered before the sun rose. That gave him two solid hours in Jason's house, and he only needed one hour at best.

After the packages were delivered, he would go to the hospital and get his arm X-rayed. After that, he'd go home, sleep, and get back up to watch the news.

"Ambulance," Jason grunted. "Hurry. I haven't got much time."

Ed watched the man bleeding out. "You killed your parents. Now you'll join them."

"Fuck you. What are you a jury now, too?"

Ed moved to the knife block and chose the serrated one. It would cut through bone better.

"What are …" Jason swallowed audibly, cutting himself off. "What are you doing?"

"I need something from you."

"You're insane."

Ed moved to stand over Jason, his swelling arm held protectively at his stomach. "I would agree. Driven there a while ago by someone like you."

"Just call an ambulance, and I'll admit I killed my parents. I'll tell them I killed that guy in the garage, too. You'll go free."

Ed shook his head. "Doesn't happen that way. I'm writing this story, not you."

He lowered to his knees and rested his back against a cupboard.

"What are you waiting for?" Jason asked.

"For you to bleed out. I'll give you fifteen more minutes, then help it along."

"Why? How could you do such a thing?"

"That's rich coming from you."

"Then do it now while I'm alive."

Ed shook his head. "Less blood when you're dead. Heart's not pumping."

"You're sick."

"I'm cleaning up the trash that the system left behind. That's all."

"Fuck you."

"Have it your way. I won't wait." Ed pushed up off the cupboard. "I'll help you along now."

He applied the blade to the top of Jason's foot and started slicing.

Jason Grant screamed for the last few minutes of his life.

Chapter 6

Parkman found a spot on Queen Street two blocks from Aaron's dojo and parallel parked perfectly on his first try. It was a hot and humid morning for late summer, the sky cloudless.

After exiting his car, he locked it and stopped, staring down the street at the Starbucks. He needed a coffee, but not until after he saw the guys to see who else wanted one. They'd called him an hour ago, asking if he'd join them at the dojo. Benjamin said it wasn't an emergency but that they needed to see him as if it was an emergency.

"What does that mean?" he'd asked.

"It means come quickly," Benjamin replied. "Stop what you're doing and meet us at the dojo. But it's not an emergency like someone's dying."

"That doesn't make much sense, but I'll be there as soon

as possible. Give me a half hour at least."

He had been getting ready to go out for a coffee and instead just drove to the dojo on Queen Street.

He wished he'd brought more toothpicks as he approached the dojo's front door. He pulled the handle, but the door was locked. He tugged once more, then checked the time on his phone.

It was slightly after nine in the morning. They were always unlocked by this time, as certain classes started at seven.

Parkman cupped his hands on the window. A flash of movement caught his eye. It looked like Benjamin was near the back of the Shotokan dojo. Parkman knocked, and Benjamin spun around to stare in his direction, then he came running.

Once he'd opened the door, Parkman asked, "What's going on? What's the big emergency?"

"You don't want to know."

Benjamin relocked the door and stared out at the busy street as if looking for something.

"What's that supposed to mean? I *do* want to know. I came as quick as I could, without coffee yet."

Benjamin turned to him, grimaced, and then touched his arm. "Follow me. Coffee later."

Benjamin led the way toward the back, then into the rear office/kitchen combination. Sitting at their lunch table was Alex and Daniel.

"Guys," Parkman said as a greeting, then nodded.

They nodded back at him.

Four boxes were spread out on the table in front of them.

Parkman edged closer and saw that all four boxes had been opened, and it seemed like they were emitting an unpleasant smell.

"What's this?" he asked. "These boxes have your Amazon orders in them, or what? Did everyone order the same pair of shoes or something?"

All three of them exchanged uncomfortable looks.

"Have you heard from Aaron?" Daniel asked.

Parkman glanced at Alex, then turned to Benjamin. "Tell me what you know." His tone had gone deadly serious now.

"When was the last time you heard from Aaron?" Daniel asked.

"It's been a few days, perhaps more. I've been giving him his space. Why? What's happened?"

A moment of silence had Parkman leaning back against the wall, crossing his arms on his chest. They'd tell him what they had to say when they were ready.

"When Alex and I unlocked the dojo this morning, these four boxes were already here," Benjamin said. "They were sitting outside our door. Two boxes at the front and two at our back door."

"And?" Parkman studied their faces. "What's in the boxes?"

Alex gestured at one, motioning for Parkman to take a look.

The expression on Daniel's face convinced him he wouldn't like what he saw when he lifted the flap.

His suspicions were correct.

Inside the first box was what looked like a man's right hand, the wrist savagely cut through.

Parkman let the flap go and stepped back as the smell intensified the closer he got.

A scary thought came to him. "I'm assuming the other boxes contain body parts, too?"

Daniel nodded.

"And you guys suspect it's Aaron's appendages?"

Alex shook his head, but Benjamin answered. "No, we know Aaron's hands and feet." He pointed at the two boxes on the right. "We've all sparred with him enough to know."

"Who would ship you guys body parts, then?"

Daniel got up from the table. "That's what we don't know." He piled the boxes, one upon the other. Several were stained dark in areas where blood had smeared the sides. "They weren't shipped, though. They were delivered, dropped off." Daniel waved a hand over the boxes, pointing at Benjamin and Alex. "When they called me, we canceled our classes for the day. We have no idea who these things belong to, and we have no idea where Aaron is. None of this makes any sense. So, we called you to see if you could talk to Sarah, see if she knows anything."

"How do you guys feel about calling the authorities, letting their people take this over?"

They glanced at each other, then Alex shook his head.

Parkman shrugged. "No one did anything wrong here. I know the cops have been unfair to us in the past, but you guys legitimately found these when you came to work. How can that play out badly for us?"

"Okay, deal," Daniel said. "You're right. We'll call the authorities on this. But not until we speak with Sarah and Aaron. They may know something. If they're involved somehow, we don't want to jeopardize that. Are we all agreed?"

Benjamin nodded, along with Parkman. Then, after a few moments, Alex nodded.

"Okay, I'll call Sarah," Parkman said. "You guys try to contact Aaron."

He pulled out his phone and strode to the sparring mats to pace back and forth. Sarah's phone rang and rang. When it clicked to voicemail, he remembered the time difference. Santa Rosa was three hours earlier. It was barely hitting seven in the morning over there. She was probably still asleep.

After canceling the call without leaving a message, he dialed Darwin in Italy using WhatsApp. Darwin picked up on the second ring.

"Parkman here."

"Is everyone safe?" Darwin asked. "You okay?"

"Not sure."

"What's that mean?"

"Aaron's missing."

"Missing?"

"Well, technically, yes. None of us have heard from him in a couple of days. The guys are trying to find him now."

"I'll see what I can do from this end."

"Thanks. There's something else, though."

"Tell me."

"The dojo got a strange delivery today."

"What was it?"

"Hands and feet."

There was a pause. Parkman hesitated on how to explain

it fully.

"Human?" Darwin asked.

"Hacked off within the last twelve to twenty-four hours."

"Any idea whose?"

"They weren't Aaron's."

Over the line, Parkman heard the exhalation Darwin had been holding after his question.

"A student of the dojo? Someone who kicked and punched there? Hurt the wrong guy, so they delivered his *weapons* back to the people that created them?"

"Shit, never thought of that."

"Police involved?"

"Not yet."

"Are you guys thinking about that? What's next?"

"Find Aaron. Talk to Sarah. Then, meet and discuss it again. Probably give the packages to forensics for testing after that unless Sarah knows something."

"Is she still in California?"

Parkman moved toward the back of the dojo as Benjamin lumbered past him toward the front, his cell phone pasted to his ear.

"Yeah, staying with her parents."

"Okay, I'll look into things over here, see if the cops found a body missing hands and feet. I'll get back to you. Keep me in the loop."

"Will do."

Parkman clicked off and thought about calling Sarah back when someone banged on the front windows.

Benjamin jumped so violently that he dropped his phone and scrambled on the floor to collect it.

Parkman lurched to stand beside the lunchroom door, waving the other guys back.

Four uniformed officers were cupping their hands on the glass, waving for Benjamin to open the door.

"Cops are here." Parkman moved into the lunch room, his eyes meeting Daniel's. "I don't think they saw me. Where's Alex?"

"He's out back on his phone trying to reach Aaron."

Daniel moved around the table and started for the door.

Parkman grabbed his arm, stopping him as harsh voices emanated from the front of the dojo.

"What are you doing?" Parkman snapped.

"Going to sort this out." Daniel jerked his arm free. "We've done nothing wrong."

"They won't see it that way." He jerked his head toward the front.

"Hey," Benjamin shouted. "You guys can't just—" He was cut off by a thumping sound.

Daniel stepped out of the lunchroom, and Parkman snuck a glance around the door's edge.

Three officers had Benjamin subdued on the mats while two other cops were striding toward the back.

"Get out of here," Daniel whispered over his shoulder. "Get to Sarah. Find out what this is about. Find Aaron. Now go. I'll stall these guys." Daniel moved away, his hands up. "I'm hoping you guys have some sort of warrant," he shouted at the approaching officers.

Parkman moved toward the door at the rear of the dojo, expecting officers to be positioned back there already. It sat slightly open, probably due to Alex being outside on his phone.

Daniel's voice filtered back to him. He shouted something about his rights. Another man's voice asked for help. Daniel was resisting, which would add to his charges and would probably get him pepper sprayed, too. But it offered Parkman a chance to get out and get to Sarah. If the situations were reversed, Parkman knew he'd do everything he could to ensure Daniel got away.

With a hand over his gut to calm his nerves, he wondered how this shit kept happening to them all. Just recently, they'd shut down a batch of ex-military assassins with heavy hardware, and before that, Sarah was in Texas. Now Aaron was missing, Daniel and Benjamin were being detained, and someone's appendages were in boxes on their lunchroom table.

They couldn't catch a break.

He eased the door open, expecting to be jumped by waiting cops, but nothing happened. After one final push, he hopped out and stopped as he saw three uniformed cops lying in a small heap beside the dumpster.

"What the fuck …"

After a quick inspection, he saw all three were breathing but knocked out cold. They could wake at any time, and he didn't want to be there when they did.

Parkman strode away from the building, turned the corner, and started up a side street. Alex was gone. He must've dropped those three cops, piled them up, and then disappeared. And now Parkman was far enough away that they couldn't place him at the dojo. Maybe there was the off chance one of the officers was at the front window early enough to see him, but he didn't think so.

A cruiser raced by, its siren off, lights flashing. A moment later, another screamed by, screeching its tires as it took the corner onto Queen Street.

The guys had done nothing wrong. This had to be about those hands and feet. Someone dropped them off and then called in an anonymous tip. And now Alex was gone, Aaron was gone, and Sarah was out of the country.

Someone was coming after them all while they were weak and divided.

An unknown enemy, a mysterious delivery.

As he approached his car, he thought about walking over to the Starbucks nonchalantly like he didn't have a care in the world, then decided against it. Whoever was coming after them could be watching. It was better if Parkman left the area and grabbed a coffee elsewhere, then got started on reaching out to Sarah and finding Aaron. Maybe she knew where he was.

He dropped into his car and checked the mirror.

No one had followed him—at least no one in uniform.

The second he pushed the button to start the engine, someone sat up in the back seat.

Parkman shouted and spun around. "Motherfucker, you restarted my heart."

"When you drive away," Alex said, "turn on the air. It got hot waiting for you."

"Yeah, sure. Fuck." Parkman turned back in his seat and got the car moving. "What did you do to those cops?"

"Put them to sleep. None of them saw my face."

"How?" He glanced in the mirror.

Alex just stared back at Parkman's eyes in the mirror.

"You want a coffee?" he asked, his heart still racing from being startled to shit.

"Yeah. But drive for twenty minutes first to ensure we don't have a tail. Find a Starbucks in Etobicoke or Mississauga."

"I know one."

"I'll watch the back." Alex turned in his seat.

After a moment, as Parkman got them onto the Gardiner Expressway heading west, he asked, "Any idea where Aaron might be?"

He waited a full minute before Alex responded.

"He's hurting. Bad."

"A location would help."

They got on the highway and left Benjamin and Daniel behind. Charges would start to pile up, especially after what the officers find in their lunchroom. There was a chance a warrant would be issued for Alex, too. Those three cops in the back would probably be awake now, and they would at least know someone associated with the dojo did that to them.

Would an arrest warrant be issued for Aaron, too, even though he'd been gone for a few days and nowhere near the dojo? What about Parkman?

"I think Aaron isn't even in the country," Alex said.

"What? Really? Where would he have gone? And why wouldn't he tell anyone?"

Alex thought out his answers because he usually took half a minute to answer.

"He's hurting bad. I'm not sure why there was a lack of

communication, but there's a reason. We're brothers, family."

"Then where did he go?"

"After Sarah is my guess."

Chapter 7

Sarah woke with the sun streaming through her window and was up and ready to go by eight, even with a nasty headache from that sweet Crown Royal the night before.

After thinking about everything that was going on before falling asleep last night, she made a few rash decisions. It was time to head back to Toronto. Her stay in Santa Rosa had been cut short. After just a few days here, too much attention was on her parents—attention she didn't want to be responsible for.

She packed her rental car and came back inside the house. Her mother was up and pouring a coffee. Sarah entered the kitchen and stopped.

"Leaving already?" Amelia asked.

"If I'm to take time away, it can't be here. It needs to be at an anonymous location."

Amelia faced her, blew on her coffee, then sipped it. "I totally understand. Are you waiting until your father wakes?"

Sarah pursed her lips, then shook her head. "I bought a flight out of San Francisco for the early afternoon. By the time I drive the hour, return the car, check-in, and get to my gate," she checked her phone, "I won't have much time to spare. And shit!"

"What?"

"I have it on silent, and I missed a call from Parkman. It's got to be almost noon in Toronto. I have to go. I'll call him on the highway."

"It's no problem, sweetie. You go. I'll tell your father." She sipped her coffee again. "Where are you flying?"

"I need to get back to Toronto." Sarah leaned against the counter, eager to get going. "How can I be certain you guys will be safe?"

"Nothing to worry about with us. The house has a good alarm system." She smiled, then set her cup down on the counter. "Give me a hug and go. Just promise you'll come back soon."

They embraced.

"I will," Sarah whispered. "Probably sooner than you know."

"Okay, little one, off you go."

Sarah pulled back from her mother, feeling twelve again —a life before she could hear her sister in her head. "You haven't called me *little one* in years."

"Sarah, you'll always be my little one." Amelia grabbed her cup from the counter. "Just wait. You'll know what I'm talking about when you have kids."

"I imagine so."

She started for the door.

"Sarah?"

Her step faltered, and she stopped.

"Why didn't you tell the whole truth to the cops last night?"

Sarah turned and met her mother's gaze, holding it a moment, thinking about what her mother could be referring to.

"You know," Amelia said, "with what happened in Subway."

"The guy who stole my cup?"

"Yeah. Sure, he claimed to recognize you, but he stole your drink and ran before anyone could catch him. He didn't look like a vagrant. And it's great that the clerk gave you a new drink, so we tipped the guy. But it's not embarrassing if an idiot bests you sometimes."

"Mom, I mentioned it, but I didn't tell them everything because I like to keep a lid on information to maintain a level of control over it. We did nothing wrong yesterday. Also, I'm not concerned if someone bests me. My reputation isn't something I actively try to protect. What other people think of me is none of my business. I never take anything personally because we're all just projections of another person's thoughts, life, and beliefs."

Her mother stared at her with fondness in her eyes for a moment. "I like that. Makes sense. One more thing. Are you sure that guy in Target wasn't Aaron?"

Sarah froze. "You saw him, too?"

Amelia nodded, then sipped her coffee. "Yeah, and he

was gone when I did a double take.”

“Same with me. I watched for him after that. Didn’t see him again. Could’ve sworn it was Aaron.”

“You think he would’ve followed you here?”

Sarah shook her head. “Why? If he wanted me in his life, I wouldn’t have left in the first place.”

“Men can be jerks, but once they realize they’ve made a mistake, they’ll go to the ends of the earth for their woman.”

It was Sarah’s turn to nod, emotion choking off her voice. She needed to call Parkman. She needed to leave. Her flight wouldn’t wait for her.

“Mom, if it were Aaron, he’d probably come here today. Just tell him I’ve gone back to Toronto. He’ll follow, and we can talk there. But I don’t think it was.”

“Okay, go, honey. I don’t want to make you miss your plane.”

They said their goodbyes while Sarah suppressed a few tears. She got in her rental car and left Santa Rosa without incident.

Impatient, she dialed Parkman first.

He answered on the second ring.

“Hello? Sarah?”

“Yes, it’s Sarah.”

“Where are you?” he asked.

“On my way to the airport.”

“You flying somewhere?”

“Yeah, I’m coming back to Toronto.”

“Something happened?”

“Long story. I’ll explain when I get there. You called me a while ago. Did you locate Aaron?” Her stomach twisted at having to ask that question. Like he was a lost dog, they were stapling posters to streetlights in the area.

"No, we haven't found him, but Benjamin and Daniel got arrested."

"Arrested?" Sarah shouted, gripping the wheel tighter. "What the fuck happened?"

"We received a strange delivery at the dojo this morning."

"Wait, what? A delivery?"

"Yeah, and you wouldn't believe what it was."

"Body parts would be my guess."

There was a pause on the other line. The noise from the car's speakers made it sound like Parkman was driving.

"How did you know? Vivian tell you?"

"No, I haven't heard from her in a while."

"Then how did you know?"

"I got a delivery last night and a visit from the cops after one in the morning."

"You what?" It was Parkman's turn to shout.

"Someone sent me a cock in a bowl of blood. I knocked the bowl over when a tarantula crawled out of the bottom of the box. Spilled the blood everywhere. My mom helped me clean it up."

"Why did the cops come?"

"I have no idea. Someone tipped them off somehow. They wanted to know where I was the day before. Like they knew everything and were waiting for me to slip up."

"What's everything?" Parkman asked.

"No idea. Tell me what happened there."

Parkman told her about the four boxes and how he and

Alex got out of there.

"Also, Alex thinks Aaron may have left the country. There's a possibility Aaron went to California."

Sarah thought about that for a moment. "When my mom and I were shopping yesterday, we both thought we saw him."

"If it was Aaron, why wouldn't he approach?"

"That's why I didn't think it was him."

They both drove in silence for a moment.

"Look, Parkman, I'm flying out this afternoon. With the three-hour time difference and the flight length, I won't get there until nighttime. I'll check into a hotel—"

"Alex and I can meet you at the airport."

"Won't the authorities be looking for you two, or at least Alex?"

"True."

"Once I'm checked in, just join me. We'll talk in the privacy of my hotel room."

"See you soon then."

She hung up and focused on her driving while thinking about the deliveries. How could the macabre deliveries occur on the same night at both places? Why was it happening, and who was behind it all?

And where the hell was Vivian? That had to be the most frustrating part. This could all be explained with a quick visit, so there had to be a reason Vivian was remaining silent. And as always, Sarah had to trust the process. It would all work out, and they would get to the bottom of it.

She dropped off the rental at the San Francisco International Airport, checked in for the flight, got through security, and then called Aaron's number. It rang several times, then went to voicemail yet again.

Where the hell is he?

The least he could do was answer her calls.

The phone in her hand rang as they announced the boarding would start for her flight.

She checked call display, thinking it was Aaron calling her back, but it was her mother. Shouldering her one bag, she got up from her seat and started toward the back of the line when she hit the answer button.

"Hey, Mom, let me put my earbuds in."

"Sarah, the officers returned."

She pushed the buds in and inserted the plug at the base of the phone.

"What was that?"

"The police have returned to speak with us. Are you almost finished at the grocery store?"

Grocery store? Why did her mother—

They were listening. And they wanted to talk to her in person. Her mother put them off long enough that Sarah could make her flight and land in Toronto without being arrested.

Sarah turned away from the crowd waiting to board the plane and moved ten feet to stand in a corner so no one could listen in. "Why did they come back?"

"Search warrant."

"For your house?" This wasn't good. Something was wrong. Terribly wrong. "Why?" Now she was getting pissed. Who was doing this to them? "Did they tell you why?"

"They want to speak with you—"

There was a shuffling on the phone, then a man's deep voice said, "Sarah? This is Officer Sherman. Where are you?"

"That search warrant you have had better be legit."

"Oh, it's legit, all right. Where are you?"

If the PA announced a flight, the cop would hear she was in an airport. She had to get off the phone.

"What's the issue?" she asked. "Why would you need a search warrant for my parents' house?"

"Come on home so we can talk about it, Sarah."

"I'm out and plan to be out until late tonight. Maybe some other time, Sherman."

"I can issue an arrest warrant if you want to play it that way."

The speaker overhead clicked. Sarah smacked the mute button on her cell phone just as a woman at a flight desk spoke about a last-minute gate change.

"Sarah," Sherman said, his voice taking on a dark tone. "We have found traces of blood in your mother's carpet. Recent blood. And if it matches the body we found last night at the Western Best Hotel across from the Subway you claim to have visited, we're going to have a lot more to talk about. Much better if you just come in on your own time."

The woman on the speaker system was now going on about the final boarding call for Sarah's flight. She needed to take it off mute but couldn't.

"Sarah?" Sherman said. "Are you still there?"

She checked the line. Less than ten people left, showing their passports and tickets. And still, the woman spoke on the system overhead.

"Sarah, if you don't answer me, I will hang up and send out a BOLO in your name. This isn't looking good for you."

Her mother asked what the problem was in the background. Officer Sherman said Sarah wasn't responding to him.

The speaker overhead clicked off.

Sarah jammed her thumb on the mute button.

"Sherman, whatever you think I've done, you're wrong."

"There you are. Tell me something, Sarah, are you on your way to Los Angeles?"

She frowned. "LA? Why?"

"We ran your plates. It was a rental car from the Los Angeles airport. We could contact them to assist in bringing you back."

"No, I am not heading to Los Angeles." At least she wasn't lying.

"Then where are you? Because we will need to discuss the blood we photographed on your clothes last night. And then there's the—"

"Sherman!" someone shouted in Officer Sherman's background.

"What? I'm on the phone."

"You have to see what we found," the other man said.

"Hold the line, Sarah."

The phone line clicked silent.

All the passengers boarding the flight had gone through. Sarah started that way, opening her passport, hands shaking. They wanted to charge her with a crime she hadn't committed. Now she knew why that large spider was added to the box. To startle her in the hopes she'd spill the blood, leaving traces for someone on Sherman's forensic team to examine.

Would she even be able to get out of the country? In the time the flight took to get to Toronto, would they have already alerted the authorities there?

Vivian, what the hell is this?

She got through the gate check and started along the elevated tunnel toward her flight. If Sherman didn't come back in minutes, she'd end the call, put her phone on airplane mode, and hope for the best when she landed.

"Sarah?" Officer Sherman said, coming back abruptly. His voice sounded slightly muffled, like the phone was against his mouth. "I'd seriously advise you to return to your mother's house as quickly as possible. It'll only get worse if we have to come after you."

"I'll reiterate, Sherman, I've done nothing wrong. So, I will return tonight as per my schedule." Okay, that was a lie. Bold-faced. "Besides, what did that other guy find?"

"The victim was missing a body part. We just found it discarded in your trash bin, along with a box that had smears of blood. Perhaps your prints are on that box? Sarah, help me understand this so it can all go away. Come on in and talk to us."

She was almost at the plane's door. She needed off the phone.

"I'll be in touch, Sherman."

She ended the call, flicked her cell phone to airplane mode, then powered down and stepped onto her flight.

What the fuck was going on? Benjamin and Daniel were arrested? Who was taking them out one by one?

She took her seat, put her head back, closed her eyes, and thought about her past. Who even knew where her parents lived?

Aaron was quite possibly in California. Could he have lost his mind and was coming after them?

No way. She wouldn't believe that, couldn't believe it.

Not after all they'd been through.

But if he wanted her to stop listening to her sister and stop being the psychic vigilante, this would definitely stop her.

She'd be in a jail cell for quite some time if they laid that Western Best murder on her.

What could she do then?

She feared whatever was going on was just getting started, and she was already running out of time.

Chapter 8

THE BONE WAS BRUISED. That was it. No broken wrist, no cracked bones. Just a nasty bruise that ached to the touch.

The doctor told Edward Sweeney that over-the-counter pain relievers would work just fine, so he wouldn't prescribe Tylenol 3s.

When he returned to his car, he connected his phone to it, dialed out, and started driving. With one injured hand, he'd be challenged to think ahead for such small tasks.

"Hello?" Steve answered quickly.

"What's happening down there?" Ed asked.

"Everything is going great. It all worked like a charm."

A car horn sounded in the background.

"Where are you?"

"Having a coffee at a café across the street from the police station. My contact here just updated me, then went

"

back to work."

"What's the update? Also, were you able to leave evidence in the hotel room?"

"Yes, Sarah's prints were on a cup I nabbed from her at a sub shop. The crazy thing was, she hit the Subway right across the fuckin' street from the hotel. What are the odds? The cops found it in the hotel room. And that spider worked, too. I just found out they're preparing an arrest warrant for Sarah as we speak."

"That's great news. I needed to hear that."

"Want more good news?"

"Sure. Hit me."

"They obtained a search warrant this morning and found our victim's thing at her parents' house. Plus, there was evidence of newly spilled blood on the front carpet area. They've got everything to make a solid case against Sarah being the one who killed Malcolm King in that hotel room."

"You sealed it up great."

"How about at your end?"

"Jason Grant is gone. His parts were delivered to the dojo, and I called it in when I saw the boys arriving. Haven't checked back yet to see what the result is. I had something to attend to first."

"How's Dale handling all this?"

Ed slowed at a traffic light and wondered how to tell Steve that Dale was dead. If this continued to work, he'd have to just tell him. Steve needed to trust his brother.

"Jason killed Dale. He got sloppy and paid the price."

"What?" Steve gasped on the phone, his voice taking on a panic Ed hadn't heard before. "That wasn't supposed to happen."

"Take it easy. Accidents happen, and with what we're doing, you can't afford to get sloppy."

Steve sniffled on the phone as Ed pulled away from the light. He decided to let it go. Dale and Steve went back about a decade. He knew it would bother Steve, but there was no way around it. Dale was a pussy. He didn't jump out of the bushes last night, and because of Dale, they both almost bit the bullet, so to speak.

"Look, Jason's gone, the house burned, with Dale in it, so it looks like Jason's place got broken into. After a fight broke out, a fire started, killing both of them. When the delivery happened this morning, along with the business card for Aaron's dojo found inside Jason's car and those boys' reputation for being vigilantes, this'll go down smooth and clean. They're all done for."

"And if the dojo boys and Sarah Roberts get off for some reason, then what?" Steve's voice faltered with emotion.

An urge to shout at Steve to grow up and get over it consumed Ed, but he let it go. He'd give Steve a pass this one time.

In ten minutes, he'd be home and crawling into bed. It had been a long night, and perhaps his nerves were frayed.

"If any one of them get off for any reason, then we'll handle them our way. Courts first, then us. It's the *Death Wish* deal."

"Okay, I'm in the hotel one more night, then I'm heading back. I'll meet up with you when you're finished work tomorrow."

"Meet me at our usual spot."

Steve sniffled again. "I'll be there. At the usual spot. I'll text a time when I land."

The line died.

At the next light, Ed dialed one more number.

"Toronto Courthouse, Miriam Sweeney speaking, how can I direct your call?"

"Hey, Miriam. Busy today?"

"Not so bad today. The usual. What can I do for you?"

"I've heard there were some arrests on Queen Street this morning."

"How did you hear that so fast? They just brought them in."

"I have my sources."

"Isn't it your day off?" Miriam asked.

"Yeah, but a friend called to tell me because of my interest in those vigilante boys at Aaron's dojo."

"Well, whoever your source is has solid info. Two of the teachers were arrested this morning. They're here being held for questioning as we speak."

"Two of the teachers?" He sat up straighter, knocking his sore arm on the bottom of the steering wheel. He winced with the pain. "I thought there were four of them."

"No, only two. Why? Did you hear more were arrested?"

"I thought my guy said four were arrested."

"Here, let me check." He heard his sister typing at the keyboard, even through the car speakers. He tapped his fingers on the steering wheel to her rhythm. How come they only got two? He'd seen three of them show up that morning. Then Parkman was let in the front door. He'd made the anonymous call, then went to the doctor's office afterward.

"Ed, it says here a man named Benjamin and a man named Daniel were arrested at the dojo. They're here now. A warrant has been issued for Alex and Aaron." She clicked something else. "Looks like that's it."

"Okay, my guy must've thought the other two were also arrested." What the hell happened that they didn't get the other two? How could Alex and Parkman escape? And where was Aaron? He knew all of them from photos and didn't see Aaron there, so where was he? Parkman and Alex had to have left before the cops arrived.

"It was a nasty bust, too," Miriam went on. "Several officers in court this morning were discussing it."

"Really? What happened?" Ed pulled into the parking lot of his building, slowed to the curbside, and stopped.

"They needed several guys to subdue each of the arrested men, and three officers were found unconscious at the back of the building. Apparently, all three claim they have no idea what hit them. Like some ghost whirled around them, and it was lights out."

Probably Alex's work. He cleared a path for him and Parkman to escape while Daniel and Benjamin kept the officers busy inside the dojo.

"Shit, that does sound dangerous. These guys are good. That's why I've always appreciated their work. Ever since Jessica and Lisa were killed, these guys were someone to watch."

"Are you okay?" Miriam's voice always softened when Ed brought up the senseless murder of his wife and daughter a few years ago.

"Yes, I'm fine. Just always wondering if those boys,

along with that girl, Sarah something, would ever find Jess's killer." He knew Sarah's name quite well. Steve's idea was to follow her to Los Angeles and then to her parents' home in Santa Rosa. Luckily for Steve, his friend at the courthouse knew about a convicted rapist being released the day Sarah arrived. There is not enough evidence to hold him on the new sexual assault charge. So Steve told Ed he'd handle it, and everything went well. Malcolm King was dead, and the cops thought Sarah had something to do with it.

It was Ed's handling of Jason Grant that got fucked up. They'd lost their friend Dale, and only two of the four dojo boys were arrested.

"Look, Miriam, I'm home now. It's my day off. I'm heading upstairs to take a nap. I'll see you tomorrow at work."

"You sound tired. We'll talk soon."

"You got it—"

"Oh wait, Ed? You still there?"

He pulled his thumb away from ending the call. "Yeah, I'm here."

"Did you hear about Jason Grant?"

"What happened to that scumbag now? Did he kill someone else?"

"He was found dead in his burned-down house. Looks like someone did to him what he was suspected of doing to his parents."

"The guy probably killed his parents and deserved what he got. Look, I should go. I'm tired and irritable."

"Okay, see you tomorrow."

Ed clicked off.

"Where are you, Aaron, Alex, and Parkman?" Ed whispered to himself.

At least the cops were looking for Aaron and Alex. That would make things easy. And Sarah was about to be picked up in Santa Rosa. Probably within six to twelve hours, his plans would be concluding.

Then, he could start to hunt for Alistair McNeil.

That man had no criminal record and would never serve a day in prison because he was filthy rich.

But after what he did to those prostitutes, it was unforgivable.

And yet, he walked. Right out of the courtroom, right in front of Edward Sweeney, and there was nothing he could do about it.

Yet, there was something he could do about it after all.

The man was going to have an unfortunate car accident soon.

Something no one would ever tie to Edward Sweeney, a courtroom security guard at the Toronto Courthouse.

If Alistair survived, he'd be as fucked up as the women he had beaten.

However, Ed planned on Alistair not surviving.

After all, it was Alistair's *Death Wish*.

Chapter 9

AARON STEVENS CLICKED OFF his phone's voice memo app and glanced down to quickly label it with a title.

The guy beside him wasn't going anywhere in the next minute. His coffee had just arrived when his phone rang.

Aaron hadn't caught the guy's name, but he heard enough to know what he had done after following Sarah and her mother yesterday.

Enough was enough. This had to stop.

Aaron had briefly contemplated taking the recording to the authorities so they'd leave Sarah alone, but he knew it would be better to take the man with him.

However, none of that mattered if someone did the same thing to his family and team in Toronto. He'd have to make sure to get the Toronto contact as well.

Whoever these people were, today was the end of it.

Aaron slipped his phone away and waited. The man's work in Santa Rosa was finished. Aaron wouldn't be following him anymore. But if Aaron wanted to land in Canada without a team of police officers waiting for him, he needed to have a personal chat with the man sitting two feet away.

His injuries still ached, but his face was healing. He'd made it to the point where he could get through a day without pain meds. Even his vision had recovered to the point where he felt comfortable driving. That guy named Hamilton had done a number on him. Aaron hadn't been that beat up in a long time, if ever.

The man beside him drank the last of his coffee and then began collecting his things to leave. He slipped his phone in his pocket, grabbed his car keys off the table, and stood to drop a few bills beside the empty cup.

Aaron watched all of this from the corner of his eye while replaying the line the man said that stuck with him.

And what if the dojo boys and Sarah Roberts get off for some reason?

The *dojo boys*? And *Sarah*?

They'd set them up for something. That much was for sure, but Aaron couldn't call any of them. He only knew Sarah's number, and when he tried it this morning, she didn't answer. Although, he didn't want their first conversation after their last fight to be on the phone. That was why he flew here —to meet her and apologize. He came in person to make it right, like a real man should. And when he drove up to park a block from Amelia and Caleb's house, he'd seen this guy staring at it, watching it.

Curiosity made Aaron sit still for a few minutes to observe the guy. Then it turned into a half hour. And when Sarah and her mother exited the house, the guy walking away from the table followed them. So Aaron followed him. To Target, Costco, and Subway, where he saw this man running out a minute after entering, a drink cup in his hand.

Maybe Sarah confronted him. Maybe they fought.

Didn't matter. Once he saw the guy race off, Aaron was so tired and in too much pain that he decided to get a room and sleep. He'd call Sarah in the morning and go see her.

And now Aaron was following the guy again. Down the street, around a corner, staying close enough to grab him if he got near a car, all the while looking in store windows, appearing to be nonchalant. There was no way the guy could know he had a tail. The man said he would be at the hotel one more night, then meet whoever he was talking to tomorrow night after flying back. But where? Toronto? And where would they meet?

Aaron had questions he needed answers to.

The tall Faraway Hotel building was a block away. The guy had to be heading in that direction.

Aaron eased back but kept an eye on him. Only once did the man turn around to check behind him. When Aaron caught a glimpse of a police cruiser, he figured the guy was just watching his back. He was definitely paranoid, feeling guilty about something.

His suspicions were correct. The man turned into the hotel's parking lot and started toward the front lobby doors. Once inside, Aaron would lose him. Trying to find his room number would be impossible. The hotel had to be fifteen stories high.

He picked up his pace and pulled out his wallet. From within the wallet, he retrieved his library card. It was the only one that looked almost like a key card for a hotel room door.

The man slipped inside the revolving doors of the lobby.

Aaron picked up his pace and entered the doors seconds later.

Perfect timing.

The man was just about to step onto an elevator. Aaron ran for it. The doors began to shut. He gave one hard push, slid along the tile floor, and pressed the elevator button. The doors stopped an inch apart and started to open again.

"Whew, that was close," he said as he jumped on.

He made to press a floor button, but the fourteenth floor was already lit up. He eased back into the corner and tapped on his phone without looking at the man. When the elevator slowed, Aaron slipped his phone away and gripped his library card in a way that allowed a small corner to be exposed.

The doors started to open.

"Do I know you?" the man asked.

Aaron frowned, a small pain flaring on his cheek. The swelling had calmed, but there was still a deformity to his cheek due to the broken orbital bone. Even his hair was askew, having had little time to worry about such things that morning.

"Doubt it," Aaron said in a gruff voice.

The man stepped off first. Aaron waited a heartbeat, then followed him, keeping a few feet back.

When the man stopped at his hotel room door, Aaron slipped past him slowly, waiting to hear the sound of the door opening. With each step, he worried he was moving too far away to stop the door from closing.

But there was no clicking sound, no key card used, no door opening.

He stopped walking away and then turned around.

The man had a gun in his hand aimed at Aaron's stomach.

"Aaron Stevens," he said. "I knew it was you."

Chapter 10

Sarah woke with a start as the plane's wheels touched down. She hadn't slept well last night and ended up sleeping almost the entire trip back to Toronto.

When she turned off airplane mode and checked her phone, Parkman had left a message that they were waiting for her outside the Welcoming Inn on Airport Road. They'd be sitting in Parkman's car.

Sarah deplaned, and once she'd cleared customs, she headed for the taxi stand with questions rolling around in her head. When would everything calm down? When would life give her a break? It was one thing to listen to Vivian and perform small tasks that led to a bigger evil, but when someone was coming at them from all sides without any idea who, it got annoying fast—especially without Vivian's help.

Once in the taxi, she dialed Aaron's cell and wasn't

surprised it went to voicemail.

It was almost ten in the evening in Toronto, and she felt like she'd lost an entire day.

At the front entrance to the Welcoming Inn, she paid her driver, scanned the parking lot, then stepped inside and booked a room. Luckily, they had some left as she hadn't reserved one.

With key in hand, she went back outside and strolled through the parking lot, looking for Parkman's car. She reached the back area before she heard him call her name.

She spun around and saw Parkman waving at her from four cars away.

At his window, she leaned down. "Where's Alex?"

Parkman shrugged. "Said he wanted to stretch his legs. He's somewhere around here. Probably watching us right now."

"It's so good to see you," she said, squeezing his arm affectionately. "I don't like being so far away from everyone when something like this happens, and Vivian is silent. A part of me understands why Aaron wanted out. When Vivian is like this, I want out, too. She started all this, and now we're in the thick of it, and she's disappeared."

"Which reminds me, have you heard from Aaron?"

She shook her head, staring across the parking lot, knowing Parkman hadn't either, or he wouldn't have asked. Where was Aaron, and what could he possibly be up to? Was his disappearance tied to what was happening?

"Have you been able to find out more about Daniel and Benjamin?"

Parkman opened his door and got out, then walked

around to the passenger seat and grabbed a bag.

"All we know is they're being held as suspects."

"Suspects for what?"

He closed and locked the car door. "Sarah, I'm not sure how to tell you this."

"Parkman, when have we ever had a preamble? You don't need to qualify it. Just tell me."

"Two men were murdered north of Toronto last night. One of the men had his hands and feet hacked off—"

"And those were the body parts delivered to the dojo?" she interrupted.

Parkman nodded as he stepped closer. "The house where it happened was burned down, although it didn't burn all the way. The fire department got there fast enough to save most of it. They suspect it was arson with the intent to cover up the murders. The problem for us is, they found evidence Aaron was there."

"Aaron?" Sarah blurted. "How?"

"The media announced the murders and house fire on the six o'clock news. Then they posted a picture of Aaron saying the authorities were looking for him as a suspect in the murder."

Sarah's stomach clenched as anxiety acid filled her gut. They needed a break, and now Aaron's face was all over the news.

Movement to her right caught her eye. She spun sideways to see Alex standing three feet away.

"If Aaron's involved in any way," Alex said, "it was a justified kill."

"Justified?" Sarah asked.

Parkman nodded. "I called in a favor from a friend on the force. The man who was killed and had his body hacked up was Jason Grant, suspected in the murder of his own parents. Their house burned down, too. The other guy was Dale something. A small-time cat burglar who was serving time until recently in a minimum security facility."

"What's in the bag?" Sarah asked, her head spinning with the trouble they were all in.

"Dinner. Have you eaten?"

She shook her head. "Slept on the plane, landed, and came right here." She nodded toward the hotel. "Let's go up to the room and talk in private."

At the side door, she used her access card. Once in the elevator, she studied their faces. Parkman always looked like Parkman, with maybe a few new stress lines by his eyes. But Alex seemed genuinely scared. Everyone he was close to was in trouble—his brothers, his men, his life. The cops were holding Benjamin and Daniel, and Aaron's face was all over the news as a suspect in a murder. This was usually something Sarah dealt with. Her heart went out to them all, and at that moment, staring into Alex's saddened eyes, she knew she had to make things right. However that looked, whatever that meant.

Minutes later, in her hotel room, while Parkman set sandwiches and a store-bought potato salad on the small coffee table, she used the bathroom, rubbing water on her face.

And like always, when Vivian showed up, it was sudden. As if she'd always been there but so silent Sarah couldn't detect her. Then, when she spoke, chills went down Sarah's arms.

She gave Sarah a name and a place to be tomorrow and told her what to do without much explanation. Then she told her Aaron would call and how to handle that.

Seconds later, Vivian whisked away like smoke blown by gale-force winds. There one moment, visible, then gone the next.

"Why the hell am I supposed to go to court tomorrow?" Sarah asked the mirror. "And get taken by security? And why hadn't Aaron called before this?"

Sometimes, Vivian said the most ridiculous things, and it felt like Sarah was supposed to understand it all, but she didn't.

"How will all that help, Vivian? Huh? Tell me?"

But her sister was gone.

Sarah had her marching orders—and nothing made any sense.

Chapter 11

"Are you going to shoot me in the hallway?" Aaron asked. "Or should we find somewhere less public?"

"A funny guy, eh?"

Aaron raised his hands to waist height. "What's next?"

"In my room for a little talk."

"Is that all you want to do in your room? Just talk? Because, you know, if you have other ideas, I think I'll just leave now."

"Fuck you and shut up." The man slipped his key card into the door and then opened it. "Inside." He motioned with the gun.

Aaron moved past him slowly, contemplating an offensive maneuver, but then did nothing.

Behind him, the lock clicked into place.

They were alone in the man's room now.

"So, what do I call you?" Aaron asked, turning around to face him.

"You don't call me anything." The man gestured with the gun again. "Sit on the floor, your back to the wall."

Aaron did as he was told, but slowly, avoiding any sudden moves.

"How long have you been following me?" the man asked.

"Can't remember." Aaron crossed his arms and debated his options. He needed the man's phone, and it was probably protected with a password. Also, he needed to know who he called at the café and how deep this went. There were so many unanswered questions.

"Yeah, sure, you can't remember." The man spun the chair around by the desk to face Aaron, then he sat, resting his gun arm on his thigh. "Why aren't you in Toronto?"

"Personal reasons."

The gun clicked. Aaron blinked.

"That personal enough for you?"

"Sure, fire that thing in here and wake up the entire floor. Then try to explain away the dead body in your room."

"Easy, asshole. You barged in here with the gun. I overpowered you. It went off. End of story. Lucky I survived." The man cleared his throat and ran a hand through his unruly hair. "Now, start giving me some answers."

What kind of man was Aaron dealing with? Several tattoos were visible under his sleeve when his hand rose over his head to comb back his hair. With no psychic ability and nothing to base it on, could they be prison tattoos?

"I went to visit Sarah yesterday," Aaron started, feeling

that prolonging his explanation would give him time to think of a way out of this. "And I saw you parked out front of her parents' house, watching it."

"So you started following me then?"

Aaron nodded.

"You saw everything?"

"What's everything?"

"All of it."

Aaron frowned. "Probably not."

"Stop talking in circles."

"Then tell me what you and your friend in Toronto have done to Sarah and the *dojo boys*, as you put it."

The man offered Aaron a smug smile. "You know more than you should."

"I know that you've set us up somehow. But I don't know why or how exactly."

"Because you're all breaking the law and never paying for it."

"What?" That was not the answer Aaron expected.

"Doesn't matter now." The man changed gun hands. "Everything is set in motion. Nothing anyone can do to stop it. You, Sarah, your dojo boys, and that guy Parkman are all going down for a long time."

"Because we help people? Is that what you're saying?"

The man guffawed, his free hand coming up to cover his mouth.

Aaron measured the distance to his chair. If he pushed off the wall, rolled, and swung his leg hard, he could connect with the chair legs. It would take too long, though. In that amount of time, the man could shoot twice, maybe more.

"Help people. That's rich. You guys have killed people, and none of you have ever gone to a court of law for murder."

"Each one was justified in some way, or we would've been arrested."

"Yeah, right. How about we tell that to a judge?"

Aaron pushed off the wall. "Great, we'll go right now."

"Get back," the man shouted, thrusting the gun outward, his aim on Aaron's face.

"Okay, take it easy." Aaron raised his hands, averting his eyes. A test of the man's resolve and reflexes proved the guy was edgy. This situation needed to end quickly. Aaron had to find a way to get the gun out of the man's hand, which meant he needed to be closer and in a better position to maneuver than on the floor up against the wall.

"You don't know what to do with me, do you?" Aaron asked when he was back in position, staring at the man. "You don't want to fire that thing unless absolutely necessary, and you don't want to kill me. Otherwise, how would I face the consequences of everything you and your partner have set up?"

"I'll tell you what," the man said, rising from the chair. "You're right, so here's what we're going to do." He pushed the chair under the desk as far as it would go and faced Aaron.

His chance was coming. And when it did, he wouldn't hesitate.

"I will find a way to tie you up, but not too tight." The man grinned, the weapon hanging limply at his side. He was still far enough away that by the time Aaron moved, he could have it up and ready. "Then I'll leave, and we'll never see each other again."

"How's that good for you?" Aaron placed his hands on the carpeted hotel room floor in preparation to launch upward. "As soon as I'm free, I'll hunt you down."

The man shook his head. "Not with the murder charge you'll be facing."

Murder? So that was it. They'd framed them for murder. How could they have done that? Why wasn't Sarah dealing with this?

"The authorities in Santa Rosa are already scouring Sarah's parents' house for evidence of the murder of Malcolm King, a convicted rapist and serial sexual abuser. He was killed in the Western Best Motel yesterday, and Sarah's prints were found in his room."

"Her prints?" Aaron asked, shocked out of his thoughts about attacking the man. "How? I followed her yesterday. They may have turned around in the parking lot after lunch at the Subway, but that was it."

The man was gloating, so happy with himself. "And not only were her prints found in the room, but DNA evidence will also uncover Malcolm's blood in the parents' house, along with his abusive dick."

"You planted blood in her house?" Aaron asked, stupefied. How the hell did they do all that? Then he thought about the man running out of the Subway yesterday with a cup in his hand. "The cup from the sub shop," he whispered out loud.

"You're smarter than you look," the man said. "But it doesn't matter what you know or don't know. Cases are all won and lost in court on evidence, and we've got all the evidence pointing at Sarah for the murder of the rapist, Malcolm King."

"Then tell me about the dojo boys shit."

"I've told you enough already. Get on your feet. Time to tie you up. I want a good night's sleep and intend to get it."

"No, tell me what you guys—whoever you are—did to my friends in Toronto."

"Get up. You're all done for. It's over, your little reign of vigilantism."

"Tell me why, and I'll get up."

"You'll get to your feet because I've got the gun." The man cleared his throat. "But I'll tell you why. Have you ever seen the movie *Death Wish*?"

"Yeah, an oldie from the seventies. Charles Bronson, right?"

"Yes, not the new Bruce Willis one. Anyway, that's what this is about."

"Now I know you're playing with me."

"How's that?"

"Sarah and myself are practically Charles Bronson in that movie. We're the ones going after people and stopping them where the law doesn't."

"Not necessarily. You and your team of ragtag dickheads go off half-cocked all the time on people who don't deserve it."

"And who decides who doesn't deserve it?"

"How about we just go back to the days of crimes and law and order?"

"Deal. You pulled a gun on me. Set it down, and let me

take you to the local police station to explain what you've done."

"You still don't get it, and I'm wasting my time. Get up." He gestured with the gun again.

This would be his only chance.

Aaron slowly got to his feet. His back to the wall, he stared at the man from over five feet away. If he were holding a knife, this would be over in seconds.

"Turn around," the man said.

"No way. You want to shoot me? You do it looking into my eyes."

"I told you, I'm not going to shoot you. If I were going to do that, I'd grab a pillow off the bed and muffle the sound. I'm only going to tie you up, then leave. Now, turn around."

Aaron stared into the man's eyes a moment more, then turned around and presented his back to him. But when he did, he angled his head to the right just enough to watch the man behind him in the reflection from the glass door leading onto the fourteenth-floor balcony.

The man appeared to turn the gun around in his hand, so he was holding it butt out and moved to within striking distance.

That was his mistake.

The man raised his hand to club the back of Aaron's neck.

When his gun hand started the downward swing, Aaron leaned his upper body forward while driving his right foot backward. The man's swing missed completely, but Aaron's foot connected with the man's crotch with all the strength Aaron could muster.

A grunt of air escaped the man's lips as Aaron was already pivoting around, his fists up and jabbing at the man's face as he leaned toward him.

When a man is kicked in the groin, he always leans forward as the body folds upon itself, exposing the face to further danger, and Aaron took advantage of that. This was his one chance to put the man down, and he wouldn't let it slide.

The gun dropped and bounced to the left, directly under the bed, which Aaron was thankful for.

By the time he had hit the man with three jabs, he was already trying to defend himself. He stepped back to get away from the blows, but then Aaron slashed his right foot out and knocked the man off his feet with a roundhouse kick to the side of the head.

The man dropped to the floor hard.

Aaron pounced on him, landing hard on the man's gut, knocking the wind from him. He secured his arms and slid a leg down to hold the man's thighs to the carpeted floor.

Panting from the quick fight, Aaron leaned down and said, "Who are you working with?"

"Fuck you," the man grunted, his eyes squeezed shut with the pain.

"What have you done to my friends in Toronto?"

"They're all going to jail, and so are you. For murder."

Aaron couldn't and wouldn't stop his hand from lashing out in a quick jab. Blood spurted from the man's lips where they split.

"You're not in such a good position to spew any more bullshit." He grabbed the man's left wrist, twisted it backward, and then added pressure to a sensitive spot in the back of his hand. He squealed. "Tell me your name, and I'll ease off."

"Steve Cook," the man nearly shouted through clenched teeth. The pain made his face redden, and veins rose on his forehead and neck. "My name is Steve Cook."

Aaron released the pressure slightly. "Who are you working with?"

"Can't tell you that."

Aaron applied the pressure to Steve's hand again, but this time he added more.

Steve howled, which made Aaron clamp a hand over Steve's mouth. He couldn't afford to get a noise complaint.

"The name?" Aaron repeated as he released Steve's mouth and yanked his own cell phone out. Using deft fingers, he brought up the voice memo app and hit record, then tossed the phone on the bed. "Tell me who you're working with in Toronto, Steve Cook."

"Okay, okay, but let go of my wrist, man. You're breaking it."

"I'll let go when you've answered my questions. Who are you working with?"

"His name is Edward Sweeney."

"His idea or your idea?"

"It was all him. After Jessica and Lisa were murdered."

"Murdered?"

"They were killed. Rueben got off at the trial."

"Rueben?"

"Are you stupid?" Steve had broken out in a full sweat, his face glistening now.

Aaron added enough pressure to the man's wrist that his arm jammed into the floor in an attempt to dislodge Aaron, but this was a hold Aaron had perfected years ago in the dojo. Only someone like Alex could get out of it.

"Rueben was the man who killed them," Steve said rapidly. "But he was able to get off in court. Once Rueben went missing, Ed came to me with a plan. And here we are."

"Where are you meeting him tomorrow?"

Steve's eyes widened as he stared at Aaron. "How do you know about that?"

"You didn't see me sitting behind you at the café. Where are you meeting him?"

"We always meet in the parking area at Sunnyside Beach."

"I know that beach. Off of Lakeshore Boulevard. Where do you park?"

"As close to that Gus Ryder outdoor swimming pool as possible."

Without removing his grip, Aaron asked, "And you know each other's cars, right?"

Steve nodded three times.

"Sure, now last question, then I'll let go."

Steve nodded again.

"Is there a code to access your phone? And if so, what is it?"

"It's 7-8-7-9-8-0."

Aaron adjusted his fingers to ensure Steve's wrist was locked in place, then slapped at Steve's pockets until he came up with the man's cell phone.

Steve's lip had stopped bleeding. Other than a small

amount of swelling, Steve would look as good as new soon.

Aaron hit the button to access the phone and then typed in the code.

It worked.

"Holy shit, you didn't lie."

Something flashed from behind the phone.

Aaron's arm moved to cover his face, blocking whatever was coming. Steve's cell phone was lost from his grip. It sailed over his shoulder and landed beside Aaron's phone on the bed.

When something tugged on his arm, he saw that Steve had pulled a knife from somewhere, and it was lodged in Aaron's forearm.

The sound of his own voice coming out in a high pitch startled him as it sounded so far away like someone else was in the room. There was no pain yet, but that would come.

Without thinking, acting on reflex and instant anger, Aaron wrapped his free hand on Steve's wrist and hand, which was still bent backward at a painful angle, and then as Steve finally dislodged the knife from Aaron's forearm, he leaned downward and snapped Steve's wrist with one hard push.

The knife was coming in for another stab but fell short and missed, as the pain of a broken wrist was immediate.

Steve Cook screamed, and Aaron wasn't able or willing to cover the man's mouth this time. He rolled off him to avoid having to block the knife again.

"You ..." Steve managed to say as he rolled the other way, "broke my fuckin' wrist." Steve got to his knees.

Aaron stayed near the bed for several reasons. He wanted

the pillowcase to staunch the blood from his arm, and he wanted to guard the cell phones and the weapon under the bed.

While Steve stared at his wrist where it dangled, his face an even darker shade of red, eyes bloodshot, Aaron wrapped a pillowcase around his bleeding forearm and tried to stuff the end piece under itself with one hand. He had to use his teeth to finish the rudimentary field dressing. He'd wrap it right when he left this room and see about stitches.

It was time to put this man down. It was time to let the authorities hear what he'd recorded on his phone.

It was time to end this bullshit and have the authorities go after and stop some guy in Toronto named Edward Sweeney, providing Steve told him the truth.

And even if he didn't, Aaron could access Steve's phone. Once he checked the last number Steve called and saw a name, he could text Edward Sweeney and make him think it was Steve. Sweeney would drive into a trap at Sunnyside Beach, providing Steve also spoke the truth about the location.

The pain was creeping into his consciousness, even though adrenaline surged through his veins.

Where the hell did he get a knife from anyway?

Steve lowered his injured wrist, thrust the knife out in front of him, and charged at Aaron.

Aaron ducked out of the way of the knife and kicked out into Steve's gut.

The man almost lost his balance but regained it before smashing into the balcony door.

With the knife out to ward off any attack from Aaron,

Steve opened the door wide.

"You're going over the edge," Steve said. "I'm done with you."

He sprinted into the small hotel room at Aaron, who drove a front kick up and under the extended knife hand. He slapped both hands at Steve's right forearm, the force opening the man's grip.

Air shot from Steve's mouth in a huge exhale as the knife slipped from his hand. Then Aaron shoved the man away from him.

Steve reeled backward, hit the opening to the balcony, and dropped hard to the concrete floor outside the room.

With two wide strides, the pain in his arm a constant buzz now, Aaron stepped out onto the balcony and kicked at Steve's forehead.

But the man saw the kick coming and laid down, making Aaron's foot glide over Steve's body, missing him completely.

Steve rolled away from Aaron and got to his knees, protecting his injured wrist by placing it near his belly.

Needing this to end now, Aaron charged him again.

Steve twisted himself in a circle like an NFL quarterback trying to avoid a sack, which caused Aaron's outstretched arm to bounce off the man.

Steve shoved Aaron toward the balcony's edge at the end of that roll. Like someone being pushed into a pool, Aaron clung to the man pushing him, thereby bringing him to the edge, too.

Just before Aaron hit the railing, he spun out of the way and rolled Steve around.

Steve hit the railing fast and hard, both of their momentum in that final push.

As Aaron bumped the edge with his sliced forearm, his legs buckled, and he dropped to his knees. Steve had thrust his hands out to stop himself from hitting the edge too fast and potentially bending over it.

When Steve's broken hand hit the railing, the man screamed like a ten-year-old girl, buckled at the waist, and didn't lose momentum as his body weight edged over the lip of the balcony.

He grasped frantically at the top ledge with his good hand, and then he was over, his feet rising in front of Aaron.

Even after everything that had happened, Aaron didn't want the man to die, but from where he was on his knees, he was too far and too slow to lunge at Steve's legs.

Although, knowing that didn't stop him from trying.

The second Aaron understood what was happening, he was already pushing upward. Slash wound or not, he shot both arms out and made to wrap Steve's legs in a hug, but they lifted by his face a second before and were gone over the edge.

Aaron twisted around and got up as fast as he could.

Steve Cook had not fallen.

The man clung to the balcony railing on the other side with his one good hand.

"I can't hold it," Steve grunted. "Pull me up."

Aaron leaned over and grabbed Steve's forearm with his good hand. The pillowcase around the wound had loosened, and blood ran freely down his forearm now, leaving his hand a mess of crimson lubrication. The arm with the knife wound couldn't handle any pressure. He had no grip.

"I can't hold you with one hand," Aaron said, grunting with the effort, moaning with the pain.

"Fuck," Steve said, his tone desperate. "Pull me up, man."

"I can't," Aaron hissed between his teeth as he tried to cling to the man's sweat-dampened skin.

"I'm slipping," Steve cried.

There was nothing Aaron could do. Both men had injured each other enough that pulling Steve back over the balcony's edge was impossible.

The man was about to fall fourteen stories to his death.

The reality of that came into Steve's eyes as Aaron struggled to hold him.

For that brief moment, Aaron's face in pain now, too, for all the effort he was expending, they stared at each other in a silent goodbye.

Man to man, once enemies fighting, now sharing a common moment of life and death.

Steve Cook's hand slipped from the railing. Gravity yanked his forearm from Aaron's grip, and Steve began the fall to the concrete surface far below.

Even before Steve hit the ground, someone pounded on the hotel's room door.

Aaron pulled back to avoid watching Steve smack the concrete.

Another heavy knock hit the door.

Then someone shouted, "Security."

Aaron needed out of the hotel as fast as he could.

But to do that, he would have to deal with the guy at the

door.

He entered Steve Cook's hotel room, closed the balcony door, and went to work.

Chapter 12

Sarah rejoined Parkman and Alex in the room and checked her phone to ensure the volume was turned on.

"Aaron's going to call," she whispered, unable to keep the emotion from her voice.

Alex whipped his head around to stare at her.

"Vivian?" Parkman asked.

Sarah glanced up and stared at them for a heartbeat, then nodded.

"She showed up?" Parkman had his trademark toothpick in his mouth. "What else did she say? Is Aaron okay?"

"No," Sarah whispered, holding her cell phone tight. "Vivian said he was stabbed, and he's trapped. But he will call soon."

"Stabbed?" Parkman's voice rose a notch, the toothpick dangling on his lips.

Alex leaped off the bed and raced for the door as if he was going to leave, then turned back and strode to the bed. Then, back to the door. The man paced with determination, like he needed to get that pacing done and over with quickly.

"Vivian doesn't always talk like we do. She's more of a thought that permeates my consciousness. Sure, sometimes I can ask a question and receive an answer, but it's always on Vivian's terms."

"What else did she tell you?" Parkman asked, then faced Alex. "Seriously?"

Alex stopped pacing and glared at him momentarily, then his face softened, and he sat on the edge of the bed again. It had to be maddening for him. To know Aaron had been missing for days, only to hear he'd been stabbed and was currently trapped somewhere.

"We got this, Alex," Parkman said. "Look, use that energy on whoever is doing this to all of us." He turned back to Sarah.

She stared down at her phone.

"I'm supposed to go to the Toronto Courthouse tomorrow morning and sit in on the process in courtroom one for some reason. When security removes me from the courtroom—"

"Why are they going to remove you?" Parkman asked.

Sarah shrugged, looking up. "No idea, but according to my sister, they will. And when they do, I'm supposed to utter the name Alistair McNeil."

"Who's that?"

"I guess I have this evening to find out."

"What else? Did she say anything else?"

Sarah nodded once again and tried to hold back the tears.

"What?" Parkman asked.

Alex got back to his feet and stared at her.

"Vivian said the only way to work toward ending all this is for me to convince Aaron to turn himself in, wherever he is."

"What?" Parkman blurted. "That doesn't sound right."

"I know." She slapped the wall beside her. "Look how long it's been since we talked, and I'm supposed to tell him that. It's so fucked."

Alex started pacing again, and Parkman didn't say a thing to him this time. He just kept staring at Sarah, the toothpick moving slightly as he contemplated Sarah's words.

"What else?"

"Something happened in Santa Rosa."

"Tell us."

Sarah told them about her delivery, and Alex stopped pacing to listen. She explained her phone call with Officer Sherman when she was at the airport in San Francisco and how the police searched her parents' house and found the item and the box it came in. They wanted to pin that murder on her and wanted her back in California, but it was too late for that.

"So, let me get this straight." Parkman raised his hands in the air, fingers spread. "By now, the authorities in Santa Rosa are looking to arrest you for murdering some guy in a hotel and committing an indignity to his dead body, and they're looking for Aaron as a prime suspect in the murders here in Toronto, and Vivian told you to go to the courthouse tomorrow and get taken by security and have Aaron turn himself in?" Parkman stopped to stare at her.

Sarah nodded. "That about sums it up."

"And that, my friends, does not make a lick of sense. We can't do that."

"Parkman, I agree. But when have we ever willingly defied something Vivian told us to do? I don't see any other way."

"I do."

"What then? What do you propose?"

"Do the opposite. Don't go get taken by security and tell Aaron to lie low until we figure this shit out."

"But what if Vivian's way is the only way out of this, as it often is?"

Parkman shrugged and glanced at Alex. "Look," he said. "I'm never one to question this, but it seems so obviously fucked that I'm confused as to what is right and what is wrong—"

Sarah's phone rang. She smacked the answer button and brought it to her ear.

"Aaron?"

"Honey, it's your father."

"Dad?" She glanced at Parkman and Alex, frowning.

"They've taken your mother in for questioning, Sarah. What did you guys do yesterday?"

"Dad, we didn't do anything. We shopped, then came home. That delivery was dropped off around one in the morning, and then the cops showed up. They think I killed some guy."

"It's been all over the news. They've issued a warrant for your arrest."

"Is that why you're whispering?"

"Yeah, they've got cops out front in unmarked cruisers waiting to pick you up when you return. They think you're coming home tonight."

"That Sherman cop was quite aggressive on the phone when I was at the San Francisco airport. I'm in Toronto now, so that'll give me time to figure all this shit out. Rest assured, Dad, we'll get to the bottom of this."

"Hope so. They haven't charged your mother with anything, and our lawyer said she'll be home soon, but Sarah, whatever is going on is serious."

"We've all dealt with higher stakes, and Vivian just weighed in."

"Good. Do exactly what she says. She's got a better view of everything than we will ever have. And stay safe. Don't worry about us."

"Thanks, Dad. We'll talk soon." The line beeped. Another call was coming in. "Dad, Aaron's calling on the other line. I have to take it."

"Okay, chat soon. Bye."

"Bye." She clicked to go to the other line but stopped to check call display. It said PRIVATE NUMBER.

"Guys, I have to take this. Then I'll explain what's happening back in Santa Rosa." On the third ring, she leaned back and held her stomach. "I feel nauseous, for fuck's sake."

She clicked the button. "Hello."

"Sarah Roberts," Officer Sherman said. "We were expecting you to arrive home tonight."

"What do you want?"

"But instead, you lied to me."

"Yeah? About what?"

"Your rental was returned in San Francisco today instead of Los Angeles."

"I didn't lie. You asked if I was headed to Los Angeles. I wasn't." She stared at Parkman while Alex continued to pace.

"Where are you?" Sherman asked. "We need to talk."

"About what? About the man who was murdered? And how I received a delivery last night? And once I saw what was in the box, I spilled it in the living room, then cleaned it up and tossed it in the bin out back? Is that what you want to talk about? Because that's what happened. My story will match what my mother is telling you."

"She's not talking much. Her lawyer shut her down. But we're not interested in Amelia Roberts. We know you were in the hotel room with Malcolm. We have a witness who saw you leave the room, and we have your fingerprints inside the room on the Subway cup you were drinking from. Sarah, we even have you admitting you went to that Subway hours before Malcolm was murdered. So, make it easy on all of us and come on in. Or, tell me where you are, and I'll come get you. Nice and easy."

Sarah was past nervousness and fear. Someone was fucking with them all in a way that could ruin their lives for years to come. How they got themselves out of this mess was a complete mystery.

In her ear, the line beeped. Another call was coming through. She pulled the phone away as she heard Sherman calling her name.

It said PRIVATE CALLER again.

"Sherman," Sarah said, cutting him off. "Gotta run. Listen, we'll be in touch soon."

She clicked over to the other line as Sherman shouted something unintelligible. Then she brought the phone to her ear once more.

"Hello?"

"Sarah," Aaron said, and she almost lost control. His voice, her Aaron, gone for days, had finally called.

"Aaron …" she whispered. "Tell me you're okay."

She felt Alex and Parkman move closer.

"I fucked up, Sarah. Steve is dead. They're looking for me. I'm in hiding. I can't get out. I've been stabbed, and I'm losing blood. It won't stop bleeding. I've got Steve's gun. Sarah, I fear this is it. I'll be charged with murder. I'm sorry."

Chapter 13

AARON GRABBED ANOTHER PILLOWCASE and wrapped it around his arm tighter than the first one. He dropped to the floor and retrieved the gun from under the bed, then slipped his phone and Steve's phone into separate pockets.

Security banged on the door once more.

"Open up, or we're coming in," a man yelled.

We're coming in? There was more than one security guard?

Aaron couldn't be seen in the room.

But where could he hide? Did it matter in the end? His blood and his DNA were in the room. A proper investigation would confirm he had been here. How he let himself get into this mess was beyond him, but he had to find a way to get out of it on his own.

The balcony offered no protection. It was a standard

hotel room with a bathroom. There was absolutely nowhere to hide.

A key card slid into the door. The handle lowered.

"We're coming in, sir," the man's voice said, clearer now that the door was opening.

Aaron jumped two steps until he was behind the door before it was only half open. The man stepped inside.

"Sir?" he asked as he scanned the room.

Aaron saw the man in profile, his left hand ready.

The second the man moved farther inside and the door slid shut away from Aaron, he jabbed at the man's face to knock it away from him.

The man grunted with the sudden impact and naturally tried to turn back toward Aaron to face his attacker, but Aaron was already anticipating that.

He gripped the man's hair, drew back on his head to elevate the man's vision and keep it off Aaron's face, then wrapped his left arm around the guy's neck and placed his wounded right arm on the top of his head to steady him and keep him from glancing back.

Then he constricted both carotid arteries in a sleeper choke hold, counting off the seconds until the man dropped asleep. Twenty seconds was the max because cutting off those arteries for more than thirty seconds limited oxygen to the brain and could lead to death. As a trained martial artist, he didn't want to kill the man.

The guard's body dropped limp at the seventeen-second mark.

Aaron held on for another few seconds, then eased the man to the hotel room floor. The door had already slid shut behind him.

Aaron patted the guard's pockets and came up with a personal cell phone and a hotel radio. He stomped on both to give himself more time, then went to the door.

The peephole in the door showed an empty hallway.

He opened the door, peeked out slowly, and saw an entirely empty corridor. Someone had probably called in a noise complaint or something, and he couldn't afford to be seen leaving the room.

After one deep breath, he slipped out of Steve's hotel room and headed left toward the stairwell. The elevators were much farther, and getting off the floor was a priority.

Five feet from the stairwell doors, voices emanated along the corridor to him.

People were exiting the elevator.

Aaron took wider steps while concealing his bloody arm with his body.

At the same second he hit the door to the stairwell, someone shouted behind him.

"Hey, you there!"

The door opened, Aaron slid around it and into the stairwell, then dropped to the next level in three measured leaps.

The soft rumbling of heavy footsteps above came to him.

At the twelfth floor, he grabbed the door and yanked.

Nothing happened. The door was locked.

He needed a room key to access a specific floor.

Without thinking about it further, he dropped down to the eleventh floor and continued leaping the stairs floor by floor as men pounded the steps above him, shouting down for him to stop.

By now, they would all know Steve was lying outside on the concrete, and their guard was unconscious in Steve's room, although that guard would be awake again soon enough.

On the seventh floor, Aaron slowed at a fire alarm button. He'd made good ground as the men above were still at least three floors above, but his legs were shaky, and he still had to drop seven more floors. Only halfway there.

The thought occurred to him that a group of officers would be waiting at the first-floor exit.

And he needed that exit cleared.

So he pulled the fire alarm.

The shrill ring wailed in the stairwell, cutting off the sound of the men above him giving chase.

He dropped another floor, then another. By the fourth floor, he had to slow down as hotel guests filed out of their rooms and avoided the elevator. On the second floor, he didn't need a room key because the door was being held open by a man as he guided his wife and two kids into the stairwell.

Aaron held the door until they were all clear, then entered the second-floor hallway and ran toward the stairwell on the other side.

Several doors opened on either side of the hallway as people took suitcases and laptops while exiting their rooms.

The fire alarm siren had not abated. It had been loud in the stairwell, but in the confined hallway, it seemed shrill.

Up ahead, people were entering the second-floor corridor instead of leaving. He eyed them for a brief moment before realizing they were more hotel staff.

Room 202 clicked open beside him.

A lone female stepped out of her room, dragging a small carry-on size bag behind her.

Aaron leaned over to hold her door, presenting his back to the people entering the second floor.

He was trapped.

Guards and hotel staff were coming from both stairwells now.

"We're evacuating," he shouted to the woman in front of him. "Head that way." He pointed down the hall.

The woman nodded and started away from him as Aaron slipped inside her room. He slammed the door closed, then applied the night lock.

Even though he was confident a key card couldn't override the night lock, he dragged the desk in front of the door anyway. Once the door was secure and there was no chance anyone was coming inside the room anytime soon, he ran for the balcony. It was only the second floor, which made it an easy jump to the ground. Then he'd get in his car and clear the area.

He'd be away in minutes, and he could leave all this behind him.

The door slid aside. He stepped out and glanced down.

At that moment, he realized his mistake. He'd made a grave error.

This room was directly below Steve's room.

The man lie broken and dead, surrounded by six men, some in uniform, directly below the second-floor balcony.

Aaron stepped back inside the room and closed the

balcony.

Someone pounded on the door.

"Open up," a man shouted. "We know you're in there. We saw you enter."

Aaron paced for a moment, thinking about his next move. He'd almost made it. He'd gotten so close to leaving. If he'd considered the side of the building he was in, he would've never chosen this room.

Feeling weaker by the minute after expending all that energy to descend from the fourteenth floor and the blood loss in his arm, he had to consider that he was caught.

How long would he be stuck here? What would Sarah do?

All he wanted was to talk to Sarah and make things right. Instead, he followed the man who was following Sarah.

He pulled out his cell phone and dialed Sarah's number at the exact same second the blaring fire alarm siren turned off. His ears rang in the silence left behind by the siren.

When she answered, he blurted everything out in a form of verbal diarrhea.

"I fucked up, Sarah. Steve is dead. They're looking for me. I'm in hiding. I can't get out. I've been stabbed, and I'm losing blood. It won't stop bleeding. I've got Steve's gun. Sarah, I fear this is it. I'll be charged with murder. I'm sorry."

"Aaron, calm down. What's going on?"

"They were following you, so I followed them."

Aaron summarized what he'd been doing for the past twenty-four hours and how he saw Steve running from the sub shop and thought it was over. But Aaron continued to follow him, and then he played a bit of the recording for

Sarah while they pounded on the hotel room door again.

"Steve is supposed to meet his accomplice at Sunnyside Beach tomorrow evening after texting a time, and I have his phone."

"Okay, so here's what we'll do. Text that number for a ten-at-night meeting. Alex, Parkman, and I will be there to find this accomplice. Then I need you to open that hotel room door and turn yourself in."

Someone in the background protested what she had just said.

"Who's there with you?" he asked.

"Parkman and Alex."

"Where's Daniel and Benjamin?"

"Long story and not enough time. Look, Aaron, I spoke with Vivian, and she said this is what you're supposed to do."

"Turn myself in and be charged with murdering this guy, Steve? That's what I'm supposed to do? That's my only option?"

"Look, by turning yourself in, you avoid murder charges in Toronto."

"What?" he shouted into the phone. Someone banged on the door multiple times, thinking his shout was directed at them. "Murder in Toronto?"

"The man Steve was going to meet is behind all of this. Something happened here last night—a double murder. And the authorities pegged you as the suspect. You have the perfect alibi because you've been in the States."

"And what about the shit I've done here?"

"You've done nothing wrong. All you did was try to protect your girlfriend, and in doing so, you were attacked with a knife and fought back. Unfortunately, Steve died. End of story. Self-defense."

"And it was Vivian who told you this?"

"Yes, she did. Even Parkman agrees now. Send a text as if you're Steve, then open that door and tell the authorities everything. Give them the phones and get that arm bandaged properly."

"Okay. I'll do it. Ten o'clock tomorrow night?"

"Yes. Text it to me, too. Maybe send the voice memos to me as well."

"I'll do it all now."

"One more question, Aaron."

"Shoot."

"Why were you out of contact with everyone?"

"I raced to the airport to catch you, but you were gone. I bought a flight to Los Angeles and then dropped my phone in the toilet while pissing at the airport. When I landed, I bought this phone and got a pay-as-you-go plan with T-Mobile. By the time I was on the highway, I couldn't recall anyone's phone numbers but yours, and since I was about to see you later that day, I decided not to call. Anyway, I pulled up in front"—the hotel room door was thumped hard enough to move inward an inch—"of your parents' house and saw Steve watching it. And here we are."

"Aaron, that's so …"

"So what? Stupid?"

"So romantic."

That caught him off guard.

They thumped the door again. It moved inward another inch, pushing the desk with it.

"I'm coming, guys," he shouted at them. "One second." Then, into the phone, he said, "Sarah, I have to go."

"Okay, text everything, then hand it to the authorities and tell them your tale. I'll call my dad and get him to send Mom's lawyer over to get you out of there. You can stay at my parents' place."

"Texting now. See you soon."

"I love you, Aaron."

"Love you, too, Sarah."

The door barged open, knocking the desk aside.

Aaron was opening the app to send the texts when three men piled into the second-floor hotel room, their weapons drawn and aimed at him.

"Get on the floor," the frontman shouted. "Now!"

He wouldn't get the chance to text anything.

He would let her down again.

Before dropping to the carpeted floor, he slipped the phone into his front pocket, then eased to the floor.

Within seconds, they were on him, cuffing him.

"You're going to fry for this," one of the men whispered in his ear. "You're so fucked."

Chapter 14

Sarah set the phone down and tried to control her emotions. They were going to be okay, Aaron and her. He'd chased after her, and when he saw potential trouble, he dove in on his own and didn't resent her for it or blame her.

Sure, the fact that he was now going to be in police custody back in California sucked for them. At least he wasn't here when Jason Grant was killed last night.

"Sarah?" Parkman said, snapping her out of her thoughts. "Fill us in."

She told them everything Aaron said and that he would text the contact to meet tomorrow night at ten at the beach. He was supposed to text her the voice memos, too.

She checked her phone, but nothing had come through. A sinking feeling coursed through her. What if they arrested him before he could send out the texts?

"I feel so helpless as everyone around us keeps getting arrested," she said. "We need to do something, but what?"

"Whoever is orchestrating this knows what they're doing."

Sarah tapped her foot while staring at the phone. "Where are his texts?"

"They'll come. Give him a moment. Maybe the voice memos are slow due to data size."

After ten more minutes, with nothing coming from Aaron, she set her phone down.

"What's next?" Parkman asked.

"We need help."

"Who're you gonna call?"

"Darwin." She opened WhatsApp. "It's morning there now. If he isn't awake, he can call me back."

She hit the phone option on his contact and got Darwin right away. After the usual quick pleasantries, she explained everything she knew to him.

Alex sat off to the side on his phone while Parkman listened closely.

"You've got the names?" Sarah asked Darwin. "Yes, that's right, Malcolm King, Jason Grant, and Alistair McNeil."

"Sarah, these are bad dudes," Darwin said.

"What do you mean?"

"Let's start with the guy in California. Malcolm has a long history of crimes. This guy barely escaped jail this time, and it looks like they were about to arrest him on something else ... one sec."

She held the phone away and then tapped the speaker

option. "Darwin, I'm putting you on speakerphone so Parkman and Alex can hear this."

"Great, hey guys."

Both men in the room said hello.

"Okay, so without going down the list of crimes Malcolm had been convicted for and the few he served time for, I'll just focus on his recent charges. He's a serial rapist. Malcolm was recently in court on charges of aggravated sexual assault. His lawyers got him off only a few days ago, even though, as it says here, he had stalked his recent victim for weeks. He's a suspect in a murder, too, but they didn't have enough to charge him. Local papers now say Malcolm King was found dead in the Western Best in Santa Rosa, and the authorities are looking to speak with Sarah Roberts in connection with the incident. I'm assuming you didn't do this, right Sarah?"

"I wish I did, but I didn't. Someone else cut off the guy's dick, then delivered it to my parents' place. They're questioning my mom right now."

"It looks like there's a warrant for your arrest, too. They seem to think you're still in the area."

"What can you tell us about Jason Grant?"

"One second, I'll switch screens."

Sarah and Parkman stared at each other for a heartbeat. Parkman's toothpick flicked to the other side of his mouth.

"Jason Grant is a rich kid, has a clean record, and a powerful list of attorneys working for him. Over a year ago, his parents were found in their house after it burned to the ground. They were able to determine both Mom and Dad were shot before the fire. Apparently, the mother had smoke in her lungs, which indicated she wasn't dead when the fire started."

"That's how he died. Last night in a fire just north of Toronto."

"Right, and they are looking for Aaron in that death."

Sarah wiped her forehead. "Happily, Aaron has been in California for the past few days. He couldn't have killed Jason Grant."

"Alibis are good when they're that solid."

"Anything on Alistair McNeil?"

"Yeah, bringing him up now."

After a moment's pause, Sarah motioned at one of the sandwiches. Parkman fetched the tuna and handed it to her. She bit into it, hungrier than she realized.

"Okay, he's the lesser criminal of them all."

"How so?" Sarah asked, her mouth full.

"No criminal record at all."

"Okay, that's something," Parkman said. "What's he do for a living? Where does he live? Anything intriguing?"

"Well, he might have a criminal record soon as charges are still pending."

"We're listening," Parkman added.

"Six prostitutes have been picked up and beaten, raped, then left by the roadside wherever their attacker took them. They all claim the man wore a disguise and drove a dark-colored four-door sedan. Two women said it was a Honda Civic."

Parkman edged closer to the phone on the corner of the bed. Sarah had set it down to eat with both hands.

"Any convictions?"

"None, but they picked up Alistair McNeil in connection

with the attacks."

"Anything come of it?"

"According to what I'm gathering here, the attacks stopped while he was in custody and house arrest awaiting trial. Only four weeks ago, all charges were dropped for some reason, and court files were sealed."

"Really?" Sarah said. "So why would I go to courtroom one tomorrow and tell security that name?"

Parkman and Alex stared at her, and Darwin remained silent for a moment.

"There are only two reasons I can come up with," Sarah continued. "One, Alistair is guilty, and by saying his name in that courtroom, I'm bringing it up again, although I have no idea how or why that would make sense. Or two, someone in the court system—specifically in courtroom one—knows about Alistair and what he's done and wants to—"

"—take him out," Parkman finished.

"That's what I was thinking," Darwin added. "It looks like we may have a vigilante on our hands."

"More than one," Alex added. "It spans North America to have gone after Sarah and Aaron like this."

"Okay, Darwin, can you email me everything you've got on Alistair? I want to find this guy before he's killed if that's their plan."

"Sure, I'll do a little more research after a coffee and send it all while you are asleep tonight."

"Not sure how much sleep we'll get, but we'll try."

After a few goodbyes, they hung up on Darwin, and Sarah grabbed another sandwich.

"By the way," she said. "This isn't just a vigilante on the

loose. This goes deeper. It's too well-planned."

"What is it then?" Alex asked.

For a man who didn't speak much, she was happy to see him getting so involved.

"We have a serial killer on the loose. One who targets criminals who got away with something violent. One who has access to court files and pays attention to who gets off and who doesn't." She leaned back and closed her eyes as Vivian's presence was close.

"A serial killer?" Parkman said. "Or serial killers?"

"Doesn't make sense," Alex said. "Serial killers are rare. How could there be two working together?"

Sarah opened her eyes and sat up.

"They're coming after us because of what we do. They don't want to kill us. They want to drag us through the legal system, to watch us pay for the crimes we've gotten away with. If we don't go to court, and if we don't pay our debt to society, they'll kill us, too." She blinked. "Vivian said it's one or the other. And that's why we saved Aaron's life by having him arrested."

She got to her feet and set the sandwich down, no longer hungry.

"I'm next on the list. Officer Sherman in Santa Rosa is already talking to the authorities here in Toronto. They're looking for both of you." She nodded at Parkman. "Apparently, you were seen entering the dojo this morning."

All three of them stared at each other, the tension in the room thick.

"Unless we find these people and stop them, all of us will either end up in jail or dead."

"Those are our two options?" Parkman asked. "That's it?"

"According to Vivian, it's one or the other."

"I'll take the third option," Alex said.

"What's that?"

"Not sure yet, but there has to be a third one."

Sarah nodded. Parkman looked from Alex to her, then back to Alex.

"So what's next?"

"I have no idea."

Chapter 15

Homicide Detective Lynda Ricigliano stared at the photo on her computer screen as she set her phone back down. This was her chance to get close to the enigma, the mystery. She had watched from afar as she came up through the ranks. She'd seen other cops, other detectives, dealing with Sarah Roberts, and she'd witnessed some fall along the way.

But that was the thing with Sarah. The woman was in touch with some other entity, something unexplainable, and for some reason, no matter how tough it got or how much trouble she found herself in, she always found a way to make it all work.

Good cops hated bad cops, and so did Sarah. Though whatever happened to Sarah over the years, Ricigliano knew her relationship with the police was tenuous. Sarah rarely trusted cops and generally refused to work with them.

Ricigliano was there when Rod Howley died in that fight at the mall years ago. She was there when Sarah dealt with a gang on the streets of Toronto and then followed her from the news when Sarah went to Los Angeles when those priests were being murdered. And even after going to Amsterdam, Italy, Denmark, and Greece, Sarah always found her way back to Canada.

Ricigliano scanned the internet when Sarah dealt with a bomber terrorizing a city called Kelowna and most recently with her situation in Texas, along with heavy artillery gunfights on the streets of Toronto. When Sarah was interviewed downstairs almost a month ago, before the Canadian military boss scooped her from them, Ricigliano had intended to go down and introduce herself. By the time she got there, Sarah was gone.

And yet now, Sarah Roberts was falling right into her lap.

A BOLO was issued in California for the American Sarah Roberts in connection with the murder of a suspected rapist. The murder made sense to someone like Sarah. Of course, she would castrate the guy, and Malcolm King did it, as far as everyone was concerned. Bad policing lost that case, and Mr. King walked.

The only issue was Sarah wouldn't have taken that castrated item as a trophy back to her parents' house. Why the authorities in Santa Rosa didn't get that was beyond her.

The BOLO was sent to the Toronto Police Service because Sarah's last known address was in the Greater Toronto Area and because they suspected she had flown back to Canada while they were preparing the arrest warrant.

Detective Ricigliano had just hung up from talking to Officer Sherman, who had reluctantly had to hand everything off to homicide. They had proof Mr. King's appendage had been in Sarah's parents' house. They had proof Sarah was in the area within hours of the murder, and they had Sarah's admission she had lunch at the sub shop across the street—they'd found a cup from that sub shop in the victim's room, Sarah's prints on the cup.

Sherman even forwarded a photo of Sarah with what looked like blood splatter on her clothes. For some reason, this Sherman guy was hell-bent on getting Sarah and was absolutely sure she'd killed Mr. King, even though she wasn't out of her mother's sight all day, and there were witnesses in the stores Sarah visited during their afternoon shopping trip.

Homicide Detective Lynda Ricigliano didn't think Sarah did it, though. She wouldn't kill and castrate a man *with* her mother, would she? That kind of team was unheard of. Although, if anyone on Earth were able to pull that off, it would be Sarah, but again, Ricigliano didn't think so.

Sarah wouldn't leave fingerprints behind at a murder scene, either. Sarah didn't randomly find targets to kill. She found evidence and fought for justice. If someone died in the course of her actions, it was their own fault, or it was Sarah trying to defend herself.

Ricigliano loved what Sarah did and what she represented but never got the chance to get close to her—until now.

Her caseload was easy at the moment. She had a week to find Sarah and help her out of her mess, and Detective

Ricigliano was determined to do just that.

What a fine mess her friends were in, too.

The dojo got raided, and several arrest warrants were issued for the missing members of Sarah's crew. Aaron Stevens was now in custody in California—proving he didn't kill Jason Grant and that other guy, Dale Williams—leaving Sarah with nowhere left to turn.

If they all did what the authorities suspected they had done, then fine. Charge them and give them their day in court. But Ricigliano didn't think they did anything.

This was an impressive setup.

That said, who could be big enough to specifically set up Sarah and her colleagues? Who could be that organized to do it in such a spread-out fashion? The government? A secret agency? An independent?

Ricigliano wasn't much into conspiracy theories and believed it had to be smaller than it was, but what was happening was over her head.

She suspected Sarah was drowning in the knowledge that her world was coming apart at the seams. The girl could use a little reassurance and some support.

Ricigliano picked up the phone and dialed Sarah's cell number. She'd had it for months now and hoped Sarah hadn't changed it.

Ricigliano leaned back in her office chair and stared out the window at the cubicles of younger, hungry detectives as the phone rang at the other end.

The ringing stopped.

Ricigliano frowned. She pushed the phone harder against her ear. It sounded like someone was breathing on the other end.

"Sarah?" she whispered.

"Who's this?" A gruff female voice asked.

Convinced it was Sarah, Ricigliano started talking.

"Sarah, I know you didn't do what they're saying you did in Santa Rosa. I also know the arrest of Daniel and Benjamin and the arrest warrants being issued for the others are all bogus."

Ricigliano paused in case Sarah wanted to respond. Maybe she'd just hang up. Blocking her number hadn't come to mind, so Ricigliano had to remain guarded. Gaining Sarah's trust was almost impossible in one phone call. This was their get-to-know-you call.

"Okay, I'll keep talking," Ricigliano said. "I'm Homicide Detective Lynda Ricigliano out of Toronto. I've followed you for years, and I know Parkman from past visits to our department. I'm here to help, but you must help me in return."

"I've heard that before." The gruffness in her voice was gone. The softer, caring Sarah was behind those words. "What is it you want, Detective?"

"I want to help, to clear you and your colleagues of these stupid charges."

"And how do you propose to do that?"

"By meeting you, talking this through, taking it to the next level."

"I've talked it through enough with people I trust."

Ricigliano paused a moment. The subtext was she didn't trust this random woman calling and claiming to be a detective, wanting to help, which made complete sense.

"Sarah, the full force of the law is coming after you, a veritable army of blue. I'm one of the few that has watched you from the sidelines. I was in the building when Officer Budnack interviewed you before that military man claimed you and then died off of Spadina. I was just a cop when you dealt with that street gang—"

"I get it, you know shit. You can only help if you know who set us all up. Tell me that, then I'll deal with him or them, and then we'll see where that takes us."

"I might know that," Ricigliano said, feeling sleazy because it was an absolute lie. She had no idea who was behind Sarah's recent troubles. "But only through the process of elimination."

"The process of elimination?" Sarah let a short laugh out. "A Toronto detective calls me and wants to bullshit with me. Look, I'm busy and hanging up now—"

"Sarah, don't." Ricigliano waited a moment, but the line didn't die. "You trusted a cop once, and look how that turned out. Parkman is like a brother to you."

"Yeah, and I trusted other cops, and look how that turned out. They're all dead."

"All I'm saying is, I can help. I have court in the morning on another matter. Then we should meet for lunch or something—"

"Hanging up now. It's been nice chatting with you, Detective."

"Sarah," Ricigliano blurted. "I will find you. We can meet, and we can talk …"

Ricigliano stopped speaking as the line died.

Sarah had hung up.

She had to expect Sarah would put up a wall, push her away, and reject any chance to talk. Sarah couldn't know that Ricigliano genuinely wanted to help, which was something she would have to prove to her.

Walls weren't meant to stop people, though. They were erected to show how hungry someone was. If Ricigliano really wanted to prove herself to Sarah, she had to push through whatever Sarah threw at her to show she could be trusted.

She would start by speaking with Daniel and Benjamin. Gain their trust, then finish her court thing in the morning, and by the afternoon, she'd find Sarah.

And she'd make her listen.

Because the alternative was something Homicide Detective Lynda Ricigliano didn't want to face.

The alternative was Sarah Roberts, charged with murder in California, and all of her colleagues accused of similar offenses in the Toronto area.

It would mean the end for Sarah and all that she did for the good guy.

It would mean the end for Sarah Roberts completely.

And Lynda Ricigliano wouldn't stand by and allow that to happen if it wasn't justified.

She got up from her desk, intent on finding a large cup of coffee, before heading down to speak with her suspects.

It was going to be a long night.

And she didn't even get to tell Sarah about Steve Cook, the man Aaron is suspected of throwing off a balcony of a high-rise hotel. She'd wait until next of kin were notified. Then they would all see why Aaron chose to kill that man if, in fact, he actually did kill him. Another case where Ricigliano thought it was self-defense.

Aaron Stevens wasn't a murderer.

It would be a long night indeed.

Chapter 16

SARAH FLOPPED ONTO THE bed and stared at the ceiling.

"Who was that?" Parkman asked.

"A woman claiming she was a detective here in Toronto. She said she wanted to help."

Parkman grunted.

"Exactly."

"Did she give you a name?"

"Lynda Ricigliano, homicide."

"Oh, I think I recall that name. Good reputation. Strong female lead."

"Well, she'll be at the courthouse tomorrow morning."

"The same one you're going to?"

"Probably."

"Shit, what's that all about?"

"No idea. She said an unrelated matter drew her there."

"Cops and detectives have court all the time." Parkman paused, his voice sounding sleepy. "Maybe you should turn off your phone."

Sarah rolled over and held the button to power it down. "I just want to sleep until this is over."

"I know how you feel."

"The difference this time is we're not dealing with an evil corporation, or a killer hunting old men, or something else insane. We're dealing with an unknown enemy who is going after us—all of us."

"Which makes it personal. And scary."

"I'll be back," Alex said.

Sarah looked up. "When? We'll be asleep soon."

"When you wake."

"That'll be the morning."

He nodded. "I know." Then Alex slipped out the door before either of them could protest further.

"Where does he sleep at night?" Sarah asked.

Parkman lay down on his bed. "I have no idea. Never asked him."

"We really should learn more about that guy. He's been part of the family for quite some time."

"Often our worlds involve us totally, consume us, and we lose focus on those we work with, those we couldn't make it without."

"I've found there are two kinds of people out there." Sarah closed her eyes, the fatigue of traveling and the stress hitting her. "There are people who think from the heart first and those who think from the head first. When dealing with emotional issues, the heart people are my kind of people. It's the head people who try to figure it all out. All serial killers are head people. A person who comes from the heart couldn't do that. And when you're overthinking something, you're head fucking it. So, don't head fuck shit, and you'll be fine."

"Damn, that makes sense. I think. Don't head fuck it."

"Alex is a heart person. Hurt him or hurt his people, and he'll hurt back. You're a heart person, and so am I. We care too much to ever stop doing what we do." Her breathing was shallow, deeper. "I can't be in a relationship, or at least a close relationship, with head people. They're great lawyers and business people but suck at relationships. All narcissists are head people. They're also the ones trying to change others. A person who comes from the heart would never try to change someone else. They'd love them for who they are."

Sarah paused, waiting for a response. When Parkman didn't say anything, she glanced over through half-slitted eyes. He had fallen asleep.

Her last thoughts before falling asleep were whether or not Alex had a room key to get back in. And why was he outside if the authorities were looking for him? Wasn't that dangerous? Did he have a death wish?

Those last two words stayed with her as she drifted off to sleep.

Death Wish ...

Chapter 17

Sarah pulled the baseball cap lower while leaning against a wall in front of the Toronto Courthouse. It was after ten in the morning, and court was in full swing. Vivian hadn't specified an exact time, and the idea of walking into the courthouse while the authorities were looking for her seemed ridiculous. Detective Ricigliano would be somewhere in the building as well. If Vivian's purpose was to set up a meeting with the detective, then why set it up here?

There had to be more at work than just that. It had to do with whispering Alistair's name to security. And, of course, that made all the sense in the world.

Darwin had emailed her everything she needed on Alistair McNeil. He'd included notes on the recent victims in his email and updated them on Daniel and Benjamin. Both men weren't formally charged yet, but charges were pending.

They had been held in custody overnight. Darwin guessed they wouldn't be charged with the actual murder of Jason Grant, but since they had his body parts in their gym, the authorities were looking at filing accessory charges.

Aaron was arrested in Santa Rosa and was being held as well. They were investigating him in the death of the man who fell from the fourteenth floor and in talks with Toronto police about the Jason Grant thing. That would take time to sort out.

Alex arrived back to their room that morning with fresh coffee and croissants. The man looked rested and showered, but neither Parkman nor Sarah asked about his whereabouts. Even if they did, Sarah doubted he'd offer up a full report. The man was becoming a mystery, one they all loved.

And now, at this time, all Sarah had to go on was what Vivian told her to do.

She pushed off the wall and started for the courthouse's front doors, double-checking her hat was low enough. Extra makeup helped to hide her eyes, and Parkman's light jacket made her look bigger than she was. Only a keen set of eyes would pick her out of a crowd, and with a BOLO out on her, the last place the authorities would expect her to be was at the courthouse.

A man in an expensive suit and a briefcase held the door for her. She entered the courthouse and was immediately taken aback by the metal detectors. She would have to take off her jacket, hat, and shoes like filing through security at an airport.

As people filed through security, she saw it wasn't as intense as at airports. Besides, she didn't have a choice.

Going ahead with this, as per her sister, was something she'd been doing for too long to stop now.

She moved into the small line, removed Parkman's jacket, and placed it on the belt. She waited until the guard motioned for her to walk through the detector. Once she was through without setting it off, she retrieved her jacket and slipped it back onto her shoulders.

The guard waved her on with a smile. Happy that was over, she ambled along the corridor for courtroom number one. People milled about, chatting among themselves. The lawyers dressed the part, their clients less so. So many people lingered near chairs outside courtrooms, tapping their fingers, bouncing a knee, so nervous about what was coming. Uniformed officers and guards strode throughout the area without paying particular attention to anyone.

Relief swept over her. She was in the nest, and not a single bee knew who she was. No one paid her any extra attention. There had to be fifty people moving through the main corridor, some hustling past, some walking, with most standing outside courtrooms. So, it surprised Sarah when a woman about forty feet away was staring at her.

Sarah stopped, saw that she was in front of courtroom three, and spun around. She moved with purpose to the corner, strode around it, and saw a woman's bathroom. Quickly, she slipped inside and then jumped into a stall, locking the door behind her.

She sat on the closed toilet and waited.

It could've been random, but she was sure that woman was watching her.

The bathroom door opened, and the din from the hallway

outside the bathroom filtered inside. When the noise calmed, she knew the door had closed.

The woman had followed her inside. She watched the bottom of her stall for shoes or any sign of her pursuer.

A door opened, then latched closed.

No one stopped outside her stall door.

Maybe she wasn't followed. This was certainly not a place where she wanted to make a scene. If she aroused suspicion here, she'd be held downtown until the California authorities got their hands on her, and then it would be months—if not years—in court, proving her innocence on that Malcolm King murder. As far as she figured, when they pegged you for something like that, and the evidence pointed to her being in Malcolm's room, along with his DNA being in her parents' house, she would have a hard time explaining she didn't have anything to do with it. Especially because Malcolm King was her profile type of kill if she was ever to take on random killings of assholes.

A toilet flushed, a stall door opened and clanged closed, then a faucet turned on briefly. Whoever had entered the women's washroom was finishing. Sarah wasn't being pursued. She was being paranoid.

The door opened, then closed.

Silence filled the void. As far as she could tell, she was alone in the bathroom.

After another half a minute, she pushed up off the toilet and went to unlatch the stall when Vivian popped into her head.

Whispered words and cautions from her sister caused Sarah to sit back down, her hands clinging to the panels on either side of the stall.

What are you asking, Vivian?

Before she got an answer, Vivian edged out of her consciousness.

Break the law? On purpose, without helping someone? While the cops were looking for her?

Vivian, when does this stop?

And why do I need a gun?

Knowing her sister was gone and unwilling to answer further questions, Sarah eased out of the stall, checked herself in the mirror, washed her hands, and moved toward the door.

A wave of nausea hit her, and she stopped beside the door, her hand on the wall, breathing in and out, hoping it would pass. Was it something she ate? Could she be coming down with something?

After a full minute, the upset stomach eased off a notch. High-heeled footsteps approached the door from the other side. Sarah pushed off the wall and adjusted the ball cap just as the door swung open, and a tall woman rushed in past her.

Before the door closed, Sarah stepped out into the corridor. The woman who had stared at her before entering the restroom was gone. Staying close to the wall, Sarah moved along until she passed courtroom two, then saw courtroom one, all the while glancing at the guns on the hips of uniformed officers. How fast could she snatch one and run? Or was Vivian looking for another gun? Like breaking into a gun shop somewhere?

Court was already in session in courtroom one.

She paused to stare at the docket, reading it for a name

she might recognize, but none were familiar.

After a single deep inhale, she whispered to her sister that she had better be right about this, then opened the door and slipped inside as quietly as she could.

A lawyer stood beside their client, reading from a document in his hands. The judge looked on, listening without glancing at Sarah. She edged to the side and stopped moving to avoid creating a disturbance.

If being uncomfortable could be measured in a beaker, hers would be full. She hated the energy and the smell of a courtroom. Something about it was so unsettling. It caused her to feel that way.

With a hand over her queasy stomach, she watched the members of the public seated randomly throughout the courtroom. Her gaze moved to the front area, where she stopped to stare at the security officer.

The tall man stared back at her.

Was he the one Vivian had mentioned? Sarah continued to browse the room, stopping on another guard standing by the prisoner box. That man watched the lawyer who rambled on about his client's need for a break.

To be less noticed standing by the doors, she moved up one row and took a seat, lowering her face to hide her eyes under the bill of the cap. At least her stomach was settling. She'd be surprised if being in the courtroom had caused her belly ache. Even though this was stressful, she'd been through much worse over the years. She was stronger than this and knew Vivian had her back, so it had to be something she ate.

After several more sentences about his client, the judge

interrupted the lawyer and recited case law.

The guard to the left of the judge continued to watch her. Whether it was Vivian or intuition, Sarah knew this was the man she would be whispering Alistair's name to.

Then she would leave and do what Vivian told her to do that night, even though it didn't make any sense. Why was Vivian sending her deeper into the trouble?

The judge announced that the court was entering a recess.

"All rise," the guard said loud enough for everyone to hear.

The soft din of rustling clothes and whispered voices filled the room as the judge left the bench and made his way to a door that led to his chambers.

Sarah remained in her seat, her eyes on the guard that glared at her.

He was definitely her target.

But why? Who was he? Could he be the one behind everything happening to them? That would make the most sense. But if he was, why not end it now? Why tell him about Alistair?

Nothing made sense to Sarah as people began filing out of the courtroom. Noise rose around her as the whispers turned to speaking voices with people debating the case or discussing lunch options.

Similar to deplaning, everyone crowded at the door and exited in clumps. Sarah scanned the front of the courtroom. The lawyers were gathering their paperwork, slipping documents into briefcases. The security officer by the prisoner box was preparing his prisoner to take him back to wherever they went during a recess.

The other guard, the one watching Sarah, had disappeared.

She checked to the right and left. He was gone.

Was this a waste of time?

She held her stomach and waited. Security was supposed to come up to her and ask her to leave. But no one was watching her, and in under a minute, she'd be the only one left in the courtroom. Even the stenographer was wrapping up and getting to her feet.

Sarah waited, but no one approached. The last four people lumbered by her seat, heading for the exit.

On her feet now, she moved toward the door, then stopped to look around the courtroom. There was one lawyer left, still writing a note of some kind. After another breath, feeling she'd screwed this up somehow, Sarah started toward the exit.

Several feet away, her hand rising to grab the handle, the door swung inward, making her step back to avoid being hit by it.

"Sarah?" the guard said. "What a surprise."

"Do I know you?" she asked.

"Why are you here?" He ignored her question.

"How involved are you?" She glared at him. "Are you the information part? Do you sell what you know to others? Or are you behind what's happening to us?"

"Why are you here?" he asked again. "There are countless police officers in this building. One word, and you're arrested. Seems a bit stupid to come here of all places."

She moved closer, her eyes boring into him. This man was involved somehow, and she needed to know how.

"What have you done?" She was less than ten inches from him now. "Here's a little friendly advice. Come clean. Tell them what you've done. Own up to your shit, and we'll go our separate ways."

"You're giving me advice. That's rich."

"Call it free advice. Take it at no cost. The price goes up from here."

"What the fuck does that mean?"

"Don't take my advice and come clean, then you'll pay for what you've done."

The guard laughed in her face. "You mean you'll pay. Because there's nothing linking me to anything illegal, as I have no idea what you're talking about. You're spouting some shit, is all."

"This isn't over," Sarah whispered. "You have underestimated who you're dealing with. A fatal mistake."

The man's face hardened. He didn't like the idea of being threatened.

With one hand, he clutched the exit door's handle, and with the other, he grabbed Sarah's arm, dragging her toward it.

"You're about to be arrested for the murder of Malcolm King in Santa Rosa."

Someone pushed the door inward, knocking his hand off the handle, the door almost hitting him. Sarah yanked her arm out of his grasp at the same moment.

A well-dressed woman had entered the courtroom. She stared at the guard, then glanced at Sarah.

"What's going on here?" she asked.

"I was escorting this woman out of the courtroom as we are in recess," the guard said.

"I was leaving anyway," Sarah added.

"Hold on," the woman said. "The both of you."

The guard shook his head. "No, you hold on, ma'am. I'm escorting and detaining this woman until I can give her over to the proper authorities."

The woman slipped a hand into her pocket, produced a wallet, and flipped it open to a badge.

"I'm Homicide Detective Lynda Ricigliano. This woman, Sarah Roberts, will be coming with me."

The guard stared at Ricigliano's ID, then stepped back. "Take her. You're the people I would hand her off to anyway."

Ricigliano? How could she know to find Sarah in this courtroom?

The guard glanced at Sarah again, with a look of fear and anger on his face, then strode away from them toward where the judge had exited.

"Excuse me, sir?" Ricigliano said.

The guard kept walking.

"Hey," the detective shouted. "Stop right there." Ricigliano moved past Sarah, but not before whispering, "Wait for me."

The guard was walking by the lawyer's benches, his pace uninterrupted by the detective's beckoning.

"Are you Edward Sweeney?" she asked him.

That caused him to pause. He slowed, then stopped and turned around before exiting the courtroom.

Edward Sweeney. Sarah wanted to pull out her phone and text the name to Darwin to see what he could pull up on it. The fact that the detective, the woman who had called Sarah last night, was already this involved impressed her. How she just showed up was still a mystery, though.

Ed's face had lost all color.

"What's this about?" Ed asked. The man tried to put on a brave stance but looked quite scared.

"Do you know a man named Steve Cook?"

Ed darted a glance at Sarah, then back to the detective. "I might. Why are you asking?"

Even Ricigliano took a moment to turn back to Sarah. She wanted to ask what the hell was going on but didn't want to interrupt what was happening in front of her.

Ricigliano cleared her throat. "Isn't Steve Cook your stepbrother? Before your parents were killed, wasn't he adopted into your family?"

Now Ed was obviously uncomfortable. He nodded, his hand on the door as if he was ready to bolt, his face ash white, his eyes darting between Sarah and Ricigliano.

"Steve Cook is my *brother*," he said, making sure she heard the lack of the word, *step*.

"I'm sorry, Edward. That's why I'm here. It seems there's been an accident."

"An accident?"

"Your brother was found without vital signs outside his hotel room in Santa Rosa, California. An investigation is underway—"

At the mention of Santa Rosa, Sarah took a step toward him.

Edward yanked the handle, swung the door open wide, and slipped inside.

"Hey, sir," Ricigliano shouted.

A lock clicked. Ed was gone, and the door he slipped through was locked.

"What the hell was that?" Ricigliano said, facing Sarah.

"He's part of everything that's happening."

"Is that why you're here?" Ricigliano asked.

Sarah nodded. "My sister told me to come here."

Ricigliano stared at her for a heartbeat, then pulled out her phone. After dialing a number, she told whoever she spoke with to lock the building down and find a court security officer named Edward Sweeney. Then she hung up and slipped her phone away.

"Is that the man who stabbed Aaron?" Sarah asked. "The one who died in California?"

Ricigliano nodded. "The one Aaron is being questioned about."

Sarah pointed at the door the guard had slipped through. "And Edward Sweeney was that man's brother?"

Ricigliano nodded.

"Then Ed's involved in all this shit, and I fucked up."

"How did you fuck up?"

Sarah moved toward the door and slipped through it before Ricigliano could catch up.

She had forgotten to whisper Alistair's name to Ed as Vivian had instructed.

What did that mean, and how bad would things get now?

Outside in the hallway, chaos filled the corridor as police officers and security ran by to secure the exits.

The building was being locked down as they tried to stop Ed from leaving.

The downside was that Sarah couldn't leave either.

Ricigliano stepped in front of her.

"You're not going anywhere, Sarah. We have to talk."

Chapter 18

STEVE WAS DEAD? ED couldn't believe it. How was this possible? They had a good gig going. Dale's death, he could understand, but what could have happened to Steve?

No wonder he didn't return his text that morning.

Aaron must have killed him.

Sweeney refused to believe it until he had solid confirmation that his stepbrother was dead.

It was obvious that detective was working with Sarah. But how? Why didn't they just arrest that bitch?

Everything was falling apart so fast he couldn't bear it.

Ed had used the stairs to drop to the basement-level parking area. He hopped inside his van, changed into civilian clothes, discarded his uniform, and then got the van rolling to exit through the judge's garage.

No one stopped him, but two officers stared at his van as

it exited the parking area. Ed always parked in the judge's garage in case he was escorting one to their vehicle at the end of his shift. Even though his shift wasn't over yet, Ed would not be returning to work today.

Sarah had gotten too close, too fast. She was supposed to be detained in California yesterday, but instead, she showed up in his courtroom when a detective came to tell him his brother was dead.

"What the hell is going on?" he asked out loud, slamming his hand on the van's dash.

How could Steve be dead?

If it was true, he had to face it. Their time had come to an end too early, much too early. All he wanted was to do the right thing, to pick up the slack where the legal system dropped the ball.

Sarah Roberts and her fellow criminals had gotten away with too much over the years. It was like the authorities had given her a free pass. The two-birds-with-one-stone idea was his *Death Wish* plan, and now it was all fucked. He could take out Jason Grant, an actual murderer, and have Sarah's friends blamed for something. Then they'd be in court. It was either the court system or him, but they'd get their comeuppance. Taking out Malcolm was a stroke of luck because Sarah had left Toronto before they could deal with Jason Grant.

Everything came together well, and he couldn't see the problem. Sure, Dale died, but that was his own stupidity. And now, if his stepbrother was dead, it led back to him, and that detective saw Sarah with him.

A spotlight was on him now. He would be investigated.

It couldn't go down like that. Steve was alive, and Sarah was fucking with him. He was sure of it.

Ed drove a few blocks north on University Avenue before he turned right onto Wellesley. Once he drove across Yonge Street, he pulled into the city parking area and found a spot.

He needed to calm down and collect his thoughts. Should he go home? Could he?

What came next?

He realized the best solution for him was for Sarah to be out of the picture.

She'd had her chance. Dozens had tried before him, but Ed knew how to remove Sarah Roberts, and he intended to do just that.

The van was the perfect vehicle. Once restrained, he'd drive out of town or find a local place. He would stick to the plan. Do what was honorable. He would see it through and be vindicated. If his stepbrother were actually dead, it wouldn't be for nothing. He'd make sure of that.

Once Sarah was gone, her body was never to be found. They could try to connect him to whatever they wanted, but nothing would stick. In the worst-case scenario, he would blame Steve for what happened in California—which was literally true—and Dale for what happened to Jason Grant.

With all the heat on her, Sarah disappearing wouldn't cause too many alarm bells. Whether any of Sarah's friends were caught up in the aftermath, he didn't care. A year or two later, he'd make them disappear, too.

Ed stared out his windshield at the back door of a Tim Horton's coffee shop and decided he needed one.

His plan would work.

Running from the courthouse and not returning to work was easily explained away. He was distraught when he was told his brother was dead. Of course, he would act irrationally when news like that was dropped on him.

He opened the van's door, grabbed his cell phone, and locked the vehicle. With each step, he felt lighter. Nothing had changed. Hit Alistair McNeil in a couple of hours, then find Sarah and take care of her. Once she's gone, he would walk back into work as if nothing had happened and apologize to his bosses for leaving them high and dry.

Worst case, he got fired. There were always plenty of firms hiring security officers. Besides, without his brother and Dale to help, he might have to lie low on his *Death Wish* mission for a while.

Steve was dead? No way.

At the door to the coffee shop, he slowed and turned away for a moment to wipe at his eye. He leaned against the brick wall and stared at the sky as dozens of Torontonians strolled by, lost in their own world.

He could do this. He *would* do this.

The determination in his gut told him he had to do it—for Steve.

But also for Jessica and Lisa. They were the main reason this all came to be. The murderer of his parents was tried in a court of law for their murder and found guilty. He was still serving his sentence.

Yet the murderer of his wife, Jessica, and his daughter, Lisa, was never found. Ed found him first and made sure he paid the ultimate price.

Just like he would do to Sarah, he'd nabbed Rueben

Ellis, tied him up in the van, drove him to a secluded spot up north, made him suffer under the knife for hours, then killed, dismembered him, and buried the pieces.

Justice done and complete.

Sarah would have the same fate.

He pushed off the wall, entered the coffee shop, and got in line as his phone vibrated.

The movement in his pocket startled him. He snatched it up and glanced at the text.

His abdomen filled with acid as he stared at it.

Steve Cook, his stepbrother, had just messaged him. So Steve wasn't dead, and that detective was just fucking with him.

He knew it. His brother was alive.

The text said to meet him at their usual spot, as discussed on the call yesterday, for ten that night as Steve's flight would get in by eight. Ed had been waiting for that confirmation. And only Steve would know to say all that.

Or would he?

He glanced up as the line moved forward.

Could his phone line be tapped? Did someone listen in on their conversation last night?

Ed thought that was highly unlikely. Also, the text from his stepbrother came from Steve's phone.

Which only left one solid answer.

Steve was alive, and the detective was working with Sarah. They were lying just to see how he'd react, and he did exactly as they predicted—he ran.

Like a fool, he played into their hands.

Sarah had been running this from the beginning, and he

couldn't see it. Without a doubt, she had to go. She'd already committed enough murder to justify his actions as a vigilante. And wasn't the definition of that word exactly what he was doing?

He was a self-appointed citizen taking the law into his own hands because the legal agencies that protected people like him and his family had failed him. They were absolutely inadequate.

But as a man, he wasn't inadequate.

"Sir?" the clerk called. "You're next in line."

Ed stepped up to the counter. "I'll have a large—" His cell phone rang. The caller ID said PRIVATE CALLER.

"Sir?"

Ed turned off the phone.

"A large black coffee," he said, the smile returning to his face.

All was not lost. He had Alistair to deal with. Then he'd meet his brother—who wasn't dead—and together, they'd remove that bitch from their lives.

Everything was coming back together rather quickly.

Edward Sweeney was smiling again.

Chapter 19

Showing her ID, Detective Ricigliano escorted Sarah outside, her hand on Sarah's arm as she led her to a black Suburban.

The detective opened the passenger door, released Sarah's arm, and gestured for her to hop in.

"Are you detaining me?" Sarah asked. "Because that won't work."

Ricigliano looked her up and down. "I want one coffee with you to earn your trust. After that, we decide together what's next. Would that work for you?"

Sarah studied the area around her. The courthouse was buzzing with activity as more police cars entered the parking lot. So many members of the legal community scoured the area for Edward Sweeney.

Ricigliano was her immediate ticket out of this mess.

There were at least two more hours before she needed to steal the car Vivian told her to take, so there was time to humor the detective.

Sarah hopped inside the Suburban. "That'll work for me."

Ricigliano closed the passenger door, walked around the front of the vehicle, then hopped in and got them rolling quickly.

"Somewhere downtown," Sarah said. "I have things to do after we talk."

Ricigliano glanced over at her. "Talk first. Those things, whatever they are, can wait."

She respected Ricigliano's confidence and strength, but Sarah had already made a crucial mistake by not saying Alistair's name to Ed. She could only hope the repercussions of that mistake weren't too damaging. She would not make another error by failing to steal the car her sister wanted her to steal, even though doing something as stupid as stealing a car made little to no sense.

From where she sat, it was easy to watch the detective drive, but her blazer covered any chance of glimpsing a holster, and Sarah still needed a gun.

"What brought you to the courthouse?" Ricigliano asked.

"On the phone last night, you said you knew me and what I do."

"That's right."

"Then you know about my sister?"

"I understand you have a way to speak with her." She glanced at Sarah, then back to the road. "Or is it the other way around? Your sister speaks to you?"

"She tells me shit."

Ricigliano hit her blinker, waited a moment, and then turned right.

"Well," she said. "Why were you in that courtroom, then?"

"My sister told me to be there." Sarah figured there was no reason to lie about it. Edward Sweeney was involved. That much was obvious. Better the detective knew sooner rather than later.

Ricigliano made another turn onto Yonge Street, then slowed to enter the parking lot at the Eaton Centre. It brought back memories for Sarah from the food court where Rod Howley was killed by the Rapturites so many years ago.

"Let's have a coffee at the Starbucks in the mall," Ricigliano said. "It'll allow us to talk about what's happening."

Wondering what motivated a woman like Ricigliano, Sarah asked, "Why talk? What's in it for you?"

"What do you mean?"

"Why not just arrest me and hand me over to the American authorities so they can take me back to Santa Rosa?"

"Because I believe you're innocent." Ricigliano slowed the Suburban and edged into a spot. She killed the engine and faced Sarah. "Well, maybe innocent is too strong a word. I'll say you're innocent of the crime they're trying to pin on you. Look, Sarah, I know you've killed people before, but I don't believe you've ever *murdered* anyone."

"Hmph, interesting way to look at it."

"I work homicide. I don't work for the accidental death

or self-defense department. If you were a murderer, I would have arrested you back at the courthouse." She jerked her head. "Now, let's go."

As she exited the SUV, Sarah checked her phone. She still had over an hour before she needed to leave. Parkman had called twice, and a blocked number had called three times.

Once inside the mall, Ricigliano led the way to the Starbucks while Sarah texted Parkman that she would call him back when she was free.

After a short wait in line, they grabbed a coffee and took a seat.

"Let me start," Ricigliano said.

Sarah nodded, watching the detective's eyes as she sipped her beverage.

"I spoke with Daniel and Benjamin last night."

Sarah watched her, waiting for more.

"I know they received a package, and after Parkman was called in to discuss options, the police arrived, and here we are."

"The same thing happened at my parents' house." Sarah went on to tell her everything up until last night's call from Officer Sherman.

"What didn't add up was the same thing happening to the same group of people at two locations in two countries. I can see how the authorities would suspect known vigilantes in having something to do with it."

"That, and the physical evidence we all had on us when the authorities arrived …"

"… as per anonymous tips being called in, I might add,"

Ricigliano said.

"So, in both cases, we received deliveries, and then calls were made so the cops would arrive and catch us with those macabre boxes."

Ricigliano was nodding.

"Can those anonymous calls be traced?"

Ricigliano stopped nodding to shake her head. "This led me to conclude that someone was behind it all, and you were the innocent one this time."

"Most times," Sarah added, sipping from her cup.

"That's debatable."

Sarah swallowed and stared back at Ricigliano, then smiled.

"Sarcastic, too. That works for me." Sarah checked how close the next table was, then leaned forward conspiratorially and asked, "You armed?"

Ricigliano frowned. "Why?"

"It's a yes or no."

After a long pause, Ricigliano nodded. "You want to tell me why?"

"Because I'm not armed, and the last time I was in this mall, a lot of cops were killed." That sounded reasonable.

"Not very comforting, Sarah."

"Wasn't meant to be."

They both drank more. Sarah's phone vibrated, but it could wait.

"I had a theory last night," Ricigliano said. "I believe someone is doing this *to* you all. But there's no way to figure it out without an intense investigation, including forensics and many hours of profiling and behavioral analyses. Then we heard Steve Cook was dead, and next of kin was Edward Sweeney, a court officer. I asked a few more questions and learned Aaron had fought with Steve and even tried to save Steve's life but couldn't. Investigating officers are working with Aaron to figure out the puzzle in Santa Rosa, while investigators here are reexamining their arrest warrants. How could they arrest Aaron for a crime in Toronto while he was in California? So, after talking to Daniel and Benjamin and then learning about Steve Cook, a few bells rang for me. I requested to be the one to tell Edward about his brother's death, and here we are. Although, I didn't expect you to be in court today."

"My sister told me to see the security officer in courtroom one." She shrugged. "I had to go."

Ricigliano leaned back in her chair, her eyes not leaving Sarah's face. "Do you always do what your sister tells you?"

Sarah met her gaze. "Always. I'd be dead by now if I didn't."

"Did she tell you anything else?"

"You mean why I was supposed to be there? Or who Edward Sweeney is? Or what he has allegedly done?" She shook her head. "My sister doesn't talk like you and I do. She speaks in demands and commands and lacks reason at all times. It all makes sense in the end, but while I'm living it, going through it, I sometimes feel like she's trying to kill me."

"Is she telling you anything right now?"

Sarah leaned forward and placed her elbows on the table. "No, she isn't, but I wouldn't tell you if she were. Not to be rude, but I rarely tell anyone what she says."

"You tell Parkman, don't you?"

"It's like the plot of a novel. If it doesn't forward the story, it isn't added."

"So, in other words, Parkman will know what he needs to know if he needs to know it."

"Exactly."

They stared at each other for a moment.

"Let me ask you something." Sarah wrapped both hands around her coffee cup, debating how to obtain the detective's weapon without much of a fight.

"Go ahead."

"You ordered the courthouse locked down to stop Sweeney from getting out. How will you know if that nabbed him?"

"I'd be called. They haven't called yet."

"Until they do, it's safe to assume he got away?"

Ricigliano nodded. "He got away. That's my gut feeling."

"What's next?" Sarah asked.

"Make me part of the story, the plot."

"What?"

"Your analogy about your sister and what you reveal. Tell me everything she's said, and let's work together to stop whoever is behind these attacks on you and your friends."

Could Ricigliano be trusted? As with every relationship, Sarah was at an impasse. Move on, get the detective out of her life, or trust and work with her. Everything in her gut told her she could trust Ricigliano, but did she *need* her?

What she needed was a gun. And to steal that car Vivian told her about. The timing was everything, too. Showing up one minute too late meant she'd miss her chance to nab the car. This little impromptu meeting needed to end soon. But would Ricigliano let her out of her sight?

"Well?" Detective Ricigliano said. "You trying to decide if you can trust me?"

"Something like that."

"So, there is more? You have information from the other side? Telling you to do something, to perform a task of some kind?"

Sarah nodded.

"Let me help you. Whatever your sister has asked you to do, it's in the interest of ending this, right?"

"It is."

"Then tell me what you feel comfortable with, and I will do everything I can to help."

"What I feel comfortable with?" Sarah shook her head. "I can't tell you any of it." She pulled off the cup's lid and twirled it. There was no easy way to do this. Ricigliano would never willingly give Sarah her weapon and let her leave the mall.

She would have to take it by force.

"Sarah, I get it, you don't know me. How could you trust me? But come on, I'm the only one with a badge going to bat for you. If what you know from your sister will end this, why wouldn't you tell me? I'm in a position to help."

Sarah withdrew her cell phone. Darwin had called now, too.

She opened the contacts app. "What's your direct line?" she asked.

"Why? You want to text celestial messages to me?"

Sarah stared at her for a moment, her fingers hovering

over the cell phone's buttons. When she didn't respond verbally, Ricigliano started talking.

Now that the detective's number was stored in her phone, she texted once to ensure it worked. Then she told her what Vivian needed first.

Ricigliano retrieved her phone from a pocket and frowned.

"What?" she asked, looking up.

Sarah leaned back and shrugged again. "Didn't want to say it out loud."

Ricigliano shook her head. "No way."

"See? A dead end. That's why I keep this shit to myself."

The detective leaned forward until she was hovering over Sarah's side of the small table. "I can't give you my gun. Are you crazy? I'd lose my job."

"Well, I need one before the next thing I have to do this afternoon."

"And what's that? Rob a bank?"

Sarah's lips tightened, and she tilted her head in a did-you-just-say-that gesture.

"I'm sorry," Ricigliano said, pulling back. "That was uncalled for."

"Then tell me where I can get one of those things." Sarah jerked her head at the detective's waistline.

"I cannot help you procure one of those *things*."

"Then your usefulness to me ends here."

Sarah pushed her chair out to stand up.

"Wait," Ricigliano stated, her voice firm, leaving little room for misinterpretation.

Sarah stopped. She still had time, but it was running out

fast.

After a long pause, she eased back down, picked up the cup's lid again, and tore it in half.

"Why do you need one?"

"I have no idea. But if my sister tells me I need one, then I *procure* one, as you say."

"What else is she saying?"

"Nope, doesn't work that way."

"What?" Ricigliano blinked hard twice. "What does that mean? You tell me one thing, and you know my career is over if I comply, so now you won't tell me more?" Ricigliano crossed her arms and leaned back. "Sounds like a temper tantrum."

"Oh my fuck, are you serious? A temper tantrum?"

"I'll tell you what, Sarah Roberts." Ricigliano offered her a cocky smile. Then she winked at her. "You want my gun? You're going to have to take it from me." She waved her arms to the left and right, then recrossed them. "In front of all these witnesses. Take my car keys, too. Shit, you might as well steal the Suburban. You know where I parked it."

Was she saying what she appeared to be implying? She would help without compliance, thereby saving herself from any hits her career would take while still giving Sarah her trust and faith.

"I could certainly try to take it all from you."

Ricigliano narrowed her eyes and smiled wide enough to show teeth. "Yes, you could try."

"But it might hurt."

"Hurt?" Ricigliano blinked. "How do you mean—"

Sarah shoved the small table so hard it connected with

Ricigliano's sternum. The detective's arms were still crossed, and she couldn't uncross them in time to deflect the blow.

While the woman was expelling the air in her lungs and bending forward, the table continued its momentum, tilting Ricigliano's chair backward.

Sarah had already launched from her chair before the detective hit the floor, and both coffee cups shot off the table. She landed on Ricigliano, her hands fishing for the holster.

Someone hollered beside them. A woman screamed, and a commotion of voices rose from somewhere deeper in the store.

Sarah's hand found the weapon. She yanked it free and almost dropped it but was deft enough to keep it in her grip.

Ricigliano put on a show of fighting back, but it wasn't much of a show as Sarah had restrained the detective's arms and was using her body weight to hold her down.

Sarah could slip the weapon into her pants, but getting the car keys was another story altogether.

Hands grabbed her arms and lifted her off the detective. Sarah was yanked away and held back while others helped Ricigliano to her feet.

"What's going on here?" a man shouted.

A passing security guard stood between them now while Starbucks patrons held them apart.

"Look at the mess they made of my store," another man said, moving closer, wiping his hands on an apron.

"Let me go," Ricigliano said. "I'm a detective with the Toronto Police Department."

The hands holding her eased off, and she pulled out her ID slowly.

"What's your story?" the guard asked Sarah after reading Ricigliano's ID.

"Let me get my ID."

The guard nodded, and the men holding Sarah released her.

"Wait," Ricigliano shouted. "My gun is gone."

Sarah was already pulling it out. "Everyone step back," she shouted, waving the gun like a mad woman.

The circle around her grew wider, with people exiting the Starbucks.

Either Ricigliano was pissed she'd had her gun stolen, or she was acting with conviction.

"Sarah, lower the weapon," Ricigliano said.

With Sarah's free hand, she waved her fingers. "Car keys. Give them up."

The detective shook her head. "No way."

Sarah flipped off the safety and moved closer. "Car keys."

"Ma'am, give her your keys," the guard said from at least ten feet away.

The Starbucks was mostly empty now, with only a few people still hiding under tables. A small crowd had formed, some with cell phones.

How this would play out in the end wasn't important to Sarah at the moment. She had forgotten to say Alistair's name to Edward Sweeney. She couldn't screw this up, too.

Ricigliano slipped a hand in her pants pocket and withdrew the keys, placing them in Sarah's palm.

Sarah pocketed them and stepped back, moving toward the entrance of the coffee shop. The dome-like half-circle of people at the front widened to give her room.

"You'll never get away with this," Ricigliano shouted.

Sarah didn't respond as she made it out of the Starbucks, the weapon still up and aimed at anyone who moved.

A clatter of footsteps pounded toward her.

Without checking whether it was cops or guards, she lowered the weapon from sight and bolted into the store across from the Starbucks. The sportswear store also had people standing and watching the commotion, but no one tried to stop her.

She ran for the rear of the store, hit the back door, and landed in a corridor that linked the stores at the back of the mall.

With an internal compass, she bolted to the left toward the parkade. After passing the backs of several stores, she hit an exit and jumped out onto the street. No one on Yonge Street paid her any attention as she jogged to the parkade entrance and ran up the ramp until she hit the level where Ricigliano had parked.

She eyed the Suburban quickly and moved toward it, wondering where everyone was. By now, Ricigliano would have told them where she parked unless she was genuinely trying to help Sarah out.

Sarah didn't take long to get inside the SUV, drive to the exit, and leave the mall's parking garage.

No one tried to stop her.

Several minutes later, Sarah drove along the Gardiner Expressway East, staying to the right to exit for the lower section of Leslie Avenue.

She had half an hour to get to the Jones Street address

Vivian told her, which was only about a fifteen-minute drive from where she was.

Armed now, at least she could steal the car even if something came up.

No one would challenge a crazy girl with a gun.

She hit the gas to cruise through a yellow light, wondering what her sister was cooking up.

Whatever it was, somehow, things were different.

Somehow, it was affecting Sarah more because her stomach was always upset.

When her phone rang, she turned it off without looking at caller ID.

Everyone could wait.

She had a car to steal now.

Chapter 20

EDWARD SWEENEY SLOWED HIS van and eased to the side of the road. He parked over a dozen cars up on Hunter Street to be well hidden from anyone on Jones Avenue.

Alistair McNeil's car was parked on Jones, aimed south toward Gerard, with only the back bumper visible to Sweeney. This would be an easy hit. Alistair left for work daily within a few minutes of three in the afternoon.

Once Alistair was in his car and heading toward Lakeshore, Ed would follow him. On the Gardiner Expressway, Ed would execute his plan, and Alistair would finally pay for his crimes—the crimes that the court system couldn't reconcile.

Over six prostitutes had been beaten, two requiring surgery to repair the damage. After a two-month investigation, Alistair was picked up by the authorities, where he sat in his car, watching the streetwalkers at midnight. Several witnesses claimed they'd seen him on the nights of at least four of the beatings, creeping around. Even his hands showed signs of healing from a recent attack on someone when the authorities picked him up. He had a history of violent crimes against women, with two separate girlfriends testifying he'd beat them because they ridiculed him for his odd perversions.

When the courtroom heard Alistair McNeil enjoyed having women watch him jerk off, there had been a collective gasp. The judge had called for order after that.

Alistair's lawyer claimed that Alistair admitted he did that particular act most nights on Jarvis while watching the women stroll the sidewalks, waiting for their Johns. A harmless act, out of the general eye of the public, sitting in his private vehicle. How could this be anyone else's business?

His lawyer fought on, proving the scuff marks the cops witnessed on his client's hands came from a fight at his job down by the lake. The other employee had harassed Alistair until he attacked him. There was a fight resulting in the scuff marks. The other employee was terminated, and within days, he flew back home to his family in Puerto Rico. During the entire court process, no one could locate the man who fought with Alistair, yet his lawyer argued that the missing witness to corroborate Alistair's story wasn't enough to conjure doubt for his client. Even his boss admitted there'd been a fight among the employees.

In the end, even though five of the women said they would pick Alistair out of a lineup, the sixth one said the man who beat her didn't have a mustache. When the court asked Alistair to shave it, she was convinced it wasn't him.

The jury couldn't convict due to a reasonable doubt that Alistair wasn't the man who had beaten those six women even though he abused his previous girlfriends and was obviously a twisted, sick pervert. Not to mention, there wasn't a single beating of a prostitute in all the time Alistair was held in custody.

The man was guilty. Sweeney was sure of it. There was no doubt about it.

And today, he would pay for his crimes.

Today was McNeil's comeuppance.

His *Death Wish*.

Chapter 21

Sarah parked and exited the SUV. Once her phone was turned back on, she checked the time. She still had eight minutes.

She sent a text to Parkman explaining she had the weapon as per Vivian and was in a position to do as Vivian had instructed with the car. She also asked if he'd received an update on Aaron, Daniel, or Benjamin.

He replied that he hadn't and would check in with her once she had gotten away clean.

There was no need to respond to missed calls and voice messages. Everyone was looking for her, but what else was new? She would take the car, drive it downtown somewhere, then taxi back to Ricigliano's SUV and meet up with Parkman before going to the beach where Aaron had arranged for Steve Cook's cohort—his stepbrother, Edward

Sweeney—to meet him.

Would Ed still show up, though, now that he knew his brother had been killed in California?

Sarah checked the time. Three minutes left. She lingered a moment longer, then started up the sidewalk, watching the traffic, the people.

What was this all about anyway?

Why was she supposed to steal a car? Why were Edward and his stepbrother coming after them in the first place? She couldn't recall their names from the past. Had they wronged them in some way?

One more minute.

This entire scenario reminded her of the St. Elizabeth Street bridge and her sister telling her to take a hammer and sit under it at 10:18 a.m. She was so young and innocent and didn't have Parkman, Aaron, or anyone else in her life then. How reckless, yet how brave at such a young age.

The address came up on the left as she strode north on Jones. She shook her head to break the reverie, which probably came from a place of fear, an unusual emotion for her.

What could she fear with Vivian leading the way?

A door opened to her left, and a man exited his home, running along the pathway toward a car parked on the road.

Sarah placed her hand on the weapon and was about to spin around when Vivian snapped at her.

Wait!

Sarah stopped mid-turn.

The man dropped in the car and started it up. The brake lights flared as he put it in gear.

It was the car she'd asked Sarah to steal. A brand new Honda Civic, dark blue, four-door. And now she was calling her off?

The brake lights stayed on.

Sarah released the gun and checked her phone as if she was engrossed in something.

A car door slammed.

The man had gotten back out and was running for his house.

The car was still running.

Now!

The man launched inside the front door of his residence.

Sarah bolted for the car. She tore open the driver's side door and dropped inside.

Even though the engine was running and the doors were closed, she could still hear the man shout something at her.

She dropped it in gear, checked the mirror, and hit the gas. She pulled out onto Jones, heading south. In the mirror, the owner of the car was running after her at full speed. A city block later, he moved off to the sidewalk, already tapping at his phone.

He was calling the police.

Good. She'd be out of his car in ten, maybe fifteen minutes.

At the bottom of the small hill, she hit the lights at Gerard. The owner of the car was too far back to see now.

It was over. She'd done it. Dump the car somewhere downtown, and she'd be ready for the evening.

Soon this would be over, and they could find Sweeney and end this shit.

At Queen Street, she checked her mirrors again, but all she saw was a van on her back bumper. He was so close she wondered if he'd hit the Civic.

She pulled away from him on Queen, cut a right on Leslie, and got on Lakeshore to take the Gardiner into downtown.

On the ramp to the Gardiner, that same van was cruising at a solid clip as it raced up on her bumper again.

"What the fuck?"

Could the driver of the Civic own a van, too? Had he given chase?

Once on the Gardiner, she swung across lanes to avoid the van.

Yet it followed.

The time to do something drastic had arrived.

She pulled out Ricigliano's gun and lowered the window while doing over a hundred kilometers an hour.

Then she slowed the Civic to ninety and eased into another lane. The van was trapped between cars and couldn't drop behind her.

She hit the brakes hard enough to slow down and drive alongside the van. Due to the height difference, she could barely see across through the passenger window to the driver.

One small move of the wheel eased her farther away.

She glanced upward.

The driver turned toward her.

Their eyes met.

Edward Sweeney was driving the gray van.

"What the fuck?" she whispered.

He was laughing as he held up something in his hand,

something she couldn't see well enough to identify.

So she held up the gun and laughed back at him. She even angled it out the window, aiming it in his general direction.

Through the window, she witnessed his hand jerk once in the air.

Then something happened to the back of the Civic.

The ass end of the Honda Civic lifted off the highway. As she grabbed for the steering wheel to avoid falling into it, the gun was lost from her grip, falling to the asphalt of the expressway.

The car lifted so high that only pavement was visible as it skimmed by the windshield.

And then the Civic landed on its roof while still going about ninety kilometers an hour.

Like a bumper car at a carnival, the Civic connected with the guardrail while sliding on its roof. Then something else rammed it from behind, spinning the car in circles before it contacted another obstacle, glass shattering everywhere.

Sarah's last thought before losing consciousness consisted of two words.

Why, Vivian?

Chapter 22

Ed had watched as Alistair exited his house. The man had disappeared from view momentarily. The brake lights of his Honda lit up, and then Ed started the van's engine.

But the brake lights stayed lit. The Civic didn't move.

He waited a moment, his hand on the gear shifter.

The brake lights dimmed, and he watched as Alistair ran back to his house.

So Ed waited.

Several seconds later, Alistair bolted out of his house, disappeared from view, and the brake lights lit up again.

The Honda Civic was on the road.

Ed dropped the van in gear, raced to the end of Hunter Street, and swung onto Jones recklessly. Luckily, no one was coming, or he was sure he would've caused an accident.

He needed to be close enough for the remote to work on

the explosive device. All this would have been for naught if he had lost Alistair on the road. Trying again another day might not work. Alistair was his last hit before regrouping with his brother and waiting for the heat to die down.

He was certainly no lawyer, but the courts worked on evidence, and it was plain to see Aaron and Sarah would take the hit for Malcolm King and Jason Grant. That ruse in the courtroom, with Sarah sitting there and that detective lying to him about his brother, really pissed him off. When he thought about it later, he needed to calm down and focus on the final job.

At the light on Gerard, he pulled up as close as he could without hitting Alistair's car. Minutes later, after staying close, he almost lost the guy as he got on Lakeshore and raced up onto the Gardiner. But a slight maneuver got him out from behind a slow-moving transport truck and back behind the Honda Civic just as they crested the top of the ramp.

Alistair noticed him, which was fine. Ed didn't mind the man seeing the van as it was probably going to be the last thing he saw as long as the explosive device went off as planned.

They danced around a couple of cars, and then he got held up between several vehicles. The Civic slowed, though. He expected Alistair would take off, but he didn't.

Then, it slowed even more and pulled up alongside him.

The window lowered, and Alistair stuck out his arm.

But it wasn't Alistair McNeil.

It was Sarah Roberts.

Ed stared in disbelief. How the hell was that possible?

He'd seen Alistair run from his house. He'd seen the man leave.

Wait, he didn't actually see him enter the vehicle.

But Sarah Roberts? His palms and forehead broke out in a sweat.

He was the one going after her. How could she keep showing up like this? And why would she steal Alistair's car? That didn't make any sense. If she was as psychic as the media said she was, and she stole the car to save Alistair, how did her psychic power not tell her about the device by the gas tank?

Edward Sweeney didn't care. Sarah had made a mistake, a fatal one. She'd played right into his hand. This was the last time they'd meet.

He laughed at her, then held up the device and showed it to Sarah, not fearing that she'd take a shot at him on the highway, even though she pointed the weapon in his general direction.

Then he pushed the button. He'd won. It was over.

The back end of the Civic lifted off the highway, and as if something out of the movie *Fast and Furious*, the Civic was propelled forward at the speed of traffic on its front bumper for several seconds, appearing to be suspended in the air like that.

As his van drove by the Civic, it dropped onto its roof.

He checked the mirror and saw it careen off the side railing before an SUV, which couldn't get out of the way fast enough, crashed into the upside-down hood and set the Honda Civic into a nasty spin.

The last image Edward Sweeney had of the Civic that

Sarah had been gleefully driving moments before was half a dozen cars braking hard to avoid careening into the upturned car that had now caught on fire.

Edward looked away to avoid getting into an accident himself. The Civic's gas tank could ignite at any moment, and Edward felt his mistakes had come to a conclusion. Fate was righting things in his favor. It was about time.

Sarah Roberts was out of his life, and no one would ever know what he had done.

At ten that evening, he would meet his brother, and they'd form a plan to make sure none of the recent shit touched them. Then he'd return to work, and everything would be forgotten.

They had been doing a public service, after all, by ridding the world of shitty people who carried out indictable offenses with impunity.

It was something the court system failed to manage every day.

And something Edward Sweeney would never stop doing.

Not since his parents and then his wife and daughter were murdered.

That was their dying wish.

Their *Death Wish*.

Chapter 23

PARKMAN HAD EATEN ICE cream. He had potato chips. Even a chocolate bar. Yet nothing seemed to calm his nerves. Alex kept disappearing from the hotel room, returning every hour on the hour for an update.

But Sarah hadn't called him back yet.

Finally, at six that evening, he texted her again. It was left unread.

When Alex returned to the room, Parkman strode to the door, affixed the night lock, and faced the man.

"Where are you going every time you leave?"

"Surveillance."

"Surveillance? Of what?"

Alex moved to the empty bed and sat on the edge, looking down at the carpet.

"Someone is hunting our family." Alex glanced up, a

pained expression on his face. "My family. They aren't using traditional weapons, things we are taught to defend. We can even take a few bullets—ask Benjamin."

Parkman suppressed a smile, forcing himself to stare at Alex as he spoke.

"This setup, this elaborate framework," Alex whispered, "is something new for us. Something dangerous. They're all in custody, but you and me and Sarah."

Parkman moved away from the door and sat beside Alex on the bed.

"I feel trapped in a room like this," he added.

"Is that where you were last night?" Parkman asked. "Out doing surveillance?"

"Yes, so you and Sarah could sleep. Mostly Sarah. She's the true warrior, the true fighter."

"Gee, thanks."

Alex didn't acknowledge his sarcasm. He just kept unloading his fears and his anxiety.

"She had a busy day and needed her rest. And even after everyone's looking for her, she didn't hesitate to walk into a courtroom."

Parkman would swear he saw a tear in Alex's eye.

"Nothing stops that woman. She inspires us all."

Alex got up and started that mad pacing again. The forceful stride, as if getting to each side of the room, was timed, and he wanted to have it filmed for Guinness.

"So all this time, you were guarding this room, watching over us?"

Alex glanced up, then looked away as he passed Parkman on another round of long strides.

"You were protecting us," Parkman said, almost to himself.

"How else could I be in service to our Sarah?"

Parkman was mystified at Alex. What was his story? Where did he come from? The man was an enigma. He was like an autistic ninja. The patterns he saw, the moments, the physics, always blew everyone away, even Aaron, who claims he was Alex's original teacher in all things Shotokan.

But who was Alex? And how had he hurt so much in his past that he would murder without hesitation for Sarah and his newfound family?

Having Alex in their fold was nothing short of a Godsend.

"Do you sleep?" Parkman asked.

Alex stopped pacing and stared at Parkman. "Of course. When I'm not required to be awake."

"What kind of answer is that?"

Alex started race-pacing again. "Sleep is like an enemy. It pulls on me, weighs me down. When I need to be awake, I fight it and win. When I choose to sleep, I will."

"How long have you gone without sleep?"

"I can't answer that with any sort of accuracy as the days blend after so many without sleep."

This was the most conversation Parkman had had with Alex in a long time.

"Okay, do you know when you slept last?"

"Of course."

Parkman waited, but when Alex didn't answer, he said, "When?"

"The night before we had the delivery."

"You didn't sleep last night?"

Alex glanced at him, then looked away, his race pacing not faltering.

Parkman had never felt safer in his life. He just wished Sarah was with them. At a minimum, he wished she'd just text or call to update them. She'd been gone all morning and afternoon now, and as the evening came on, he was increasingly worried for her.

Alex moved toward the room's door. "I'll be back in an hour."

"Alex, wait."

He stopped by the door.

"No one knows we're here. Wait with me in the room."

"I can't. This room feels like a trap to me."

"What if Sarah calls and I have to run? How will I notify you?"

"You wouldn't be able to leave the building without me being aware of it."

Alex slipped out, and the door closed so silently that if Parkman had his eyes closed, he'd assume Alex was still standing there.

Beside him, his phone rang. The number wasn't familiar.

He snatched it up and started for the window to watch Toronto below while he talked.

"Hello?"

"Parkman?" a woman asked.

"Who's this?"

"Hanging up on me could cost you your freedom."

"I'll take my chances."

"Wait!"

Parkman paused a moment, then placed the phone back to his ear. "Say something important, something that'll make me want to keep talking to you."

"Sarah's in the hospital."

Parkman suppressed his gasp by clamping his lips closed. He leaned his forehead on the window pane and closed his eyes. That's why she hadn't reached out. That's why they hadn't heard from her.

A hand rested on his shoulder, and he jumped back, the phone launching from his hand.

Alex was back in the room. His hand snapped out, catching Parkman's phone mid-flight.

He extended it out to Parkman.

"My fuck, you scared the shit out of me." He took the phone back. "Keep talking," he said into the phone.

"What was that?" the woman asked.

"Nothing. Tell me about Sarah." He placed the call on speaker so Alex could hear, then held the phone out in front of him with one hand, the other on his chest.

"Sarah was in a car accident on the Gardiner Expressway."

"How about you start by telling us who you are?"

"Us?"

"Doesn't matter. You're on speaker. Just talk."

The woman cleared her throat. "Are all you people this brusque?"

"Fine, fuck it. I'm hanging up."

"Wait."

Parkman hadn't moved. The phone was still suspended between him and Alex. How the hell couldn't he hear the wiry little bastard reenter the room? One day, Alex would give him a coronary.

"We're listening."

"I'm Detective Ricigliano with Toronto Police."

"You called last night." It wasn't a question.

"I did."

"What happened to Sarah? How bad is it?"

"Not sure yet. Come meet me at the hospital. We can speak with the doctor together."

"Where?"

"Toronto General."

"Okay, we'll take a taxi."

"Would you like me to send a cruiser?"

"Absolutely not. Tell us the worst, though." Parkman set the phone on the bed beside him and started putting on his shoes.

"I met with Sarah after the courthouse. We had a talk, a coffee. After she stole my gun and my police-issued vehicle —"

"She stole your gun?" Parkman blurted, stopping what he was doing and staring at Alex. He knew Sarah had a weapon from her last text shortly before three that afternoon, but he didn't know she had taken Ricigliano's.

"Well, sort of."

"How does someone *sort of* steal something?" He started on the second shoe.

"Long story. Look, she stole a Honda Civic, which crashed on the Gardiner."

"Any idea why Sarah's running around Toronto stealing weapons and vehicles?" Parkman asked, even though he knew Vivian had told her to.

"Not a fucking clue," Ricigliano said. "But I know her sister is behind it all. And I need my weapon back."

"Broken bones? Missing parts? Anything you can tell us about her condition?"

"Unfortunately, nothing at this time. But I was at the accident site."

Parkman jumped up and grabbed his wallet. He lifted the phone and started for the door. Alex was already there.

"How bad was it?"

"Bad. Jaws of life bad. A fire, too."

"Sarah burned?"

"Not that I'm aware of."

"Okay, we'll be there inside thirty minutes." They stopped at the elevator and pushed the button.

"There's one more thing."

"What?"

"It was an explosive device. The car was rigged to blow."

Parkman and Alex stared at each other. This was getting worse by the hour.

"Are you saying Sarah stole a car that was sabotaged?"

"Yes."

"Before I hang up, how do I know you're on the level? What guarantee can you offer that we're not walking into a trap with arrest warrants and shit?"

"Turn on CP24. It's all over the news from several hours ago. Your girl has a name, a reputation. She's under police protection at the hospital now. Paperwork has already been started to fly her back to California to face murder charges."

"That'll never happen." The elevator doors opened.

"Let's hope not because I don't believe for one minute that—"

Parkman ended the call and stepped onto the elevator.

"What the hell is going on?" he asked Alex.

The martial arts master stared back, a tear slipping over his eyelid, his hands in such tight fists that they were stark white clumps at the ends of his arms.

"I will never stop," Alex whispered as the elevator descended, his voice cut off with emotion.

"Me neither," Parkman said, knowing what Alex meant.

Then he wrapped his arms around Alex.

It was the closest he'd ever been to the young man, and he wondered for the first time if anyone had ever hugged him.

Chapter 24

SARAH ROLLED OVER AND opened her eyes. A hospital room. Sterile smell, white walls, and a bustle of activity in the corridor beyond her room.

The car accident. Edward Sweeney had done it. He caused the accident somehow. It all came back to her in a flash.

She did a quick inventory of her body, moving her toes and her fingers. Certain areas had minor aches, but nothing felt broken.

Her wrist caught on to something when she tried to lift her right arm.

It didn't hurt much to lift her head and see the handcuff that bound her to the steel pole on the side of the bed.

She rested her head back on the pillow.

Why Vivian? What was the point?

She'd stolen Alistair's car so she could have the accident. Was all that to spare the car's owner the unpleasantness of flipping upside down on the highway? And if so, her sister has set her up to be arrested now. She'd stolen a weapon from a detective at the mall, absconded with her SUV, then stole the Honda, only to drop right into police custody.

Brilliant work, sis. Now what?

Nothing made sense in almost all of her dealings with her sister until whatever was going on was over, but this one seemed to worsen. The entire scenario offered her a glimpse of what Aaron must've felt after his face was disfigured by a military man named Hamilton. And it was all because of the tasks Vivian sent them on.

Sure, Aaron explained on the phone why he was in Santa Rosa and that he'd come after her. They would be okay, but how long would it be before they would see each other?

Vivian, tell me what to do. We need to fix this and bring our team home. This is getting stupid now. I'm losing my patience.

The door to her room popped open.

A red-haired woman in a white lab coat entered. "Ahh, you're awake."

Before the door closed, Sarah saw a uniformed officer on a chair just outside her door.

"How are you feeling?" the woman asked.

"Who are you?"

"My name is Vicki Herald. I'm your doctor." Herald checked a computer screen affixed to the wall, then made a few notes on a paper beside it.

"So." She looked up. "How are you feeling?"

Sarah jerked her cuffed hand, making sure the clanging was loud. "Not doing so well. Any chance you could get this removed? It's cutting into my circulation."

Herald leaned over to examine Sarah's wrist. "You'll be fine, Miss Roberts. This restraint isn't on too tight."

"Why am I cuffed to the bed?" she asked, knowing the answer.

Herald stepped closer to her. "I'll tell you what. When we finish our little chat, I'll have that officer come in and explain the handcuff to you. How's that sound?"

Was that judgment in Herald's tone she detected or sarcasm?

"Sarah, do you mind if I call you Sarah?"

"Sure, if I can call you Vicki."

"Works for me. Now, Sarah, you were in a car accident, and luckily, you were able to walk away from it."

Sarah lifted her wrist, the cuff clanging against the side. "Not necessarily."

Vicki seemed to hold back a smile as she turned away. Her finger ran down the page she'd been writing on, and then she faced Sarah again.

"We did some X-rays and found no broken bones or fractures."

"Good to know." It was a relief. Getting through this recent shit would've been extra hard if she had broken her legs or something worse like her back. There would have been no coming back from that with Vivian if it had been the case.

"The accident was bad, as far as I understand it," Vicki said. "They had to extract you from the vehicle. Then they brought you here, and once the X-rays were completed, we were able to take off the neck brace. Consider yourself lucky that your injuries are so minimal."

Sarah stared at the ceiling with images of Aaron, Daniel, and Benjamin going through her mind. "Yeah, feeling so lucky right now."

"Well, I'll continue explaining what tests we did and then tell you what we found."

Sarah fixed her gaze on the doctor. "What you found?"

"In a moment." Vicki went back to the computer on the side and tapped the keyboard. "Okay, we did a CT scan and made sure there was no internal bleeding and no organ injuries. All good on that count." She stared at Sarah a moment. "I have no idea how you were able to flip a car on the Gardiner, get hit as many times as it did, and show up here with fewer injuries than if you fell off a bicycle. I would venture a guess that you have someone looking out for you."

Some of her animosity for her sister ebbed. "I guess you could say that."

"Finally, Sarah, we checked your bloodwork, and everything is good. You're fit, in shape, strong, and minus a few bruises, you're good to go."

Sarah watched Vicki's face. The doctor was holding something back.

"Except?" she asked.

"Well, we found elevated levels of the hCG hormone in your blood."

"Can you explain? Not sure what an hCG hormone is."

"Sarah, when was your last period?"

She frowned. It had only been a few months since she

started having regular periods again. The miscarriage from last February and the stress from the loss of their baby had thrown her entire system out of whack. She wasn't even focused on when they came and went. Before she got pregnant last year, she was able to nail down the day her cycle started and often when it ended. When she was on the pill, it was like clockwork, but lately, her inner workings were a mess, literally.

"I have no idea. Four weeks, maybe six weeks at least."

"Sarah," Vicki said, her tone serious. "This is probably the first you've heard this then, but you're eight weeks pregnant."

Chapter 25

PARKMAN RESTED A HAND on his sick stomach the entire ride to the hospital. For the first time in a long time, he actually felt like everything was coming apart. Was this the end of over a decade of vigilantism for Sarah and the men in her life? The only good thing that came out of this was that Aaron and Sarah were back together. Well, sort of. They were in opposite countries and both in custody but were back together.

Alex had stopped speaking again, lost in his own world of thought.

The taxi pulled up to the hospital. Parkman handed the driver several twenties, and they hopped out.

"You may want to make yourself scarce," he said to Alex. "Your name is on their list."

Alex nodded and strode in the opposite direction along a

sidewalk, headed toward the back of the hospital.

"Stay close, though."

He detected a slight nod as the man vaulted over a railing and disappeared behind a wall.

"Parkman?" someone called.

He spun around as a middle-aged woman approached. He had to raise a hand to ward off the setting sun to see her face.

"I thought that was you," she said, extending her hand.

They shook.

"You're Ricigliano?"

She nodded. "Your Sarah is something else."

"How bad are the injuries? What else have you learned?"

They started toward the front entrance.

"I checked on her in an official capacity and was told she has no injuries from the accident."

"No injuries?" Parkman's step faltered. As much as he was grateful to hear that, it didn't make sense. "Wasn't she in a car accident?"

"She sure was. Extracted from the vehicle with the Jaws of Life, too. Other than a few minor bruises, Sarah's ready to go."

Relief swept over him as they entered the front of the hospital.

"There's just one small wrinkle I can't fix," she added.

"What's that?"

"The arrest warrant in California."

Parkman stopped walking and faced her. "You're kidding?"

"I wish I were, but it doesn't stop there."

Parkman crossed his arms. "Whatever she has done can

be explained away. The rest she didn't do."

"And the authorities south of us want her in custody so they can allow the courts to figure it all out."

"Which is something I understand from my time on the force, but I'm telling you, Sarah had nothing to do with Malcolm King's murder in that hotel room in Santa Rosa."

"Which is why Sarah and I went for coffee today." She tapped Parkman's arm. "Follow me to the cafeteria. We'll get a coffee and head up to Sarah's room."

Parkman allowed himself to be guided to the hospital cafeteria, where he got a large cup of coffee.

"Take a seat," Ricigliano said.

"I don't want to sit. I'm heading up to get Sarah."

"Parkman, sit down. Five minutes. And prepare yourself. There's no *getting* Sarah."

"We'll see about that." Parkman started away from her.

"We know who is behind everything that's been happening to you and your friends," Ricigliano said from behind him, her voice rising to be heard over the minor clatter of the cafeteria.

That stopped him. He turned around, walked back a few steps, then said, "Who?"

"It's a man named Edward Sweeney."

Parkman frowned. "I don't know that name."

"Please, sit for a few minutes. I'll explain what I know."

Parkman studied her face for a moment. Her kindness seemed genuine, which helped him decide he could give her five minutes of his time at least. After all, she was the one who called to tell him Sarah was here. As much as it seemed Ricigliano was trying to help, his nerves were rattled, and he wasn't playing fair.

"You're right. Let's sit. Sarah will still be there when we're through."

After finding a corner table, Ricigliano told him everything, starting with the courthouse meeting, the Starbucks in the mall, and Sarah taking her weapon after Ricigliano expressed her interest in helping. She even showed Parkman the text Sarah had sent her when they were sitting across from each other at the Starbucks.

"And so, I feel Sarah stole Alistair McNeil's car because that man was Sweeney's next target."

"You think she took the car to avoid McNeil getting behind the wheel?"

Ricigliano nodded. "He called in the theft. He'd started it and went back in the house for his wallet. Sarah jumped in and raced it to the highway. Witnesses claimed a gray van was playing Frogger with her before they drove alongside each other, and then boom, the car Sarah was in lifted off the highway and flipped after the explosive device blew. It had been planted under McNeil's car. Some of it detonated, but through pure luck, one section of it didn't. That's what caused the fire."

"The fire?"

"Everything's fine, Parkman. The SUV that was following too closely took on some damage. They had an extinguisher with them. And McNeil had his car insured. Everything will be back to normal soon enough."

"I'm guessing this Sweeney guy owns a gray van."

Ricigliano nodded.

In order to hear what Ricigliano knew, Parkman

continued. "Do you know why Sweeney would go after McNeil?" Parkman recalled last night's call with Darwin and how Alistair had been accused of several beatings.

"Alistair McNeil was recently released from custody after facing numerous aggravated assault charges. Prostitutes were beaten, and witnesses placed him at the scene. The beatings stopped when he was picked up. Not a single hooker was attacked while he was in custody. Everything points to it being him—along with his admission, he spent time in the area where these women work nightly. He watched them from his car, but the jury returned with a not guilty verdict."

"After what you told me about Sweeney's stepbrother's death in Santa Rosa, and that Sarah was in Sweeney's courtroom this morning, along with him owning a gray van and what people saw on the highway before the accident, it sure looks like Edward Sweeney is our guy."

"You know how this works, though, Parkman. Evidence. Can't do shit without it."

Parkman drank more from his coffee. "Sarah knows something."

"What does she know?"

He shrugged. "She has to know something. Otherwise, why steal Alistair's car? Why be in that courtroom?"

"Okay, how about asking her why she took my gun and when she'll return it?"

Parkman pushed his chair back and stood. "You want evidence. That's something I'm sure Sarah will be able to give you."

Ricigliano stood, too. "Unfortunately, that's where you're wrong."

"Why?"

"She's upstairs in a guarded room."

"Police officer guarded?"

Ricigliano nodded. "Once the doctor clears her for travel, tonight or tomorrow, they're shipping her back to California to face murder charges."

Parkman's mouth dropped open. "You can't let that happen."

"Out of my hands."

"Then we take her out of here and get you that evidence. Once we have everything we need, Sweeney is arrested, and it ends."

"Not that easy."

"It is if you just say fuck it."

He pivoted on his heels and started away.

"Parkman, wait up."

He didn't slow on his way to the elevators.

Ricigliano caught up. "What do you mean, fuck it?"

"Sometimes in life, regardless of risk or consequences, there are moments that you give in, or you say, fuck it. This is one of those moments."

They got to the elevator banks, and he hit the button to call the lift down.

"Are you saying I should risk everything I am and my career just to say fuck it and join the Sarah Roberts team?"

"Something like that. You don't have to join. Just help with this. Daniel or Benjamin didn't do what they're suggesting. We could use your help." The elevator opened. Luckily, it was empty. They stepped on, and Ricigliano hit a button. "All I'm saying is," Parkman continued, "you want evidence, we can figure a way to get it. But we can't do shit with Sarah bound en route to California when we both know she didn't murder that guy."

They rose several floors, then slowed, and the doors opened.

Ricigliano leaned in close to Parkman as they stepped off the elevator. "I already stuck my neck out. She took my weapon and SUV with only mock resistance. Do you know how that looks for me?"

"I do. But what's worse is the half-ass job. You want to help, stick your neck out all the way. What you did was risky but still safe."

Ricigliano shook her head. "I can't. I won't. I'm a detective first, Parkman, not a vigilante."

He slowed to look at her, then stopped walking. It felt like their world was falling apart now that Sarah was in custody. "What room number?"

"The one with the cop out front."

"Oh, right. Got it." He heard the sarcasm in his voice but didn't regret it. Now, it was his turn to lean in close. "Sure, Sarah stole McNeil's car, but she probably saved his life with that device on it. This isn't about just being a vigilante. This is something bigger, greater, something no one else could do. Only she can because she's Sarah Roberts. And with us, you're either part of the problem or part of the solution. You don't want to help, fine, leave. We appreciate what you've done so far. Oh, and when you're ready to have a fuck it moment, call me. We could use you. Otherwise, stay out of the way."

Those words were unfair considering all the help she'd

offered so far, but he stormed off anyway, leaving her standing alone in the corridor.

He didn't want her to be culpable when they took out the cop guarding Sarah's room and helped her escape the hospital. If Ricigliano weren't in all the way, she would only get hurt, and he felt she was far too special for that.

Even after all these years, he was still learning from Sarah.

Sometimes, you have to be mean to teach something.

Sometimes, you have to hurt and suffer a little to enact change.

And there was something about Ricigliano that could be counted on, trusted.

He'd bank on that when the day came.

Chapter 26

The tears came freely. The memories of her previous pregnancy, the loss, swept over her. Her love for Aaron and their baby growing in her belly made her heart swell. Why couldn't he be here with her?

She couldn't believe it, wouldn't believe it without the doctor, Vicki Herald, showing her the results on paper.

Could that have been why it felt tighter than usual when she wore Kevlar recently? How about her feeling nauseous, too? Like in the courthouse bathroom that morning.

Overwhelmed with emotions, she had asked to be alone for a bit. Doctor Herald said to expect detectives to discuss some transfer to the United States within the hour. Most of the other stuff Doctor Herald said before she exited, the room was lost to Sarah as her focus became elusive, her mind wandering.

It wasn't until the hospital room door closed that she truly wept for her new baby.

Then, like a tsunami, it hit her that she had put her unborn child at risk because of a car accident today.

Sarah rolled onto her right side and stared at the wall, her back to the room's door. Anyone passing by her room wouldn't be able to see her face through the little window.

"What were you thinking, Vivian?" She clenched her teeth, barely moving her lips as she spoke in a whisper. "How could you recklessly send me to steal that car, knowing full well it was rigged to blow? The danger you put my baby and me in is unforgivable."

Her sister hovered in her consciousness, but she remained silent.

"I know you're listening, so allow me to tell you that if I had lost this pregnancy because of what you—"

HEY! Vivian shouted so loud in Sarah's head she jolted, the handcuff clanging against the metal bar. *How many bones are broken? How many internal injuries?*

In rare moments like this, it was as if Vivian was in the room. But there was something different about her voice. It seemed more emotional.

I knew exactly how that car would land. I saw it and was given a pass to offer you the information.

"Given a pass?" Sarah wiped at her eyes. "Someone controls you? Manages the information?"

There are things at play here that are bigger than you and me, and I can't discuss them. Just know that your safety and your baby's safety are guaranteed. Now, fuck off with your lack of trust in me! I'm family first. Always!

As the last word was spoken, her sister seemed to calm down, and then, after a few hurried instructions, she vanished from Sarah's head. Her sister slipped away like a soft puff of air through her consciousness.

What the hell did that mean? What things were at play? Sarah was no one's puppet. Or was she? Hadn't she been doing her sister's bidding all this time?

This all had to stop when the baby came, though. How could she continue living this life with a baby?

And those new instructions? How was she supposed to be at the Sunnyside Beach by some outdoor pool by ten tonight? And then that stuff for two in the morning. There was no way Ricigliano would agree to be there, no way in hell, and what for? Not after Sarah stole her weapon and lost it on the Gardiner somewhere.

How would she tell Aaron about the baby? *When* would she tell him?

There was so much to handle, so much to do.

And yet, she was shackled to a hospital bed and scheduled to spend the next year or more in custody in California.

The room's door opened. Her hands clenched, grasping at the white sheets, drawing them into a tiny ball in her fists. If they thought they were going to drag her to jail in California for a murder she didn't commit, to spend a year or more in custody during a lengthy murder trial, they had another thing coming. There was no way in hell she was having her baby while in custody. No fucking way in hell.

"Sarah," a man whispered.

Parkman?

She spun around and looked up into his face. "Oh, Parkman," she said as a new wave of tears formed in her eyes.

"Sarah." He leaned down to hug her. "What's wrong? Why are you crying?"

Sarah clung to him with her free arm, holding him close to her. After a few moments, she inhaled deeply and let him go.

"They said you were in a car accident." Parkman stood to his full height.

The expression on his face was one of terror. He probably hadn't ever seen her this emotional before.

"I'm fine," she said. "But this is a problem." She held up the cuffed hand.

"You aren't crying because of that." Parkman pointed at her cuff.

Sarah looked away for a moment, then turned back to him. "I need out of here. We have a meeting to be at tonight, and we need Ricigliano's help."

"She won't help. I just had a talk with her."

"I need to have that talk with her. There's new information."

"What's going on? Tell me."

"There's a chance we can stop this tomorrow."

"How?"

"Not sure yet. I just have locations and random times. No idea why it's all important."

"For now, consider Ricigliano is out. And she wants her gun back."

"Tell her to charge me with stealing it."

"What? Why?"

"So I can stay here longer before they try to fly me back to the States for a murder I didn't commit."

"Yeah, but if this is all over tomorrow …"

"There's only a chance."

"I'm willing to work with that."

"But we need Ricigliano."

"Why her, specifically?"

Sarah shrugged. "Vivian used her name with an instruction."

Parkman nodded. "Okay, so why the tears when I came in?"

She stared into his eyes for a few heartbeats, then pointed at the paperwork on the side counter by Doctor Herald's computer.

"Check my bloodwork."

"Oh no …" Parkman whispered.

"It's nothing negative like cancer. Just check it."

Parkman picked up the paperwork and scanned it to the bottom. "It's a lot of mumbo jumbo to me. Elevated hormones and white T counts are normal."

"The hCG hormone."

"Wait, why have I heard of that?"

"Parkman?"

He set the paperwork down and moved closer to the bed.

"Yes, Sarah?"

"I'm pregnant again."

His eyes widened, and then a moment later, he smiled so wide. "Oh, Sarah, I'm so happy for you and Aaron—"

He must've realized the predicament they were in at the

moment. Several chaotic thoughts had to have raced through his brain because he glanced around the hospital room and then refocused on her face.

"The accident," he whispered.

"I know. I thought the same thing. Vivian assured me they"—Sarah pointed toward the sky—"knew what they were doing."

"They?"

"I don't know much more than to say that someone manages Vivian somehow. The information was approved, as Vivian called it."

"Holy shit. That's a new development."

"What freaks me out is where it's leading."

"What do you mean?"

"I mean, is all this just a training ground for something larger, something bigger? Like I'm to have my baby, raise them to a certain age, and then the two of us stop a nuclear war or something?"

"You're nobody's pawn, Sarah."

"Well, I can tell you one thing for sure."

Parkman leaned closer, placing a hand on her shoulder. "What? Tell me."

"All this stops when the baby comes. Actually, it stops sooner. Can you see me chasing an asshole down some back alleyway at eight months? Nope, not this girl."

"I'm sure they've taken that into account." Parkman nodded toward the ceiling. "Whoever they are."

She grabbed the hand on her shoulder and squeezed it. "I'm glad you're here. I need your help."

"What kind of help?"

"I need out of here."

The door swung open, and three men in suits barged in without knocking.

"Sarah Roberts," the lead man in the dark suit said.

Parkman moved in front of her to block their way. "You guys got some form of ID?"

"Step aside," the man said. "Or I will have you removed."

Parkman moved to within an inch of the man. "Produce some form of identification, or I will have you removed. Who the fuck barges into a woman's private hospital room without knocking?"

The door opened again, interrupting the man as he went to grab Parkman's arm.

"Parkman," Ricigliano said. "Let them pass. They're federal agents."

"What's the issue with identifying themselves?" he asked.

The man in front moved around Parkman. "We are cleared to move the patient into custody and remove her to a secure facility. Our prisoner is of no concern to you."

The other agents moved past Parkman, one bumping into Parkman on purpose.

If she weren't handcuffed to the bed, a fight would've ensued, agent or no agent. No one treats her Parkman like that.

"I wonder what your unprofessional side looks like," Sarah said, glaring at the lead man. "Because your professional manner isn't fit for the badge you supposedly carry."

"And your bedside manner leaves something to be desired—"

"Excuse me," a woman shouted from behind the agents. "Who are you, and how did you get in here?"

Doctor Vicki Herald stepped farther into the room. Parkman moved up alongside the bed to place himself bodily between the people in the room and Sarah.

"I haven't cleared my patient for travel yet," Herald said.

"We won't be requiring that, Doctor." The lead man nodded at the other agent, who strode around the bed and stuck a key in Sarah's cuff, releasing it from her wrist.

"Sarah Roberts is our prisoner." The man turned back to the people now assembled in her room. "We are taking her to the airport. She will leave this evening for California. Detective Ricigliano has seen our paperwork." He faced Doctor Herald. "If further medical treatment of Sarah Roberts is required, that will be handled south of the border. I assure you, our doctors are quite capable. Now, if you will all leave so Sarah can get dressed." The agent waved toward the door.

Herald caught Sarah's eye and mouthed the words, *I'm sorry*.

Then Ricigliano winked at Sarah and left the room.

What the hell did that mean? Why wink? This wasn't good. She had to leave, get away from them.

Ricigliano held Parkman's arm as she led him out of the room. The last person to leave was the lead agent.

"You have two minutes," he said, then closed the door.

Sarah bolted from the bed, grabbed her pile of clothes, and slipped into them. A few muscles protested, but she ignored them. She was only eight weeks pregnant. Getting to the bottom of this was more important than anything, but being out of the country and in custody did nothing for her.

She grabbed her cell phone. Less than ten percent battery power. There were a dozen missed calls and over fifteen texts. Many of them were from Darwin in Italy. She would read them when she could, but she wondered if he had learned something new. Was he coming to join them? She sure wished he was here.

The door would open at any moment, and she wanted to be ready.

At the side counter, she snatched the bloodwork document off the desk, and after folding it, she pocketed it. Vivian said proof she was pregnant was important, yet Sarah had no idea why.

And there had been no chance to speak with Ricigliano.

The one thing that drove Sarah crazy more than anything else when doing things Vivian asked of her was how meddling the authorities got. It was always their show. If they'd just leave her alone, they would have all their answers by tomorrow, perhaps sooner.

But by carting her off on a plane to face charges of murder she had nothing to do with, wasted everyone's time and allowed the real murderer to roam free.

Ready to go, she opened the drawers in the cabinet beside the sink, lifting out a few packets of syringes.

"You won't need any of those," the man said as he stepped inside her room.

Sarah jerked around to stare at him.

"Drop what's in your hands and come with us willingly."

He moved farther into the room, his other agents following him. "Don't make me have to restrain you."

"Where's Parkman?"

"What matters is your transport to the United States for the alleged crimes you've committed there."

Sarah let go of the packages in the drawer and crossed her arms as she faced him. "What about the charges here? Don't I need to face them first? I stole a car. I wrecked it on the Gardiner. Oh wait, I stole a homicide detective's gun, too." She nodded. "I think I'll stay here to deal with that first."

Something changed in the man's eyes, like he had a gleam of respect for her at the mention of stealing a detective's weapon.

"We were informed the car's owner was thankful for your sacrifice and did not want to press changes. The detective's weapon is being sorted out, and there are no pending charges here in Toronto. You're free to travel, Miss Roberts." He held out a hand. "Please, don't make this hard on yourself."

"I can't leave," she said.

"You gave up your right to decide that when you were in California."

This wasn't happening. It couldn't be happening. How was she supposed to get out of this?

"Where is my friend, Parkman?"

"He left the hospital. Now, please, come with us."

"Left the hospital? Yeah, right."

"Look, Sarah." When the man tightened his jaw, muscles protruded under his ears, giving him a chiseled face. "You are leaving with us regardless of how you feel about it. We are leaving now. If you don't want to walk, we can strap you to a wheelchair or carry you. But we are leaving."

"What's the big hurry? When's our flight?"

The man sighed, exhaling loudly. He shook his head and glanced at the floor, mumbling something under his breath. "He said you would be difficult."

Sarah closed the gap of four feet between them and pushed the man back once. He staggered a few feet, regained his composure, and adjusted his suit jacket.

"Who said I'd be difficult?"

The lead agent glanced over his shoulder at the open door. Sarah followed his gaze.

The cop guarding her room was in a deep conversation with Ricigliano. The cop was shaking his head. They were obviously disagreeing on something.

"Time is short, Sarah. Our window is closing."

Our window? What the hell was he talking about?

She met his gaze and stared into his eyes. "You're not a fed, are you?" she whispered.

He returned her stare for over five seconds, then said, "Sarah, please come with us."

"Who sent you?"

The man glanced over his shoulder again.

The cop outside the room was on the phone now. Ricigliano shot Sarah a worried look.

Were they breaking her out, and she was causing too much resistance? If so, who sent them?

"I'll go," she said.

The lead agent—if that's who he was—sighed again.

"Gentlemen." He waved at the two men who were with him.

They stepped out into the corridor and walked shoulder-to-shoulder away from the room. The lead agent led Sarah in behind them.

"Wait," the cop who was guarding the room said.

"We're not waiting," the man holding Sarah's arm shouted back over his shoulder. "She's our prisoner now. The paperwork is coming. You've been relieved of duty."

At the elevator, the four of them got on. Sarah turned around and peered down the corridor as the cop beside Ricigliano pulled the phone away from his ear, a look of shock on his face.

"*Wait!*" he shouted and started for the elevator. "Nobody has cleared this—"

The doors closed on his pleas.

"That was too close," the man said, releasing her arm.

"Who are you guys?" she asked.

"We've been paid to be in your service for twenty-four hours. What would you have us do next?"

Sarah smiled.

"Have I got a job for you guys." She breathed a sigh of relief. "And now the fun will start."

"Good, because that wasn't any fun at all. We hate pretending to be the good guys. Too stressful."

Chapter 27

WHEN HE WEIGHED HOW much had gone wrong versus how solid his *Death Wish* plan was coming together, Ed realized everything would still work out.

Sarah had to be dead. Who could've survived that car accident? In his mirrors, he had seen the flames. He saw the car sliding on its roof, smashing into the guardrail, the SUV behind it knocking the Honda into a nasty spin.

With Sarah Roberts finally out of his life, he would plan another final hit on Alistair McNeil and then lie low for a while.

All the evidence still pointed to Sarah and her friends. The police knew nothing about him. The only detective who had spoken to him in the past week was that woman in his courtroom, and it was just to tell him his brother was dead.

Was she even a detective? Was that all a lie to get to him?

Because after she said that, Steve texted him, and only Steve would know their usual meeting spot. No one else on earth would know that particular beach.

So why lie to him about Steve?

As much as he couldn't figure any of it out, he knew Sarah was behind it all. Somehow, she'd figured out what Steve had done in California and came after him here in Toronto. That had to be it because how else did she know about Alistair McNeil?

Also, there was no way Sarah had his stepbrother's cell phone because he had talked to him, voice to voice when Sarah was in Toronto.

No, Steve was fine, and it was Sarah who was dead, and rightly so.

Once Alistair was gone, they had no further intended targets at the time. They could spend six months or a year and wait for more targets. Next time, they wouldn't involve outsiders like Sarah and her team of martial arts rejects. Next time, they'd just make a clean break, do the job, and move on.

When Steve got home, Ed would apologize to him. It had been his idea to go after Sarah. She had done so much damage over the years. How many assaults was she guilty of? How many deaths were because of her, and how many crimes were in her name? And then, when he added how many times she'd been in a court of law to realize some consequences for her crimes, he came up empty.

The authorities had tried many times, but not Sarah Roberts.

She was an untouchable.

Ed had read an article in a Toronto newspaper that Sarah had once gone to the roof of the CN Tower and shot a woman who then fell off the roof. After that, Sarah jumped, a parachute tied to her back.

How the hell she got away with this shit was beyond Edward Sweeney.

"Well, not anymore, you little bitch," he said to himself as he drove along Front Street, downtown Toronto. "If you're not dead, you will be soon."

A country had laws for a reason, and who was Sarah that she could disregard them at will? What boggled Ed's mind was why the authorities didn't just shut her down. He'd sometimes read that they'd even *asked* for her help.

He shook his head at the absolute stupidity of it all.

Sure, she was good. He'd give her that. Otherwise, how could she have caught onto him so fast? To keep showing up like she did was impressive, but she wouldn't show up anymore. He made sure of that.

He passed John Street and slowed to make the right onto Windsor Street. As soon as he turned, he set the blinker to turn again and entered the underground parking lot.

He had to hide the van until everything was settled in a day or two. Where better to hide it than in the basement of a busy parkade?

He drove down to the lowest level and found a spot in a corner unit. Once the van was backed to within an inch of the wall, he cut the engine, grabbed his things, and hopped out the passenger side.

One quick look around confirmed he was alone.

It didn't take long for him to drop to his knee in front of

the van and remove the front license plate. He retightened the two screws in their holes and tossed the plate inside the back of the van.

Now, it was just an empty van, commonplace, without visible markers, parked backward in a corner spot in the basement level of a Toronto parkade. Virtually impossible for anyone to find and report to the police.

It was just one more safety measure in case anyone who witnessed the accident on the Gardiner with the Honda Civic claimed a gray van was dodging traffic, too. Not to mention the shit Sarah knew. He couldn't rely on the fact that she would know what he was driving and would tell the authorities if she survived the accident.

Edward started for the parkade elevator. Once he was back at the street level, he felt completely free of all the shit Sarah had caused him.

He would meet his stepbrother that night, then hit Alistair tomorrow.

After all that, he'd go back to work, and that would be the end of it—for now.

And the people that were supposed to die would be dead. For that was the way of the *Death Wish*.

Just like Rueben Ellis, Ed's first kill.

Nobody deserved it as much as that man.

Once his first was dealt with, Ed knew he could do it again. Killing Reuben felt so good that he *had* to do it again.

Deep down inside, he knew he wouldn't stop, couldn't stop.

But he'd stick to only people who deserved it. People who beat the system. People like Jason Grant, Malcolm King, and Alistair McNeil.

People like Sarah Roberts.

One block from the parkade, he slipped inside a coffee shop and grabbed a large one with a few donuts. He needed the caffeine and sugar.

Then he'd rent a car, have dinner, and wait for his meeting with his brother.

Everything was finally coming together well.

Edward Sweeney couldn't be happier.

Chapter 28

The foursome exited the hospital and headed toward the parking area.

"We must be quick," the lead man said. "That cop will make phone calls."

"I need a name," Sarah said. "What do I call you?"

"Call me Disco. Those two don't need names." He nodded at the two men who came with him.

"Okay, why Disco? Where did it come from? And why don't they need names?"

Disco glanced at her, then turned to watch the parking lot as they strode across it. "They don't need names because they only take orders from me. And I use Disco for several reasons. It's an old nickname from my teens. I love the music, and I can often dance my way out of messes. So, the name stuck."

Something caught Sarah's eye about seven vehicles away —a small movement just above the lip of a trunk. Did Disco and his men see it?

In the few seconds before they passed that area, she decided to say nothing.

Steps away, she slowed.

A black form launched upward, and the first man escorting them dropped to the concrete. The second man buckled at the waist, then slowly fell.

Sarah took a step back to a place of marginal safety.

Disco jumped forward, a weapon already in his hand.

All this occurred in mere seconds, and then Alex disarmed Disco. The man was bent forward at an impossible angle as Alex clung to the man's wrist, twisting it to a spot where Sarah feared it would snap.

"Alex, I think these guys are with us."

"You think?" Parkman said, moving alongside the car to her left.

"Hey, hey," Disco grunted. "Take it easy."

"Who hired you?" Parkman asked.

Disco hesitated a second, and Alex moved an inch. The man shouted once in a high-pitched voice.

Parkman bent down to look in Disco's face. "Last chance before he does some real damage."

"Some guy out of Italy paid for all three of us. I don't get names. All I know is the Italian connection came recommended. The deal was," Disco winced, then continued, "get Sarah out of that hospital. Act as FBI agents, and there'd be a large bonus." He dropped to a knee. "We were told someone close to Sarah would know we were coming."

"You said he came recommended," Parkman said. "Who recommended the man who hired you?"

"A guy we did a job with a year ago."

Sarah glanced around the immediate area, but they hadn't created too much attention yet.

"A name," she said. "We need something substantial to include you guys here."

"Big fucker. All muscle, all business. His name was Bruno. That's all I know. I can't tell you if it's a code name or a real name. But it was Bruno who recommended the guy in Italy."

Sarah and Parkman exchanged a glance. Then they looked at Alex.

They nodded, and Alex released Disco.

"Holy fuck," Disco said, massaging his wrist. He glanced down at his men, who were still sleeping on the pavement. Then he fixed his gaze on Alex. "What the fuck are you?"

Alex's eyes didn't budge. The man stood in his stance, feet shoulder-width apart, hands near his hips, always at the ready. He didn't answer Disco's question.

"If I'm still part of this *shit*," Disco said. "Then we need to leave. Now."

"Where's your vehicle?" Sarah asked.

Disco pointed at a black H2 Hummer.

"Bruno didn't talk to you about discretion?"

"We didn't deal with Bruno. He was the recommendation. As I said, the man we dealt with in Italy—I don't have a name—transferred funds less than two hours ago. That's my personal vehicle. I brought it because this job was supposed to be a girl in a car accident needing to be released early from the hospital. We had no idea we were walking into a fucking ninja convention."

No one laughed.

Sarah gestured at the Hummer. "Let's go. Get your men up. We can talk on the way."

Alex shot a hand out for Disco to stop. The man literally jumped back one foot even though they didn't touch each other.

Alex slumped to the ground, lifted the first man, clamped a hand on his nose and mouth, then slapped him several times. When he released the man to the ground, he snapped awake. Alex duplicated the action on the other guy, snapping him awake, too.

"What the hell hit us?" the first guy asked.

"A dock in pay," Disco said. "Get to the Hummer. Now."

Both men, slightly sluggish from their encounter, got to their feet and forged ahead to open the Hummer's doors.

Alex moved along with them, staying one foot to the right of Sarah.

She lightly punched his arm in thanks, which was something no one ever got to do. Alex's reflexes were always in combat mode, but when Sarah reached out to touch him, it was like he welcomed it.

"Thank you," she whispered. "I'll always be in your debt, my dear friend."

Alex heard her, she was sure, but the man turned away and scanned the parking lot. It wasn't until they reached the Hummer seconds later that she saw a small tear in his eye. He had looked away because he didn't want her to see the emotion on his face.

It reminded her of the talk they'd had before she left for California and how he said he would take several beatings for her, even die for her, if it meant she'd be okay.

It wasn't love in the romantic sense, but love just the same. Alex had dedicated his life to her, and she knew in that moment that she could count on him to the end of days. It was something worth treasuring, something money couldn't buy. Loyalty to a loved one, a friend, at this level, was earned, and along with that came a level of unprecedented gratitude.

She wondered if she could say the same of her man, her Aaron.

They filed into the Hummer. Sarah sat between Parkman and Alex in the back seat.

"You okay to drive?" Disco asked his man from the front passenger seat.

The driver nodded and started the vehicle.

As he eased out of the spot, three police cars raced up to the front of the hospital.

"Get us clear of the area," Disco said.

Parkman nudged Sarah. She glanced over and stared at his cell phone. Darwin had texted him. It said: Sending an extraction team for Sarah.

She nodded and withdrew her phone. Scrolling through the missed texts, she opened one from Darwin: Sending friendlies. You'll be good to go soon.

Alex nudged her, and she saw his phone had a similar message.

Sarah shrugged and whispered, "Who knew?"

"All good back there?" Disco asked.

"All good," Parkman said.

The Hummer exited the hospital parking lot and headed south toward the lake.

"Where are we going?" Disco asked.

"Dinner," Sarah said. "We eat and plan. We have a ten o'clock meeting tonight down by the lake, then one more job to deal with after midnight."

"I'm assuming details are forthcoming."

"They are."

Disco shot a glance back at Alex.

"Are we good?" he asked. "We cool?"

Alex didn't move. He just stared at Disco.

"Does he talk?" Disco asked.

"Only when required," Sarah volunteered.

Disco spun around in his seat to look at Sarah. "Isn't it required when someone asks him a question?"

"Sure, if the question *required* an answer."

"What? I asked him if we were good."

"You're all good right now because if you weren't, he wouldn't be sitting calmly watching you like that. When you're not good, you'll know. These are things that don't require conversation."

Disco looked from Sarah to Alex, then back to Sarah.

"He reminds me of a loyal wolf sitting quietly beside you. Yet, without expression or much effort, he could murder us all in seconds."

"You'll be good to remember that. Stay on our side, and he'll protect you with those skills. Wrong us, and he enters combat mode. No one ever walks away from that but Alex."

"Trust me," Disco said, rolling his wrist in circles while

staring down at it. "I won't forget. My men and I have fought the best of the best, been shot, stabbed, and killed everything from experienced street fighters to top-level black belts. What he did today I've never seen."

"Most who do aren't here to discuss it."

Disco turned back in his seat and faced the front.

"Does he come with a price tag? We could use those kinds of skills."

"Loyalty can't be bought."

After a moment's pause, Disco said, "I'll remember that, too."

They all sat in silence as the driver aimed the Hummer for the lake and the restaurants in that area.

Chapter 29

Positioned five hundred meters from the outdoor pool, Sarah sat on a park bench and watched the waves of Lake Ontario calmly trickle in.

Detective Ricigliano had called her cell phone an hour before and apologized for allowing Sarah to be taken by the FBI.

"It's fine," Sarah had said. "I'm safe now."

"I tried, Sarah. I called Doctor Herald and talked her into refusing the release of her patient. I did everything possible, even arguing with the cop guarding your door to check their paperwork."

"As it turned out, they helped me. So, we're all good. But there is one thing."

"What one thing?" Ricigliano asked.

"I need one small favor."

Ricigliano didn't speak for a moment. Then she said, "I'm hesitant, Sarah. You have to understand. There are questions I'm unable to answer with my superiors. Like, where's my gun? What happened in the mall's food court? What happened at the hospital? Also, what—"

"Lucky for you, with the incident at the hospital, you were on the right side of things. You were working with the cop. No one can discipline you on that count."

"Look, Sarah, I want to help, but within the limits of my job. Meaning, when this is all over, I'd like to keep my job."

"Great, then what I have to ask of you will do just that."

"It will?"

"Absolutely."

There was a short pause, and then Ricigliano said, "Ask away."

"I need you to come to the Toronto Courthouse at two fifteen exactly. But come undetected and remain that way."

"Undetected, how? Like in disguise?"

"Undetected, as in don't set off any alarms."

"Alarms?" Ricigliano laughed. "Why would there be alarms at two fifteen in the afternoon? The building is filled with people at that time."

"Not two fifteen in the afternoon."

There was another pause, then, "You mean two fifteen in the morning?"

Sarah stared at a boat out on the water as it raced toward shore. "Yes, roughly five hours from now. My life depends on it."

"What?" Ricigliano's tone dropped a notch.

"If you fail to show, I might not make it." Seagulls flew

in circles over the water and sand, watching, searching for their late evening dinner.

"What about Parkman? Can't he show up?"

"Sure, but it won't work."

"What won't work?"

"I have no idea. I'm not told everything. All I know is it has to be you."

Ricigliano sighed on the line. "In other words, you need a cop?"

"Could be, but one I can trust would be best."

"Are you saying you trust me?"

"Ricigliano, will you come or not?"

"Enter the courthouse in the middle of the night without tripping alarms to save your life without backup or any reasons why or what I'm facing?"

"Yeah. That."

"Sarah, are you serious?"

"Deadly."

"Then I'll come early. I'll be there at one in the morning. Maybe earlier."

"Don't. He'll know. It has to be two fifteen."

"Who will know? What's going on?"

"I have no idea."

Sarah listened to Ricigliano's breathing on the other end for half a minute.

"Okay, I can live with that. What I mean is, I'll have to live with that because you're not going to tell me anything else, are you? Two fifteen in the morning, Toronto Courthouse. No sooner, no later. Otherwise, you might not make it."

Without confirming or denying anything the detective just said, Sarah whispered, "So, I guess we'll see you then, Detective."

"I guess so." After a moment, Ricigliano added, "Be safe, Sarah."

"I'll do my best. Be on time, Detective."

"I'll do my best—"

She had ended the call and then stared out at the expanse of Lake Ontario. The men were in position in two vehicles now.

They were ready for Edward Sweeney, provided the man showed his face at all.

And if not, they would see him tomorrow.

But something told her—well, Vivian did—that Ed would show at ten and that somehow, some way, by two in the morning, Sarah would have to deal with him at the courthouse, even though none of that made any sense.

It wasn't looking good for her, according to Vivian. Sarah swore that this had better not affect the baby, or she was out, and Vivian assured her that the baby would be fine. But how much was Vivian leaving out? How much was she *authorized* to tell Sarah? Who was in charge of Vivian?

All this new information scared Sarah because she'd always assumed it was just the two of them, and now more were involved.

What was the overall purpose in the end? To stop a criminal? To stop bad guys, one by one?

If that was the case, then fine. Yet, it seemed as if something bigger was coming.

But what could it be?

Vivian, am I being trained for something in the future?

With a baby coming, how useful would Sarah be going forward?

She shuddered to think of having a baby in her current world. That wasn't possible. Too dangerous. Changes would have to be made.

"Sarah," Parkman said from behind her. "It's time."

Sarah got to her feet, stared across Lake Ontario again, then turned and walked back toward the Hummer with Parkman.

Where the fuck are you, Vivian?

"Does everyone have the description of the van?" Sarah asked when she got back to the Hummer.

Disco nodded. "We know what we're looking for. Gray van, older model."

"How about Ed's hairstyle and facial features?"

"All good. We see him, we'll nab him." Disco moved closer. "Sarah, we got this."

"Yeah, well, I've heard different."

Disco frowned. "What have you heard?"

Parkman stepped closer, and Alex slipped in beside her.

"I've heard that it all might end tonight."

"Oh, well, that works for us, as our contract ends in slightly over twelve hours anyway."

Sarah nodded and moved away from the group. "If you're alive."

"What's that?" Disco asked.

"I'm going to wait by the fence." She pointed at the pool area.

The men moved into two different vehicles. Parkman,

Alex, and Disco in the Hummer, and Disco's two unnamed men in a Jeep. The Hummer would stay back as it was large and easily noticeable, and the mercenaries in the Jeep would patrol the parking area from end to end, looking for the gray van.

Sarah glanced over her shoulder as she approached the fence of the pool.

Edward was there somewhere. She could feel him.

It was happening tonight, that much she knew.

There was no going back.

And if it didn't finish tonight, Alistair's life was in danger tomorrow.

Before Sarah reached the fence, she glanced up at storm clouds as they moved in from the east. Rain would fall within the hour.

She placed a hand on her stomach, hoping one day she would bring her baby into a better world, but already knowing that wasn't going to happen.

Why couldn't Aaron be there?

What will he think when he finds out?

Sarah stopped at the corner of the fence and then made her way to the center, stopping and studying the area.

And now she would wait.

If Edward were out there, he would make sure it was safe before attempting to approach.

But Ed wouldn't see the trap she had set.

He would never escape from Disco's men, Parkman and Alex.

So then, why was Ricigliano supposed to be at the courthouse for two fifteen in the morning?

Nothing made sense, and Vivian wasn't around.

"Welcome to my life," she whispered, her hand still on her belly.

Chapter 30

Edward Sweeney rubbed the protective vest that covered his abdomen and upper body. Then he checked his government-issued weapon. Now armed, the gun loaded, he was ready for whatever or whoever waited for him at ten o'clock by the outdoor pool at Sunnyside Beach. He even had white zip ties that could be slapped on quickly as restraints.

Was it going to be his brother who showed up? He thought so, and then they would continue with the *Death Wish* pact.

Yet, it could be Sarah Roberts, but he had no idea how that was possible. However, if it were, he would take her by gunpoint and learn what she knows and how she was able to manipulate him, staying a step ahead. What mistake had he made that led her to his courtroom to steal Alistair's car?

Or it could be the authorities.

If that were the case, then he'd deal with it. Since he couldn't be tied to Jason Grant, Malcolm, or even Alistair—unless they relied on Sarah's word, which couldn't possibly be allowed in any court of law—the authorities had nothing on him.

Being in a public place, going for a walk as the sun set, wasn't against the law. And if it was Steve who sent the text and it was Steve who would be showing up, then why wouldn't he go and meet him?

Tonight marked the final stage, regardless of how it turned out. That was why he was going, and that was why he had the gun.

Edward chose a spot where he could parallel park with the nose of his rental aimed toward Lakeshore Boulevard. If he had to leave quickly, he wanted nothing in his way.

Lucky for him, the car rental agency had a minivan available. He'd already folded all the back seats into the minivan floor, so now there was just a flat carpeted surface behind the two front seats. With tinted back windows, he'd hit the jackpot.

The dash clock said it was fifteen minutes to ten.

People were out for a late-night stroll. A few were on rollerblades—do people still do that? Over on the grass and farther still on the sand, others milled about playing Frisbee, tossing a ball, playing tag.

It was late, but at the end of the summer, people wanted as much outdoor activity as possible.

The Gus Ryder swimming pool was closed and empty.

Ed eased his driver's seat back and watched his mirrors

for anything untoward. There were no police cars anywhere and no vehicles that resembled an unmarked cruiser. He couldn't see anyone who looked like Sarah in any way, and he wasn't concerned that any of her friends would show up. They were either in custody or soon would be.

Everything appeared calm and relaxed, and he reminded himself to stay that way. He was the one doing the right thing. Otherwise, none of it would've worked out.

Thinking about things working out, he massaged the wrist area where Jason smashed him in his kitchen the other night. That fucker could've broken it. Lucky for Ed, he had bested Jason and got out of there.

But that was one more example of how he knew he was in the right. If he weren't supposed to be doing the *Death Wish* pact, fate would have intervened a while ago—fate, God, karma, or whatever people called it.

Divine intervention hadn't stopped him. It had helped him to continue his mission, his arrangement. So, even if there was someone or something of greater power looking down on them all, that entity was grateful for what Edward was doing. Otherwise, why allow him to continue?

Edward Sweeney didn't believe in some higher power, though. You make your own fate, your own future. And that's what Ed was doing.

Besides, if there was a God, why would he allow a monster like Rueben Ellis to exist? A man who could stalk his wife and then decide to take her and rape her. His daughter died, so she couldn't place Ellis at the Sweeney house. Wife raped multiple times, then both of them murdered. Absolutely senseless.

If there was a God, then Ed did not accept this because there couldn't be a God and a Reuben Ellis in the same world.

Humanity was nothing but a cosmic mistake, and Ed planned on fixing as many human mistakes as possible before he was finished with the life he still owned.

A dark-colored Jeep slid by his minivan, going too slow for the area. Ed could see a driver and a passenger even with the tinted windows on the Jeep. Both men reminded him of the mafia or gangsters. Neither of them would be interested in a middle-aged man driving a family-oriented minivan.

The dash clock said it was a few minutes before ten now.

He leaned forward and stared at as many people as he could. With the sun down and dark clouds rolling in, the only light was from streetlights, so searching faces from the minivan was challenging, but he would know his brother upon sight. He knew the man's walk, his usual gait.

Ed checked his cell phone. No calls, no texts.

He glanced at the clock once more.

One minute to ten.

A lone woman stood by the fenced-in pool when he peered out the windshield again. She moved along the fence, stopped momentarily, glanced over her shoulder, then moved several more steps, her hand on her stomach as if she was about to be sick.

Was that Sarah Roberts?

Ed leaned forward and squinted.

It had to be, but he couldn't be absolutely sure from where he sat.

And if it was, then he was done playing cloak and dagger

with her. Or was the term cat and mouse?

It was time to have a deep conversation about her role as a criminal.

After one last check of his mirrors, Edward exited the minivan, leaving it unlocked.

If that was Sarah, then he needed her in his van.

Tying her up, kidnapping her, would be easy.

Once he drove her out of the city, he'd decide what to do with her then.

Maybe an eight-hour drive north to Timmins would work. He could kill the criminal bitch and bury her in a field. Not a single soul on earth could ever connect him to that crime.

Along the way, they could have a court of their own. He would play a one-man jury and find her guilty.

Something stirred deep inside him, and he enjoyed the feeling as it made him smile.

Sarah would stand trial for her crimes with him instead of the traditional court process. He knew she was guilty. That's all that mattered, wasn't it?

Besides, if she went to an actual court of law and got off because of some sympathetic jury, they'd be right back where they started, which was where they were now.

Edward closed the door quietly and watched his back. There was no one watching him. Still no police cars and none of Sarah's friends.

Why was she making it so easy for him?

Unless the woman by the pool wasn't Sarah.

Only one way to find out.

Edward Sweeney started forward, putting one foot in

front of the other, anticipation rising with each step. *I'm coming for you, Sarah. I'm coming …*

Chapter 31

Edward Sweeney was less than fifty meters away when she noticed him. Without jerking left or right, she scanned the immediate area for the roving Jeep.

How did they miss his gray van?

Then it dawned on her. Ed wasn't driving his van.

So then, why couldn't Vivian have given them a heads-up?

They stared at each other for a moment. Sweeney took a few more steps before stopping again.

She frowned. Something was in his hand.

Not once had it occurred to her to carry a weapon as Disco and his men were well-armed, and she had an Alex with her. They were all watching her at that moment. Weren't they?

She stared past Sweeney, watching vehicles over his

shoulder as the first peal of thunder reverberated over the lake. Where was the Jeep? The Hummer was about twenty vehicles back. Due to its size, Disco parked it out of the way.

In the end, none of that mattered as much as where Alex was.

Sarah pushed off the fence and took a couple of steps toward Sweeney.

He lifted his hand slightly to show her what he carried.

She wasn't surprised to see it was a gun.

"We should talk," she said loud enough for him to hear from where he stood.

"Not here," he shouted back. "Come for a ride with me." He gestured toward the parking area.

What was he driving? Where was everyone? She could jump him herself, hold him until Parkman or Alex came, but he had a weapon, and she didn't. That made things more challenging.

There were still a lot of people around, too. Luckily, no one seemed to notice the weapon stashed in the shadow of his thigh.

"Where's my brother?" Ed shouted.

She didn't want to taunt the man with the gun, but her mouth opened, and she said, "He's dead," before she could stop herself. Then, "It's over, Sweeney. Drop the weapon and give it up. You're surrounded."

Surrounded? Where did that come from? Whoever had them surrounded had to be invisible. She knew they were out there, but even she couldn't see them.

Sweeney took a few steps back, glancing left and right.

Sarah moved forward in an attempt to shorten the

distance between them. Her comment had spooked him. Now Ed spun in a full circle, staring at all the people and vehicles nearby.

Sarah moved closer until she was only twenty meters away, taking advantage of his bewilderment as he glanced around.

She didn't think he'd shoot her or Vivian would tell her. Ed wouldn't kill her in such a public setting, and none of her team seemed to be in the immediate vicinity.

"Why us?" Sarah asked. "Why did you send those deliveries?"

Sweeney snapped his head around to glare at her. "I have no idea what you're talking about. I was out here enjoying the park when I saw a wanted criminal." He stepped back toward a row of vehicles. "But it's obvious you're too much for one man to handle. I'll just use my cell phone in my car to call the proper authorities."

Something spooked him. Was it the understanding that his brother was actually dead? Was that why he showed up tonight? Because he didn't think it was true, and he'd find Steve Cook here?

"You thought your brother would show, didn't you?"

Sweeney moved backward until he bumped into a light-colored Camry. Was that his vehicle?

"You will pay for what you've done, Sarah."

Someone strode swiftly by her, so close she flinched.

Alex.

"Wait," she said to him, but Alex kept moving toward Sweeney. He'd be on the man in seconds.

Sweeney raised his weapon and aimed it at Alex's chest.

"Stay back," Sweeney shouted at him.

There was a quality of panic in Sweeney's voice.

Still ten feet from Sweeney—the man was retreating backward and was about to bump into a dark red minivan—Alex jumped.

The weapon fired.

Alex twisted in the air, then dropped to the ground to lie flat out.

It was as if he jumped to draw the first bullet, twisted, and dropped to the ground to make less of a target of himself.

If Sarah didn't know him any better, she would assume Alex was insane or suicidal—or both.

When the weapon fired, she dropped to her knees and bowed her head, but the bullet didn't come anywhere near her.

She glanced up as over a dozen people in a twenty-meter radius were startled by the gunshot. Some shouted, others scattered, while others ran toward Alex and Sweeney, not aware the weapon had fired from that direction.

Sweeney had circled the dark red minivan. Before Sarah got to her feet, he was behind the wheel.

Alex was already up and running at it.

An engine revved in the distance as more thunder split the air. Several people screamed as the noise was so abrupt.

The Hummer was racing toward their position.

Where the fuck was the Jeep?

Sarah ran after Alex toward the minivan as it backed up a couple of feet.

Then Alex jumped on the hood and crawled over the windshield, his left hand clinging to the black roof rack.

Sweeney jammed on the brakes so hard that Alex was jerked off the front of the minivan. He launched several feet and smashed into the back window of another car, the glass shattering from the impact.

Sarah screamed as Alex slid into the back seat of the car.

The minivan was already moving forward again, its back wheels screaming on the concrete.

She was running at it when she changed course and ran toward Alex. The minivan was several cars away when she saw Alex climb out of the broken car.

The Hummer stopped with all four tires locked up. The back door popped open.

"Get in!" Parkman shouted.

Alex got there before Sarah, and then she hopped in. The second her foot touched the floor mat, the Hummer accelerated forward, the door slamming shut behind them.

"Do you see them?" Disco shouted.

"Yes," one of his men from the Jeep shouted over the Hummer's speakers. "He just pulled up to the lights at the crosswalk by the tennis courts. We're six vehicles behind him."

"Stay on him," Disco yelled as he maneuvered out of the parking area and onto Lakeshore Blvd.

Sarah grabbed Alex and yanked on his arm. He spun around to stare at her, his forehead glistening with sweat.

"You could've gotten shot," she shouted at him. "Why did you do that?"

"I read the situation," Alex said, just loud enough for her to hear.

"He talks," Disco yelled from the front seat.

"Fuck off and drive," Sarah shouted back at Disco.

No one responded or said anything for a moment while Sarah glared at Alex.

Parkman put a reassuring hand on her shoulder. "He needed to get close enough to—"

"Close enough to what?" Sarah asked, without taking her eyes off Alex. "There is no *close enough* if we lose you."

"Where is he now?" Disco asked.

"He's hard to catch up to. He's driving erratically."

"Where is he?" Disco shouted as he jerked around a slow-moving pickup.

"The left lane. Looks like he wants to enter the Gardiner."

"I know where that is. Stay on him."

The Hummer's strong engine revved as they raced along Lakeshore Boulevard.

With each breath, Sarah calmed down a bit more.

"It just seemed reckless, Alex."

He shook his head. "I guessed he was primed to shoot. I jumped to draw his fire, already planning to spin and land flat. The odds of him hitting me were much lower doing that as opposed to running at him in a predictive manner."

"You just confirmed it."

"What?"

"You are insane. Who does shit to have people shoot at them on purpose?"

"Yeah, fucking insane," Disco said from the front seat. "But you did it."

"Did what?" Sarah asked. "Broke your back on that car's window?" She tugged his arm slightly to examine his back.

No blood or markings were visible, but the back of the Hummer was dark.

"I'm fine, Sarah. It's all good."

"Wait, Parkman, you said close enough to do something. What was it?"

"You calm now?" he asked.

The Hummer jerked left, then right, all their heads swaying with the action.

"No, I'm not. I'm pissed. I hate when people shoot at us."

"Alex slapped a tracker on the roof rack of Sweeney's minivan."

She eyed Alex a moment. "That's why you landed on it the way you did?"

Alex nodded.

"Why didn't I know about this?"

"Last minute decision," Disco replied. "You were already on the way to the pool when Alex volunteered. We needed the insurance in case this Sweeney guy got away."

Everything made sense to her now. Alex had stayed close to her to be able to identify Sweeney. When Sweeney showed the weapon, Alex intervened and drew his fire, then jumped on the minivan to plant the tracker and allowed himself to be thrown from the vehicle as he didn't need to be clinging to it anymore.

They'd been doing shit like this for years, but for some reason, it bothered her more now. Was she getting too old for this? Was she softening? Or was it the pregnancy that was working on her emotions?

"The target has accessed the Gardiner Expressway from

the left lane," the guys in the Jeep said.

Disco tapped something on the screen of his phone, and a map lit up the small area, a red dot blinking as the map moved.

"We've got him. Tracker activated."

Up ahead, the sign for the Gardiner Expressway came into view. They weren't far behind Sweeney now.

It came as no surprise that Sweeney didn't drive his van to the meeting at the beach. Why would he when everyone knew his vehicle?

But he had come armed and ready to kill.

She glanced back at Alex, wanting to hug him and punch him in the same breath. He was uninjured, though, and that was what mattered.

He took her hand, squeezed it reassuringly, then released it and turned forward to stare out the windshield.

Sarah followed his gaze.

A light rain started, making everything shine under the streetlights.

Up ahead, the Jeep was visible now as it dodged back and forth through traffic.

"Update?" Disco said.

"He's in the right lane, possibly in preparation to exit soon. Passing Spadina now."

Disco kept the Hummer under control well as he sped past car after car, bringing the Jeep closer and closer.

The rain fell harder now, the Hummer's wipers fighting the onslaught. Lightning lit up the downtown area ahead, followed by violent thunderclaps.

The cars ahead were slowing due to the conditions. The

brake lights were brighter because of the rain.

"How close are you?" Disco asked.

"Four cars back, but it's getting thick out here."

"We see that. Stay on him—"

"Fuck!" the driver of the Jeep shouted.

"What?" Disco asked.

Sarah leaned back and rested against Parkman. It felt like everything was falling apart. She was a couple of months pregnant, sitting in the back of a Hummer in the middle of a thunderstorm while they chased a man downtown—the same man who was responsible for having Daniel, Benjamin, and Aaron jailed—and Aaron didn't even know he was going to be a father.

"We lost him," the guys from the Jeep said.

"You what?" Disco shouted, slapping at his phone.

"He jerked to the right at the last second and got off on the York, Bay, Yonge Street exit. Cars blocked me, and we must continue until the Jarvis exit another kilometer up."

"Then you guys had better thank Alex for that heroic fucking placement of the tracker," Disco said, slapping the phone button on his steering wheel.

The line clicked off, ending the connection to the other vehicle.

"We're on our own," Disco said. "But I can see where he's going seconds after he makes the turn. We won't lose him."

"Will the rain affect the tracker?" Sarah asked.

No one answered her as the Hummer barreled down the exit ramp, staying on the left to turn onto York Street.

"He just took a left onto Front Street," Disco said.

The light was red as the Hummer skidded to a stop on the slick pavement. Disco checked each way, then hit the gas and ran the red light. They raced up to Front Street and encountered another red light.

"Shit," he said under his breath.

"What?" Parkman asked.

Sarah leaned forward.

"The light disappeared."

"What light?" Sarah asked.

"The tracker light. The one on the minivan's roof. It just died." Disco glanced at Sarah in the rearview mirror. "I'm sorry, but we lost him."

Chapter 32

Sweeney had noticed the Jeep staying on him all the way from Lakeshore. So he slowed enough to allow the Jeep to calmly edge closer. And he waited for the driver to make a lane change, then jerked right and bolted down the exit ramp at York Street.

They knew his burgundy minivan now. He needed to dump it and get back in his van. At this hour, that was his only option.

During the storm, in the darkness and rain, he could leave the area better in the gray, nondescript van while they tried to find his rented minivan. In the morning, he could either come back and return the van to the rental agency or call them and tell them where it could be found.

Once he turned onto Windsor Avenue, he found a spot a block from the parking garage. He'd be soaked before he got underground, but none of that mattered. He needed out of the area. Sarah's friends were not people he could beat one-on-one, let alone in a group. That was why he came up with the deliveries in the first place. To be able to get to Sarah from afar.

He killed the engine and cut the lights. Then he sat for a moment to collect his breath, the rain pounding the minivan's roof. That always reminded him of camping when he was a kid with his parents when the rain would pitter-patter on the roof of his tent.

Edward Sweeney looked at himself in the rearview mirror and shook his head. That guy Alex was insane. He had run toward him and jumped. Of course, he would fire at the guy. Ed had read all about Alex and knew he was the ninja of them all. Then he'd jumped on the front of the minivan, clinging to the roof. What the hell was that all about?

In the end, Sweeney was just happy he made it out of there. He had been stupid. Of course, Sarah would bring friends with her this time. Of course, a couple of thugs in a Jeep would follow him.

But again, how did she know he would be there? Steve was in California, which probably meant Steve was dead after all.

Did Sarah do it?

He shook his head. The timing was off. If Steve was dead or if he got arrested, it was something he had done.

Sweeney would grieve later. He was in survival mode now. He needed to leave the downtown area, and the rain wasn't letting up.

He cracked the door open a notch, took a deep breath,

then exited the minivan and ran for the sidewalk.

A black Hummer drove along Front Street at the end of Windsor directly in front of him, cruising by slowly, looking for something.

They were looking for him.

Grateful he'd parked so far up Windsor they wouldn't have been able to see the minivan from Front Street, he started jogging toward the parkade.

In under a minute, he would be underground and out of sight.

Five minutes later, he would be leaving the area in his van.

Sometimes, it was better to survive the battle to be able to fight again another day. This was one of those times.

With this much heat on him and Steve potentially gone, he would have to give Alistair a free pass for now.

Sarah had become too much to handle.

She had become his priority.

He would regroup and come after Sarah.

Ending her life would free him—which translated to liberty or death.

When they met again, he would be certain to make sure she was taken care of.

Twenty feet from the parkade entrance, soaked through completely, his Kevlar vest heavy with wetness, shirt sticking to his skin, he witnessed a blond woman step around the corner up ahead and start in his direction.

He slipped to the right to hide behind a pillar.

How could he be so lucky? The stars really were aligned for him. He was meant to do this.

Sarah Roberts was walking toward him in the pouring rain—alone.

He remained hidden, waiting for her to pass him, thanking the God he didn't believe in for delivering her unto him.

With his weapon in hand now, he clicked off the safety.

He counted his breaths, then on the third, he jumped out, gun raised at Sarah's face from four feet away.

Sarah stopped and stared at him.

"Got you now, bitch," Sweeney whispered.

Chapter 33

"W‍HERE DID WE LOSE him?" Sarah asked as Disco turned onto Front Street.

"Right up here somewhere," Disco said, slowing down and easing to the right to let a car pass him.

"Can you tell where the tracker had him last?"

Disco pulled over and hit the hazards. "One second." He yanked the phone from its holder on the dash and tapped several buttons. Then he glanced up through the windshield. "The signal died somewhere up ahead, just past John Street."

"Then pull over half a block after John Street and let me out."

"No way, Sarah," Parkman said. "I'll do it."

She didn't argue because they could all be dropped off, one by one, in different areas.

Disco did as he was asked, dropping Parkman first. Then

he dropped Alex off a little farther on, and finally, he slowed and stopped just past Windsor Street when his phone rang.

"Where are you guys?" Disco asked. He nodded at Sarah after they told him. "They're a few blocks behind us now."

"Good. Have them circle the area looking for the minivan." She opened the door and dropped outside into the pouring rain. "You too. The three of us will be on foot for a block or two."

"What if Sweeney kept driving?" Disco asked. "What if he's gone?"

"Then we'll know in the next ten minutes or so, won't we?"

She slammed the door and looked up and down Front Street. Her decision made, she started for the side street called Windsor. In an attempt to keep as much rain off her as possible, she ran up alongside the building, hugged the corner, and then started up Windsor Street, studying the cars parked along the side of the road.

She passed a parkade on her left, the garage door sitting ajar.

Could the tracker signal get lost because Sweeney drove the minivan underground?

She figured she could backtrack and check, but not until she continued up the street a little more.

Head down, hands in her pockets, feeling somewhat pissed that they'd lost Sweeney in a downpour—especially after what Alex risked to plant the tracker in the first place—she shuffled ahead.

Someone stepped out in front of her, startling her to a stop.

Edward Sweeney glared at her, his eyes lit with some sort of mad glee, his weapon aimed at her.

"Got you now, bitch."

Chapter 34

HE COULDN'T BELIEVE HIS luck. Sarah Roberts walked right up to him after all the shit at the pool and all the shit on the highway.

"How is this possible?" he asked out loud, gawking at her.

Sarah eased her hands out of her pockets slowly. Rainwater ran down her forehead and dripped into her eyes.

"How is what possible?" she asked.

"That you would walk right up to me like this. Like the fly to the spiderweb."

She fixed her gaze on the weapon. "You're going to want to lower that," she whispered, just loud enough to be heard over the din of the constant rain.

His free hand thrust something white toward her. "Wrap these around your wrists."

"Fuck you."

"That's not very polite, Sarah." He leaned closer. "Wrap your fucking wrists. You know I'm trigger-happy. I tried to shoot Alex, but the wiry fucker got lucky."

She took the proffered ties and held onto them.

"Do it," he said, thrusting the tip of the gun toward her stomach.

Something changed in her face, and she quickly cinched the ties as best she could. He clutched the end piece and tugged hard, effectively securing her wrists as tight as handcuffs.

"Now move." He gestured toward the underground garage. "What's that old cliché about bullets running faster?" He pressed the weapon into the small of her back. "Just don't try to run Sarah. Convince yourself now that I have no issue with murder, and we'll get along well."

They entered the garage and started down the concrete ramp. He kept her close, the gun closer. With an eye on all the cameras, he tried to keep the weapon hidden between their bodies in case he had to shoot her down there. If that happened, the cameras would be watched, and they'd see his face. It would be much better for him if the cameras weren't watched. Meaning that if he shot her, he'd have to take her body with him, leaving only blood behind.

"Why are you doing this?" she asked.

"Shut up."

Sarah glanced over her shoulder. "Really? Shut up? That's all you've got after sending body parts to my parents' house?"

"You'll face your day in court, and everything will

become clear then." He nudged her forward with the tip of his weapon. "Keep going."

In the time they'd been in the underground garage, only two cars had moved. One finding a spot and one leaving. Sarah didn't scream or act out. He wondered why because she was done for once she was in his van.

Footsteps pounded close.

Ed spun around, swinging the gun with him, but no one was there.

Sarah moved away from him. He grabbed her hair and yanked her back. A small yip escaped her as she almost fell to her ass with the force. She danced several steps backward until she regained her balance.

"Getting your hair pulled hurts, doesn't it?" he whispered, keeping the gun trained on the empty spaces behind him.

"Not really," she whispered through clenched teeth. "I've had my hair pulled before."

"Keep moving."

"Where?" she asked. "You have some kind of dungeon down here?"

"My van. Over there in the far corner."

"What are we going to do—"

"Be quiet," he snapped. "I'm listening."

"Listening for what?"

He pulled her back and, this time pushed the tip of the weapon into her cheekbone.

"The safety is off. One bullet will ruin this pretty face." He moved so close he could smell her breath. "Now shut the fuck up and move toward the van."

"Spineless," she said. "Dickless. Feeble. Weak-willed, inadequate piece of shit."

"Okay, that's it." He shoved her so hard she stumbled to stay on her feet.

Something pounded the pavement behind him again.

"Who's there?" he shouted, waving the gun back and forth.

He backed up, keeping an eye on Sarah, who had tripped into a car three vehicles away from the van. The vile look on her face held pure hatred.

Ed's problem could be defined as kindness. He was being too nice. Sarah struggled with his orders, with his directness. She thought he was spineless and ineffectual. But he wasn't. Look at Jason Grant. Look at Reuben Ellis. He was a man who kept his word and did the right thing, no matter how hard. A little respect would go a long way.

He moved over to her. Hatred and anger radiated off her like a radio signal, and he needed to change the channel.

With the gun in his left hand, he faced Sarah.

"We need to move faster." This time, he used his more authoritative voice. "Move toward the van and get in the side door. Do it now."

She hesitated.

Someone was stalking them—probably Alex—and Sarah was stalling for time.

Before he paused to think about it, he did what he thought was right and drove his fist into Sarah's left cheek.

The sucker punch was so sudden and fast that she flattened across the hood of the car they leaned against.

The car's alarm sounded due to the sudden vibration, and

someone was yelling now.

But it wasn't Sarah.

Someone was shouting behind him.

Edward spun around and saw Alex running at him across the hoods of several cars lined up on the other side of the narrow lane.

Without thinking, acting in survival mode, Ed spun and fired with his left hand.

Being right-handed, the bullet went wide, but it didn't deter Alex. The insanity of the situation was that the gun coming up and firing did nothing to slow Alex down.

It was like the man had a death wish of his own.

Ed went to switch gun hands for better aim, but Sarah grabbed his right arm and pulled him off balance.

On his way toward her, he shot an elbow up and was grateful to connect under her chin, the corner of his elbow hitting her in the throat.

She released him and gagged as she dropped back onto the hood of the car with the alarm still wailing.

Alex was ten feet away.

The gun slipped comfortably into his right hand.

Six feet.

The gun came up.

Three feet.

Ed pulled the trigger, then dodged left.

Alex sailed by him, rolling into a ball, drops of blood smearing the pavement where he had just been, leaving a crimson trail.

The car's alarm went silent, Alex's banshee animal screech died, and Sarah's choking calmed as she was breathing slightly better.

Ed's ears rang as she moved toward Alex, the gun extended in his hand, ready to fire multiple times.

"Wait," Sarah groaned.

She pushed off the car with her elbows, her hands still locked together.

Ed glanced back at her and shrugged. "He has to die. This asshole will never stop coming for me. Alexander the Great is great no more."

He spun back, already applying weight on the trigger.

A small circle of blood stained the concrete two feet away.

But Alex was gone.

Chapter 35

Sarah couldn't stop swallowing. The blow to the throat really bothered her. At first, she choked, but then, as her airways opened, she felt hoarse, her throat partially restricted. The constant swallowing wasn't alleviating it much, and the throbbing cheek from the sucker punch only fueled her anger, her hatred.

This definitely ended tonight.

Edward Sweeney shot Alex.

Sweet, kind, loving Alex.

The only one who would joke about this day for years to come would be Benjamin, and only because he didn't get shot—provided Alex survived the wound.

Well, he'd better survive it, or Vivian could find another puppet because Sarah would be through, finished, completely done.

Alex had come out of hiding because Ed had sucker punched her. She knew what drove Alex and how he melted into the landscape when needed. Striking Sarah must've pushed him over the edge, and he sprung from hiding.

Bullet or no bullet, if Sarah's hands were free, Edward Sweeney wouldn't have made it out of that garage in one piece.

But he'd pushed her toward his van. Once inside, he bolted the doors and slipped behind the wheel.

The car alarm hadn't drawn too much attention yet, but it was going off again.

Sarah laid back in the rear of the van, her hands now attached to a chain suspended from the ceiling. Without strong scissors or a way to break the chain, there was no getting out of her restraints.

Ed started the van and slipped it into gear. Advancing slowly out of the parking spot, he started toward the exit signs. Alex didn't jump out or attack the van. Alex didn't try to break a window or gain entry in any way.

Alex was nowhere to be seen.

Sarah feared the worst.

Did Parkman know where he was? What if Alex followed Sarah and Ed to the bottom of the parkade without telling anyone, and now he lies bleeding out? How long would he be there? How much time did he have?

"Hey, Sweeney," she moaned, her throat still protesting.

"Keep your mouth shut, bitch."

"That the best you got?"

"Just shut up."

"You're dead, Sweeney. You're a walking corpse."

They were approaching the exit ramp now. Sarah could only hope the Hummer was parked across it, blocking them from leaving.

Then precise shots fired through the windshield would end it all.

"Use your cell phone," she said. "Call an ambulance."

"For Alex?" He laughed. "No fuckin' way. Hope he dies down there. If he lives, I'll always wonder when he's coming for me, sleeping with one eye open." Ed shook his head. "No fuckin' way."

Sarah stared out the windshield as the van rose to the street level.

There was no Hummer, no Parkman, and nobody waiting for them. How had the tables turned so fast? She was his prisoner tied to the inside of his van while Alex bled out at the bottom of the parkade. Not to mention, Ed had changed vehicles. Even though he was in his personal vehicle again, Disco and Parkman would be looking for the minivan.

At the street level, Ed paused and stared up the road to the left as the rain beat a rhythm on his windshield.

"Looks like they found the minivan."

"They?"

"The Jeep and a large Hummer are parked beside it. Also, that looks like Parkman, who just jumped out of the minivan."

Ed turned to the right and drove down to Front Street, where he turned left.

"You're clear," she said. "Call in for Alex."

"No. Stop asking for something that'll never happen."

"I'll offer you a truce, a deal. If he lives, I'll get Alex to forget about you, leave you alone."

Ed shook his head. "You're so fucking stupid. There is no way in hell I'm calling anybody to save Alex's life." He glanced at her in the mirror. "I'm hoping the bullet tore an artery, and he's already dead."

"You know the rest of us will come after you for what you've done to Alex, right?"

"The rest of you will be jailed or dead, Sarah. No one is coming after me. It's supposed to be this way. It's ordained, and I'm not even religious."

She swallowed several times, adjusting her weight to manage the movement of the van better.

"How is it ordained?"

"You know, holy orders and shit."

"What?"

"Everything is working out brilliantly. The fact that you walked right up to me outside that garage. The fact that I'm driving away unharmed after the Cirque du Soleil of martial arts himself attacked me—twice. No, this shit is *supposed* to happen. Which means I've changed my mind on killing you."

"Oh really? Gee, thanks."

"You're going to court first. You'll be sentenced in a courtroom where you will have a jury, a defense lawyer, and a prosecutor. The judge will hear everything, and the jury will decide your fate."

Ed stopped at the light on University Avenue and then turned left.

"You've completely lost your mind." She swallowed, her throat feeling slightly better. The cheek throbbed less, too.

Sweeney focused on where he was going as he turned

into another parkade of some kind. He withdrew a white card to access the garage and swiped it on a reader. Ahead, through the windshield, Sarah watched as the garage door lifted.

"Court is in session," Ed whispered.

Sarah squinted at the time on the dash. "It's nearly eleven at night. Court is *not* in session, asshole."

"This one is," he whispered as he drove the van down one level and pulled into a parking lot. He killed the engine and climbed out of his seat to kneel before her.

"We're finally alone without fear of anyone coming to interrupt us."

"Great, is this where you try to have your way with me?"

He scrunched up his face and looked her up and down. "You're disgusting. Not at all. If that were what I wanted, I would've taken it already."

"No, you wouldn't. You can't *take* from me. You would be dead if you tried."

"Sarah, let's get something clear. I'm not a rapist, and I'm not a criminal. I right wrongs."

"This is righting a wrong?" she asked, jerking her tied wrists.

"You still have no idea what's going on, do you?" He shook his head and blinked a couple of times, offering a sad face. "It's okay. You'll know everything soon enough."

He unclipped her from the chain and swung open the side door. After he hopped out, he guided her out and then sat her down.

"Wait here." He moved to the front of the van and grabbed a wheelchair. After unfolding it, he wheeled it over.

"Get in."

"And if I don't?"

"I'll break an ankle, a kneecap, a femur, one by one until you get into the wheelchair. Then you'll be bound there anyway but in much more pain."

Sarah eyed him a few moments more, deciding to play this out. She got to her feet, pivoted, then dropped into the chair.

"Where are we, exactly?"

"In the judge's parking area of the Toronto Courthouse."

She laughed. "As soon as security sees me and I tell them what you've done, you're through, Sweeney."

"Won't happen. You know why?"

"No, but I'm sure you'll tell me."

"Because this building is armed to the teeth. This pass card"—he held up the white card—"gives me access to the entire place. I'm court security and have been for years."

"So there's no night security?"

"The place is armed. Access is authorized only. If an alarm trips, a security company receives the call and responds. Besides, who breaks into a courthouse? This is the kind of building people want to break out of, not in."

He leaned down and wrapped a zip tie around her ankles. "Don't kick me, or I'll make you bleed."

"How long have you worked here?" How else could she stall for time? No one knew where they were and couldn't access the building if they did. It wasn't even midnight yet, and Vivian told her to have Ricigliano come at 02:15 a.m. But how would the detective gain access to the building?

"Too long, but I stay because I need to continue my

Death Wish pact with my brother."

"Your dead brother."

The final tug of the tie shot a pain up her leg. "Too tight," she whispered.

"Too bad." He got up and walked around behind her, then pushed her toward the elevator. "I've seen degenerates getting off on technicalities. I've watched as weak judges let people go with a slap on the wrist, only to re-offend."

"So what, you're the lone crusader now, out seeking justice through vigilantism?"

"Something like that. But none of that matters to you because your court session has started, and they won't wait much longer."

"Who are they?"

"You'll see, Sarah."

He pushed her along a corridor, swiped his card, then onto an elevator. After swiping his card again, the doors closed, and they began to ascend.

"Using your access card leaves a record behind," she said.

The doors opened on another level.

"I'm aware of that and can explain it away. Remember, I work here as security and have been in the building after hours. No one questions their own security team."

"They will when I disappear and the cameras filming us tell a tale."

"Sarah, Sarah, Sarah, you are really stupid. Do you think I haven't thought of that? I'm security. I have access to all the cameras. The time stamps, the older images, everything. I will finish your court session, and once your jury finds you guilty, we'll deal with you. Then I'll remove the footage of our entering the building."

"You won't get it all. The courtroom footage, all these people waiting for us. This does not end well for you, Sweeney."

"It's been ordained, Sarah. It not only will end well, it will end the way I want it to."

After swiping his card again, magnetic locks disengaged, and the doors to courtroom number one popped open. Ed pushed the wheelchair inside, then paused until the doors closed and the magnetic locks engaged again.

"Where is everyone?" she asked. A tingling rose up her leg, where the circulation was cut off from the zip ties on her ankles.

"You'll see." Ed pushed the chair to the defendant's table on the left. He parked it, set the wheelchair's locks, and then produced more ties.

"More?"

"Can't have you crawling away in the dark."

"Dark?"

"Shhh, Sarah. No more questions. Honor the court process."

He slipped a tie over her wrist and secured it to the arm of the chair.

"Fuck your court process."

His gaze met hers. Then he backhanded her. "Watch your mouth, or I'll hold you in contempt of court."

She tasted blood as it oozed onto her tongue. A sharp sting accompanied her probing tongue. The inside of her lip had cut against her teeth. It was no bother. A slight cut, the sting of the slap already fading to numbness.

"You've lost your mind." She licked the blood, then swallowed.

"And you've lost your way."

Both wrists were bound now. Sweeney got to his feet and glanced around the large courtroom.

"Almost ready," he said. "I'll be right back."

While he was gone, she tested the strength of her restraints, but there was no getting out of them. Everything was too tight, too secure.

Sweeney slipped back in through a door in the back wall. He cradled several candles in his arms.

"The courtroom from the past," he mumbled as he set a candle on the judge's desk, one on each lawyer's table and one in front of the twelve seats where the jurors would sit.

Then he produced a Zippo lighter and went about lighting them all.

"Spooky," she mumbled.

Sweeney didn't respond. He exited the room again once the candles were lit, leaving the main doors propped open.

Sarah mentally assessed the time and figured it was getting close to midnight. She had two more hours until Ricigliano was set to arrive.

A lot could happen in two hours.

How she got out of that office in Texas while the head of a human procurement company held them hostage was a mystery—until it happened. How she got out of an attack with automatic weapons and bombs in northern Ontario several weeks ago was a mystery also—until it happened.

But this one seemed more challenging for some reason.

Tied to a wheelchair, deep inside a building meant to keep people out with magnetized heavy doors, made her feel she was on her own.

No one knew where they were. And even if they did, launching any sort of rescue mission would be fruitless. They'd literally have to find the exact people with access and get inside the building without tipping off Sweeney.

She was completely on her own.

What could he be up to? What was taking him so long?

And since the entire courtroom—the entire building—was empty, who was attending this mock court session he was prattling on about?

She glanced around at the four candles.

What were they for?

Even before she finished the thought, she knew the answer.

The lights clicked off, and the courtroom descended into darkness. The pit in her stomach grew larger and twisted.

What if she got the time wrong from Vivian? What if instead of 02:15 a.m., it was supposed to be 12:15 a.m.?

If she died here, would Aaron ever know he was supposed to be a father?

The doors opened. She spun back and watched the black figure stroll toward her. As he neared her position in the wheelchair, he smiled.

"We're finally ready. The electricity has been cut. Which means all doors remain locked because those magnets need power to disengage."

"You propped the door open when you left."

"So I could get back inside once the power was cut. The

good news is, it's impossible that we can be interrupted now. So," he clapped his hands, "let's get started, shall we."

He angled the chair to face the raised judge's desk.

Then he strode to the side where he usually stood as a court officer.

"All rise as Judge Edward Sweeney enters the courtroom."

He nodded in the creepy candlelight at Sarah.

After a moment, he jumped up to the judge's chair and sat down.

"In the case of Sarah Roberts versus the people of Canada and the United States, I hereby ask the prosecuting lawyer to read the charges and get this court underway."

Sweeney jumped down from the judge's chair and jogged over to the other lawyer's table as a shiver shook Sarah's shoulders. Her clothes hadn't dried yet. They were cold and wet in the air-conditioned courtroom. But that wasn't the only thing that gave her the chills.

It was being locked inside a candlelit courtroom with a madman who was intent on delivering a guilty sentence.

Tied to the wheelchair as she was, there was nothing she could do about it.

Nothing at all.

Chapter 36

Parkman tried Sarah's phone, then he tried Alex's phone. No one was picking up.

"Fuck guys, what happened to them?"

Disco stared back at him. "We dropped them off within a block of you."

"Well, something's happened." Parkman turned in a circle, studying the area. No one was out walking in the rain, with only a few cars braving the wet streets at this late hour.

"Okay, I'll walk along here. Let's spread out and try to find them."

"You seem worried," Disco said. "I wouldn't be. That Alex guy can handle ten men."

"He was shot at tonight already. Sweeney won't hesitate again. And sure, he can handle ten men, but one bullet could still put him down."

One of Disco's men whacked his arm, then pointed.

Parkman turned as a police car spun a hard left and disappeared down a ramp under a building.

Then, another cruiser turned the corner and followed the first one.

A siren wailed in the distance.

"That's got to be Sarah and Alex," Parkman said, breaking into a run.

"Parkman," Disco shouted after him. "Shouldn't we check it out? The cops aren't looking for us."

He wasn't waiting. They could follow him or not, but he needed to see what was going on. What if they had trapped Sweeney? Or what if Sweeney had Sarah or Alex trapped? Too many scenarios raced through his head, all of them not good.

He reached the entrance to the parkade and turned so fast he almost wiped out on the wet pavement. Disco and one of his men were right behind him.

Down one level, then another, and still Parkman couldn't see the cruisers.

Tires screeched above as another car entered the underground parking.

The trio continued lower to the final level, where they saw lights reflecting off the walls.

With Parkman in the lead, they strode toward the cluster of cop cars. One of the uniformed men was on his phone, offering some sort of description of wounds or something.

Panic welled up inside Parkman as he got closer.

A large cop heard them coming and turned to block their way.

"You can't come in here."

"I might know these people," Parkman said, trying to scurry around the cop.

The man was able to grab Parkman and restrain him.

"Hey, hold up, sir. None of you are getting any closer."

Parkman stared at the cop. "What happened here?"

"You tell me," he said, easing back, arms out to ward off further advance. "You said you may know them."

"Parkman," a feeble voice called from behind a car.

"That you?" the cop asked him.

Parkman nodded and started forward.

The cop didn't try to stop him this time.

He rounded the front bumper of a car and glanced down at Alex. The man's face was white as snow, and blood covered the front of his shirt on the left side.

Parkman dropped to the pavement, tears already welling in his eyes, clouding his vision.

"What happened?"

"Sweeney took Sarah. In his van."

"How bad?" Parkman asked, nodding at the wound.

"I'll live. It just clipped me. Bled bad. Can't move much. Keeps bleeding."

"How were you able to call the cops?"

"I didn't. Car alarm. Some guy called them for me when he came to check his car."

"Smart play, setting it off."

"I didn't. Sarah did when Sweeney hit her."

Parkman tightened his fists. "I'll kill him."

"I tried."

"Sir," the cop said, leaning down. "Paramedics are

arriving to take your friend to the hospital."

"Did Sweeney say where he was taking her?"

Alex shook his head.

"Shit." Parkman got to his feet.

"We're going to have some questions for you, sir."

Parkman faced the man. "Look, the man who shot him kidnapped a woman. First, we find them, then you can ask all the questions you want."

The cop shook his head. "Parkman, right?"

Parkman frowned. "How did you know …" He glanced at Alex. The police had been looking for them since they escaped when Daniel and Benjamin were picked up at the dojo.

"I'm afraid you'll have to come with us, sir. You can tell us all about the shooting and the kidnappings when we get where we're going."

Parkman faced the man, knowing what he was about to say would do no good but needing to try anyway.

"Look, you don't understand. The man who shot him has Sarah Roberts. We have to find her first."

"Sounds good, but Parkman, we are going to talk about this elsewhere, okay?"

He fumbled with his cell phone and tapped on it quickly. "Since I'm not under arrest yet, I'm making one phone call, and then I will go willingly."

"Look, Parkman, make your call later—"

The phone rang at the other end. "When this phone call is over, I'll go without complaint."

The cop glanced over his shoulder at the other officers. They both nodded, and the cop in front of him crossed his arms and waited.

She picked up on the fourth ring.

"Detective Ricigliano," Parkman blurted.

The cop lowered his eyebrows at the mention of the detective's name.

"Is this Parkman?"

"Alex was shot, and Sarah was taken in Sweeney's gray van."

"What?"

"We're in a parking garage off of Front Street. Toronto Police are on the scene. They're taking Alex to the hospital and me downtown to be questioned. But Sweeney took Sarah in his personal vehicle, the gray van."

"Okay, Sarah asked me to be at the Toronto Courthouse for two-fifteen in the morning—"

"She did?" Parkman cut in.

"Yes, but I decided to come early and watch the place, so I had an idea of what to expect."

"And?"

"About ten minutes ago, a gray van pulled into a private access parking area under the courthouse."

"That's Sweeney," Parkman nearly shouted. "You have to get in there. He's got her."

"Okay, but there's nothing I can do. I can't access the building. I don't have an access card."

"Shoot your way in."

The cop in front of him uncrossed his arms and stared hard at Parkman.

"Parkman, listen to yourself. Shoot my way into the Toronto Courthouse. That'll look good on my résumé because helping Sarah is already killing my career."

"Look, you're not listening. Think probable cause when I tell you Alex was shot. They are taking us in now. Sweeney took Sarah. They are inside that building. Do whatever you must, but don't wait for two more hours."

"Even if I wanted in, I can't get in anyway. The power went out."

The cop waved an arm at Parkman to move aside as paramedics arrived to tend to Alex.

"Off the phone," the cop said. "Time to go."

"You hear that?" Parkman asked. "They're taking us in for questioning. Ricigliano, since the power is out in the courthouse, call the sheriff, call the security company that monitors the courthouse, and call somebody, but get inside. I fear Sarah's life depends on it. Her entire support group is paralyzed now. We're all in custody. Just fucking do something, and you'll have your answers, your arrest, and your career back." Parkman ended the call without waiting for an answer.

Alex was being lifted onto a stretcher.

The cop led Parkman to a cruiser.

No matter how hard they tried to make things right, the authorities always got in their way. If Parkman could get to the courthouse, he could help Detective Ricigliano, which would help Sarah.

But instead, he was being driven downtown to be asked endless questions.

What a complete waste of time.

I'm sorry, Sarah. We all tried.

I tried …

Chapter 37

The prosecuting lawyer—Edward Sweeney—had finished reading all the charges against Sarah.

Then he ran back to the judge's desk to sit down again, browsing fake notes as if considering all the charges.

The man had done his research. He brought up stuff from the days of Armond Stuart. He knew about the street gang she dealt with before heading to Italy. Sweeney pushed hard on the crimes committed in the Canadian area, covering her alleged attack on a cop in Kelowna when it was actually that cop's wife who killed and dismembered him. He listed over fifty charges leading up to and including a misunderstanding between Sarah and the authorities when a group of militants attacked and killed people off of Spadina over a month ago. Sarah was the lone survivor of that attack, and some suspect she was in on it to win her freedom.

To have a stranger like Sweeney, a madman in every sense, list crimes from her past as if she were a long-term fugitive gave her a creepy feeling. It was like she had just undergone a life review, the kind one would see after one dies when faced with the light at the end of the proverbial tunnel.

Was this the end? Was that the justice she would receive when she was so close to having a life with Aaron, a baby, and a family?

How was her life so public that Sweeney could know as much as he did about her? Or was he privy to specific information because he worked court security?

Sure, Detective Ricigliano was supposed to arrive to save the day slightly after two in the morning, but it couldn't be past twelve-thirty yet, and Sweeney was fast-tracking this process as the candles wore down.

Her shirt had dried considerably, but her jeans were still wet. Although, it didn't really matter how wet they were because she couldn't feel her right leg below the thigh. Her foot was completely asleep, which worried her. The zip tie was too tight, and Sweeney wasn't loosening it.

"It appears you've got a considerable list of charges, Miss Roberts. How do you plead?"

She stared up at him without speaking.

He clasped his hands together in front of his face. "Miss Roberts, please understand that you may feel justified in helping all kinds of people over the years, but you're not a government employee. You did not earn a badge nor a rank of any sort in any Canadian police force. You are not some international assassin, spy, or intelligence agent. You're an

American citizen who spends considerable time locally here in Toronto, causing havoc because you pretend to hear someone speaking to you from the other side." He raised a finger. "Do not attempt a plea of insanity, Miss Roberts. For over a decade, you have shown a tenacity to commit these crimes willfully. If anyone knows right from wrong, that's you, ma'am, yet you continue on your destructive path. So, I ask you again, how do you plead?"

Sarah glanced away. She wasn't going to give him the satisfaction of an answer. If there were a way out of the zip ties, she would show him what the crime of murder was all about.

The judge's chair shot back and bumped the wall behind it.

Sweeney ran down from the desk and over to the defendant's table, where he skirted around and glanced back up at the desk he had just vacated.

"Your Honor, my client pleads not guilty."

"You're an asshole," Sarah mumbled.

"Your Honor, may I confer with my client?"

After a moment, Sweeney nodded at the empty desk. Then he lowered to whisper in Sarah's ear.

"We can fight this and try to win. Are you willing to take that chance?"

"What the hell are you doing, Sweeney? Untie me so I can commit first-degree murder."

"Are you threatening a member of the bar?" He reared back, appearing shocked at the notion.

There was a twinkle of madness behind his eyes. The man was truly gone.

"You're no such thing."

"Your Honor, my client has decided to change her plea."

"What?"

"My client has decided to plead guilty on all counts, and unfortunately, we are recommending the harshest sentence allowed under the laws of this nation."

"Fuck you," she said. "You're making a mockery of the court process and an ass of yourself. The defendant's own lawyer doesn't recommend harsh sentences for their client. What's next? The death penalty?"

Sweeney hustled over to the jury box.

"Ladies and gentlemen of the jury, have you reached a verdict?" He scanned the empty chairs of the courtroom. "Can we have silence?"

Sweeney had lost his mind. Or he was doing this because he knew he had the time and had decided to kill her anyway.

He hopped over the railing and stood facing the judge's desk.

"We, the jury, find the defendant guilty on all charges and recommend the death penalty." Sweeney affixed his gaze upon her. "We recommend Sarah Roberts be executed immediately because she has resources, friends, and ways out of situations like this one. We, the jury, feel that if Sarah Roberts were to leave this building to be executed at a later date, she would find a way to escape." Sweeney pivoted enough to stare up at the judge's desk again, the candlelight giving him an eerie glow on one cheek. "Without prejudice, we recommend death by gunshot in this courtroom so the jury will see this case to its natural conclusion."

"You're fucking insane," she shouted at him.

This was getting out of control. She had to find a way to stop or slow him down. Yelling at him wouldn't help, but how could she control her anger? The man had her bound to a chair, and she was about to be executed for crimes she didn't commit. Well, she committed them, but they were pardonable crimes, what the military would often call non-culpable.

Sweeney hopped over the railing again and pulled his gun. He checked the chamber, nodded once, and then set the loaded weapon on the small table by where the stenographer sat.

"Your Honor," Sweeney said, his eyes locked on Sarah. "I'm ready to execute as per your orders."

Then he blinked and ran around to sit in the judge's chair.

"I've heard all I need on this case at the moment. I want to thank the jury for their duty in this case and will take their recommendations seriously. You are all dismissed."

Sweeney stared over at the empty jury seats as if waiting for people to rise and leave the courtroom.

Sarah's mind raced. How could she get out? There had to be a way. If Judge Sweeney agreed with himself—the jury— she could be shot in moments. And if so, how did two-fifteen in the morning help her?

Come on, Vivian, what the fuck is going on here?

Sweeney faced Sarah. "I'll take a short recess and deliver my verdict. If I come back with the death penalty, you shall be executed in front of me as I sit here at this desk. You are to remain where you are, Miss Roberts, for the duration of my recess as I, like the jury, feel you are a flight risk."

From the corner of his mouth, Sweeney shouted, "All

rise." Then he got up and exited from the side door the judge would use.

A moment later, he returned and ran over to stand beside her.

"Sarah, it's not looking good for you. And wow, what an asshole of a lawyer you have. You might have hired better." Sweeney shook his head. "And wasn't that jury brutal?"

"Sweeney, it's you, it's all you." She watched him for a sign that he was putting her on, but he revealed nothing. "What are we doing here?"

"We're living out the final moments of your death wish."

"The final moments of my death wish?"

He nodded. "Most certainly."

"But I don't have a death wish."

"Actually, you do. Let me explain how it started."

"Sounds great. Go ahead." By keeping him otherwise occupied, the *judge* couldn't return and declare his sentence of death, which was obviously what was about to happen. So she would keep him talking for as long as she could.

Which might amount to ten minutes.

Maybe five.

She prayed she could keep him talking for an hour or more but doubted that to be the case.

"Tell me all about the death wish and how it came about."

"It all started with a murder," Sweeney said, gathering a chair to take a seat.

"Of course, it did." She smiled.

Moments later, she wasn't smiling anymore.

Chapter 38

Ricigliano set her phone down. The power company said the grid was fine and someone cut the power inside the building. The security company had alarm codes and pass cards but was woefully under-equipped to access the building without power.

The emergency contact list for the courthouse had two unanswered calls so far, one where the sheriff was on holiday in Europe, and the other where the man's wife answered saying her husband, the key holder, was in the hospital with a lung infection.

It was going on one in the morning, and she was no closer to gaining access to the building.

The only upside was that the rain was tapering off.

Ricigliano got out of her SUV and began a walk around the base of the courthouse, trying every door on the off chance that one was left open by accident. She had tracked her SUV to Jones Street, where Sarah had left it, which was good because losing her vehicle and having her weapon stolen was a much harder sell to her bosses. Now, she was just missing her gun, which she hoped would turn up soon.

This was her last attempt at gaining entry before she broke a window pane and began an internal search of the building. At least breaking a window wouldn't trigger an alarm as the electricity was cut to the building.

Or would it?

She had no idea what kind of alarm system the courthouse had.

Door after door, none of them budged. Once she got back around to the parking area, she stopped and stared at the new vehicles in the lot.

A Jeep and a black Hummer were parked near her SUV.

Who were they?

Something touched her neck, and her heart rate tripled as she jerked away.

Hands grabbed her arms and subdued her. She grunted, the urge to scream overwhelming, but she suppressed it in case Sweeney was close enough to hear.

"What the hell," she mumbled.

"Calm down," a man said by her left ear. "Name. We need a name."

"I'm a homicide detective with Toronto police."

"That tells us shit. What's the name?"

"Lynda Ricigliano."

The men nodded to one another and released her.

"We thought so, but we had to check."

Ricigliano straightened her shirt and stepped back a few feet to examine the men who surprised her. "Wait, you're the feds from the hospital. What are you doing here?"

"Sweeney reacquired Sarah after shooting Alex."

"By the way, the gun in the neck—is that how you boys ask a girl her name? Can't imagine what you do to ask for ID."

The tallest man stepped forward. "We deserve that. Call me Disco. These two don't need names. And we're not feds."

"Okay, how do you know my name?"

"We work for an interested party in making sure Sarah remains alive. That's why we organized her release from the hospital."

Ricigliano studied all three men with a new eye. "In other words, you're hired guns."

"Call us what you want, but we are paid a certain sum to attain a result. Today's payment was to guarantee Sarah's life. Failing that, we …" He paused and glanced at his men, who suddenly sported worried looks. "… don't want to discuss failure."

How would these men know Sarah was inside if they weren't working for Sweeney? She hadn't told anyone— she'd only spoken with Parkman.

"Then why are you here?" she asked.

"We understand Sarah Roberts is inside this building with Edward Sweeney, and he's armed."

That's impossible. They tapped her phone. She told Parkman, and then he was taken by the police. At least, that was what he had said.

"And how would you have come by this sort of

information?"

"We are wasting time." He sighed. "We were working with Sarah, Parkman, and Alex on an operation when we lost the target. While attempting to reacquire Sweeney, he shot Alex and abducted Sarah. We overheard Parkman speaking with Detective Ricigliano. Because he knew we were listening, he repeated your words to give us the lead. We heard about the courthouse and the power outage. He told you to call the sheriff and the security company or something. And here we are to help."

That made a lot of sense. "How do I know I can trust you?"

"You don't. But that doesn't matter to us. We're going inside this building to get Sarah out and to stop Sweeney from whatever it is he's doing—"

"You mean arrest Sweeney?"

The men exchanged a glance.

"Our priority is Sarah. Once she's safe, Sweeney can be arrested. But we can't guarantee his safety."

She studied them for a moment. "How do you propose we enter the building?"

"Are you familiar with the interior at all?"

She nodded.

"Where would Sweeney take her?"

She shrugged. "No idea, really."

The men stepped away, mumbled a few words to each other, then Disco returned.

"My men will get a few things from the vehicles, and then we will breach the perimeter."

"How?"

"We will climb the fire escape ladder on the side there." He pointed. "On the second floor, we will cut a hole in the glass and enter that way."

"Inside the building, many of the doors are secured with magnets, as far as I recall."

Disco turned and looked at the darkened building. "Which means they won't work without power?"

"Exactly."

He snapped his fingers. "That won't be a problem."

He turned and headed toward the Hummer.

"And why won't that be a problem?"

"Because you can take us to the utility room or wherever the power to the building is turned on and off. I'm sure we'll find what we're looking for in that room."

"Oh, fuck yeah," she whispered to herself. "Shit, didn't even think of that."

She started after him. "Did you guys bring guns?"

"We have many of those things."

"What the fuck am I doing now?" she mumbled to herself. "Breaking into the Toronto Courthouse with hired mercenaries? For real?"

She shook her head.

"My career is surely over."

Chapter 39

"REUBEN ELLIS STALKED MY wife for over two weeks," Sweeney said. He had taken a seat usually occupied by one of the lawyers. Ed crossed his arms and stared at Sarah.

She watched him closely. A change had taken place. The moment he spoke of his wife, the man's veneer softened.

"It all started with a job application."

"A what?" she asked.

"Her résumé. My job pays well, but she wanted to work. She was a stay-at-home mom ever since our daughter Lisa was born. But after ten years, she thought she'd return to the workforce. I encouraged her to do it."

Sarah didn't take her eyes off him.

"After all the usual preparations for job interviews and researching who to talk to and so on, she dropped her application off at C&S Accounting. She was never a certified accountant, but she could sign off on tax returns as if she were certified back in the day. Of course, she was willing to start at the bottom and work her way back up, but she never got that chance."

"What happened?" She genuinely wanted to hear his story but to get him to talk until after two in the morning, she added, "Tell me everything."

He shook his head. "I can't. Not enough time for that." He checked his watch. "It's slightly after one, and the judge will return soon. I'll give you an abbreviated version." He inhaled deeply, then let it all out. "Jessica got called in for an interview, but it wasn't legit."

"Was it Reuben?"

Ed nodded. "He'd taken her résumé and kept it. HR at the accounting firm never got it, which helped them in court from escaping any sort of blame."

"But wouldn't she see it wasn't legit as soon as she showed up for the interview?"

"The HR guy—well, Reuben, not the actual HR guy— said he was swamped and wanted to perform a more casual interview. He asked if she would mind if they met at a café two blocks down for a small lunch."

"And your wife agreed?"

Sweeney nodded. "She agreed and showed up, and from what I remember her telling me, the interview went well. He really liked her and promised good money and a serious position and on and on. But she couldn't start for a few more weeks, and he would be in touch."

"And?"

"Then the shit started. Late-night calls to the house. She

bumped into him twice at the grocery store. Reuben claimed to live a few blocks from us. All the while, he was stalking her, following her."

"I'm sorry."

Sweeney rubbed his face, checked his watch, and then stared at the door the judge used.

"It was a Monday morning. Lisa, our daughter, wasn't feeling good, so she stayed home from school."

Sarah wasn't sure she wanted to hear more. And why did he keep saying things like *our daughter* and *my wife*? She knew who they were. Something wasn't quite right.

"Reuben clocked in at work, then slipped out a back door. Court was in session, and he knew that. Jess and Lisa were home alone. He showed up at the house in a suit, a twelve-inch knife stashed in the back of his pants. And flowers to welcome her to the C&S Accounting family." Ed wiped a tear off his cheek. "The man was sick. When he heard Lisa was home, he punched my wife so many times he knocked her out, then tied up my little girl."

"I'm so sorry …" Sarah whispered, completely disgusted with humanity at times like this.

"Then he raped my wife repeatedly for hours while I was here, in this courtroom, watching criminals get light sentences."

Sweeney sat up and rested his elbows on his thighs, covering his face in his hands.

"He raped her while she was still unconscious, then woke her up to hear her screams when he violated her from behind."

"Ed," Sarah whispered, her gut-wrenching at the details.

"I get it. You don't have to go further."

"Reuben Ellis used her until mid-afternoon that Monday, then cut her throat wide open, like a canyon of blood."

Now, Sweeney was openly crying. All the pain was oozing out onto his cheeks.

"Sometimes people breathe in too much hatred in their lifetime," Sarah said. "And this is a result of their exhale. They literally become the hate."

He seemed to get himself under control for a moment before standing and pacing in front of the lawyer's desk.

"The man couldn't leave a witness. His alibi was the accounting office. So, knowing my ten-year-old would have to die, he tried to make it look like a hate crime—"

"A hate crime? Like a racist thing?"

"No, like he had a prior relationship with Jess and Lisa and hated them. The profile of a murder. So he cut her face to pieces. Slashed and slashed until her face and neck were destroyed, bone exposed everywhere. He cut out her eyes, slashed at her hands and feet, and just kept cutting." Sweeney was working himself up, but Sarah was too shocked to stop him. If her hands weren't tied, she would place them over the baby growing inside her. "And on his way out the door, he stopped to slash apart my wife, even inserting the knife in her vagina and cutting backward."

"Okay, Sweeney, I've heard enough." Sarah spoke firmly to get through to him. "Tell me, how did they catch Ellis?"

"He'd done it before. Seven murders in total. At first, they thought it was a taxi driver. Focused all their attention on him. Searched his home twice and followed him. But then Ellis struck once more. In the end, a single fingerprint nailed

Ellis down as the killer. When the authorities arrested him at the accounting firm, he lawyered up and pleaded not guilty."

"I'm guessing he was found not guilty?"

Sweeney nodded. "But it was him. He told me everything as I cut him into tiny pieces." He stopped pacing and wiped at his eyes. "I enjoyed every single scream as my blade tore that man to small shreds of skin. I even castrated him before he died. And on his last breath, I shoved my blade up his ass in anger, tearing him open like he did to my wife."

The images in her head were like watching *Saw* meets *Hostel*. How could humans exist like Rueben Ellis and Edward Sweeney? Or was Sweeney one of the good guys who got pushed too hard? Where was the line, and did she ever cross that line?

"So," Ed continued. "My brother and I decided people like Ellis had a death wish, and we formed a pact. We called it *Death Wish* after that 1970s Charles Bronson movie. When people vouched for Ellis at work, and they had to let him go, we sentenced him to death. When Malcolm King got off on all those rapes, we sentenced him to death. Jason Grant, too. And I will continue the *Death Wish* pact without my brother." His attention snapped, and he stood straighter.

One of the candles flickered, threatening to go out. Another lit the side of his face in a grotesque mask of madness.

Something died in Sweeney when his daughter and wife were taken from him in such a brutal fashion. And it wasn't enough that he got his revenge and got away with it.

He wanted to continue his vigilante justice on all those who broke the law without regard or got away with it.

"I assure you, Sarah Roberts, that I made a pact on purpose. And this pact was only ever to harm those who deserved it. Never hurt the young, as they may not know right from wrong yet, and always give the courts a chance first. That's why the deliveries were sent. You and your group of hooligans needed a court process. But since you constantly show up to thwart me, I offer you this courtroom as your judge and jury."

After one clap of his hands, Sweeney ran over to the side and shouted, "All rise."

Then he shot through the door, waited a moment, opened it, and strode to the chair at the judge's desk.

"After reviewing the case of Sarah Roberts against the people of Canada and the United States and considering the jury's statement regarding punishment for your crimes, I will offer you this. You have had a fair trial. A jury of your peers judged you. And you have been found guilty. I don't want to do this to a nice young lady, but the people have spoken." Sweeney pointed at the empty chairs in the jury box. "So, as everyone in this courtroom believes, and as I see no other choice, I sentence you, Sarah Roberts, to die in the chair. By gunshot."

"In the chair? Really? You made it sound like the electric chair."

"Well, you know, the wheelchair."

"So, what's next?" she asked. "You're going to just walk down here and shoot me while I'm tied up and can't defend myself?"

Sweeney stood and stared down at her. "No, I'm going to get a large roll of plastic, lay it out like a carpet, roll you onto it, then shoot you in the face until you are not breathing. Once, twice, or the entire magazine. Doesn't matter to me. Once you're dead, I'll wrap up the brain matter and shit, wheel your body out to my van, put the wheelchair back where I got it, and dispose of you where Ellis's body is. I'll be home within the hour and ready for work in the morning. And no one will be the wiser."

He dropped down to the side door, disappeared for half a minute while Sarah tugged at her restraints, then reappeared with the plastic.

"I'd ask you if this is necessary, but I feel that would be a waste of breath."

"It would be," he said as he rolled out the plastic.

"Watching too much *Dexter*, I fear."

Sweeney smiled. "Unlike Dexter, I have scruples. I prefer the court system first. He went after his victims before court."

Sweeney moved around behind Sarah and pushed the wheelchair to the edge of the plastic, then angled her back toward it.

He would shoot her in the face, and the plastic would catch it all from behind her.

"This isn't a good situation I find myself in," she whispered.

"Solid conclusion and befitting."

"In your opinion."

"Who else's opinion would I be offering? Of course, it's my opinion."

"I said it in more of a *that's what you think* way."

He stepped over to the stenographer's table and grabbed

the gun.

"So, tell me one more time about the rules for killing," she said.

Sweeney stepped in front of her, the weapon partially raised, a questionable look on his face.

"Why?"

"Before I die, as per my sentencing, I'd like to know your personal rules. For instance, would you kill me if there was a mistake and I could prove it?"

Sweeney laughed. He laughed so hard he bent over and clutched at his knees, then straightened and placed a hand on his chest.

"Trust me," he managed to say. "There's been no mistake."

Sarah wasn't amused but had to appeal to his righteous side. "I realize that. But suppose for a moment there was. Would you still go through with it?"

Sweeney got himself under control, then stared down at her, a smile the only remnant of the laughing fit. "If you were innocent, I would be forced by my pact to release you and face the consequences for my actions. But, Sarah, I've followed your exploits for years. You are guilty, and this court proved that. Therefore, you must die."

He raised the gun.

Sarah didn't flinch.

She calmly said, "My back pocket. Read the paper in there and then shoot me. That's my dying wish."

Sweeney hesitated, his gaze penetrating, his eyes swimming in madness.

Then he blinked, and the weapon lowered.

Sarah inhaled, all that time thinking a bullet would enter her skull.

"Which pocket?" he asked.

"Back left."

Sweeney got behind her and fished into her pocket. He withdrew the paper from Doctor Herald, unfolded it, and then moved closer to the candle on the lawyer's table to read it.

"What am I looking at?"

"You'll see the hCG hormone in the blood has increased. After the car accident on the Gardiner, they checked me over and gave me that."

He scrunched up the paper and slipped it into his pocket.

"What do I care?"

Sweeney stepped in front of her again and raised the weapon.

"The increased hCG hormone means I'm pregnant, Sweeney."

He seemed to hesitate a moment, the weapon now less than a foot from the bridge of her nose.

"If you kill me, you're killing a baby. An innocent baby, one who has done nothing wrong. The baby growing inside me has committed no crimes and does not comply with anything your *Death Wish* pact states."

"Then I'll have to assume you're lying, and there's no baby."

"Sweeney, there is a baby."

"I don't care. You die. Whisper a prayer, Sarah."

The lights flickered on in the courtroom.

Chapter 40

TRUE TO THEIR WORD, Disco's three-man team breached the building quietly by carving a circular hole in the glass. They had all climbed inside a main corridor instead of a room or office to avoid using doors as much as possible. Once inside, they ran as quietly as they could in search of the electrical room, the entire time moving with caution—they could happen upon Sweeney and Sarah at any time as they were inside the building as well.

In the end, Disco found the room in the far corner of the first floor.

But the door was locked. One of Disco's men used a lock pick set on the handle while Disco and Ricigliano kept watch in the hallway.

"Got it," he whispered a minute later.

Inside, Disco found the master switch and placed his

hands on it, about to lower it to give the building full power again.

"Wait," Ricigliano said quickly.

Disco paused, eyebrows raised.

"We should find them first. Then, once they're located, turn the power back on, and we'll be right there. Turning it on now alerts Sweeney we're in the building and allows him to extricate himself."

Disco nodded. "Makes sense."

He ordered one man to remain back and guard the power. Even after he turned it on, it remained there in case Sweeney returned to kill it again.

Then Ricigliano, Disco, and his other man began a search for Sweeney and Sarah.

"He works in courtroom one," Ricigliano whispered.

Disco nodded. "We should start there, then."

He followed her toward the doors of Sweeney's courtroom. Minimal light filtered in through the windows high up, causing wild shadows. Emergency lighting due to the power being out illuminated the exits and stairwells with a red-and-white glow.

They stopped in front of the doors to courtroom one and placed an ear to the wood. Ricigliano heard a man's voice from within.

She pulled Disco away, drawing him to the other side of the corridor.

"They're in there. We found them."

"I heard."

"Okay, tell your guy to hit the lights."

"Then what? Won't we need an access pass for the door?

It's after hours. Most of these magnetic doors have timers. What happens when we hit the lights but still can't get in?"

"Shit," Ricigliano mumbled, glancing away to think. "What if Sweeney exits the courtroom to see what's going on?"

"Could be. But that's a chance I don't want to take. If they're talking, Sarah's still alive. If he panics, she may not be."

She nodded. He was right. There had to be a better way. Waiting for the security company to come with their pass cards and codes would take too long. They needed inside now.

"We'll have to take our chances," she said. "If Sweeney thinks someone is in the building, would he risk killing Sarah until he investigated? It's nearly two in the morning. He'd have to assume it was a cleaning company or something."

"I've got a better idea," Disco said.

He withdrew his phone and called the man in the electrical room.

"Look around for timers for the magnetic locks."

Disco stared at Ricigliano for several moments, then nodded.

"Can you reset them? Try for two in the afternoon instead of two in the morning." After a moment, he nodded again. "Okay, flip the switch in one minute." Disco ended the call and turned to his other man.

"In one minute, we go in there." He pointed at the main doors. "You go around and find a back way into this courtroom. If we encounter something we can't deal with, I'd like to know you're coming up from behind."

Without a word, the man trotted off around the corner.

"You ready?" he asked Ricigliano.

She nodded. "Let's end this shit. Remember, I want both of them alive."

"As I said outside, I'm only interested in Sarah's life. I can't have fucking Bruno hunting me, or I'll have to commit suicide. That would be more pleasant."

"Who's Bruno?"

"Never mind. You don't want to know."

"I'm a detective. I make arrests, not bodies."

"I'm not interested in bodies, either. But I will fire if fired upon."

She waited a heartbeat, knowing they were down to less than ten seconds.

"I'm the same. Fire if fired upon."

He tapped her shoulder. "You're all right for a female cop."

She didn't respond, then the lights flicked on, and she yanked on the doors.

They opened without resistance.

Before bursting into courtroom one, she blurted out, "It's detective, not cop," then ran inside, gun raised.

Chapter 41

WHEN THE LIGHTS FLICKERED on, Sarah squinted and then closed her eyes. Sweeney moaned and dropped behind the wheelchair.

"Freeze," a woman shouted. "This is Detective Ricigliano. Get to your feet, Sweeney. It's over."

Sarah didn't like those kinds of demands on a man who had already lost his mind, not to mention he was armed.

"This isn't what it looks like," Sweeney shouted.

Sarah was able to open her eyes further. Ricigliano was taking big strides straight up the middle between all the seats, a weapon extended with both hands in Sarah's general direction.

A movement to Sarah's left made her turn that way. Disco was hugging the far wall as he moved toward the front by the jury box.

Disco was with Ricigliano. Sarah frowned. How the hell did that happen?

"Stand up, Sweeney," the detective said. "I need to see those hands."

What Sarah expected and regretted was the small indent of Sweeney's weapon being placed at the back of her neck.

"Get back," Sweeney said, still hiding behind the wheelchair. "You," he shouted, the gun jerking against her skin as Sweeney no doubt pointed at Disco. "Stay where you are."

Scrunched behind the wheelchair as he was, Sweeney remained completely hidden from Disco and Ricigliano.

"You can't walk out of here," Ricigliano said. "Lower the weapon and come out."

"How about you both leave and let Sarah and I finish our conversation?" When Sweeney talked, his voice was muffled by his clothing. It added to the creepy feeling of the candles that were still lit and the way he had described killing Reuben Ellis.

All that, mixed with her thinking she was going to be shot, along with the emotions running through her at being pregnant and never getting to be with Aaron to raise their baby, made her want to run from the courtroom screaming. Yet she sat in the wheelchair, bound by the limbs, and waited while others negotiated her freedom.

She opened her hands and waved them.

Ricigliano glanced down and saw the restraints, then nodded at Sarah.

"Sweeney, we can talk about this," the detective said. "Don't do anything rash."

Disco had stopped by the edge of the jury box and was leaning against the wall, arms crossed. The man looked too nonchalant for a tense scene, unnervingly so.

"I'll tell you what," Sweeney said. "Leave my courtroom and close the doors behind you. One minute. That's all you get. I'll take my chances if you don't leave within one minute."

"Take your chances? How would you do that?"

"I shoot you."

"Not smart, Sweeney."

"Sure it is. What, you want to return fire? Go ahead, you'll hit Sarah and do my job for me."

"You kill Sarah. I don't stop shooting until you're dead."

"Uh, uh, uh, Detective, I don't think so. That would be murder. You can't murder a security officer of the court in his own courtroom."

"How ironic, you preaching justice in a court of law. Since when is justice ever served here?" Ricigliano lowered her weapon.

Then she winked at Sarah.

Sarah frowned. What the hell was going on?

"Okay, Sweeney, maybe you're right."

Ed moved behind her, edging out to stare at Disco. Then he moved farther to look at Ricigliano.

"You believe that?" Sweeney asked.

Ricigliano nodded. "I've been working with this man since the beginning." She pointed at Disco and holstered her weapon. "As a detective, I couldn't nail Sarah down. Not enough evidence on anything. But then you came along and did my job for me. You provided evidence on all the guys at the dojo, Sarah and her boyfriend, Aaron. Now, give her to me so I can take her in and arrest her. Then I will offer you a commendation, and we'll all return to catching the bad guys."

"You'd do that?" Sweeney said, slowly rising to his feet. "You'd arrest her?"

The gun moved with Sweeney but stayed pressed into Sarah's flesh. She didn't like it one bit. The man could snap at any second, knowing his life was over, and pull that trigger.

"Of course. I have the authority and will arrest her right this minute. I'm a homicide detective. I'm trying to stop you from killing her for two reasons. One, she gets her day in court, and two, you don't get charged for murder. It's Sarah who is the murderer here, not you."

"Ahh, but I've told her too much, I'm afraid."

"What did you tell her?"

"About Reuben Ellis."

Ricigliano frowned. "Wasn't that man charged in the gruesome murder of a woman and her child?" She glanced down as if recalling a memory. "He was found not guilty, only to disappear days later." She snapped her fingers. "Right, I know that one now. He was the one with the alibi that came up later. They'd arrested the wrong guy. That case is still open. It wasn't my case, but I recall it well now."

Sweeney nodded, the tip of the gun bobbing slightly. "You have the right case. That was my wife and daughter Ellis murdered. He got away with it, so I killed him."

Ricigliano's mouth opened slowly, then closed. "Sweeney, I know the detective working that case." She shook her head. "It wasn't Reuben Ellis who murdered your family. I can guarantee that. I work homicide. I know these things."

"No, you can't guarantee shit," Sweeney shouted. "He did it. He even confessed to me before I killed him."

"A lot of people will confess a lot of shit to avoid being killed."

Sweeney pulled the gun away from Sarah and pointed it at Ricigliano.

"He did it." His voice cracked.

What if Sweeney had actually killed an innocent man?

Ricigliano raised her hands. "They had video coverage of Ellis at work. Some accounting firm. He used his passcode to file something on his computer and had a receipt from a Starbucks at the time the murders took place." She frowned again. "Wait, wasn't that a Jess Cook and her daughter, Lisa?" Ricigliano paused, staring at the carpeted floor as some other thought came to her.

Sweeney stepped forward, the gun wavering. "You don't know anything!" he shouted, the madness leaking through his voice.

"There were rumors of an affair. She was raped repeatedly before she was killed. And Steve Cook is your stepbrother—"

"*Shut up*," Sweeney screamed.

Disco pushed off the wall, ready to do something. Ricigliano stepped back.

"You're dead, pig," Sweeney said.

The gun fired in courtroom one.

Chapter 42

TWO WEEKS LATER ...

Sarah sat at the dojo's back kitchen table as all her men sat around her. It was so good to have everyone back together again.

Shortly after that rainy night in the courthouse, Sweeney was arrested for the murders of his stepbrother's wife and daughter, Jess and Lisa Cook. He confessed to their murders and the murder of Reuben Ellis, who he knew was innocent, but had convinced his stepbrother that Reuben was the real murderer of his wife and daughter.

They'd found Sweeney's prints all over the Cook's house, but he was family, and no one ever suspected the man.

Sweeney was charged with the murder of Jason Grant as well.

But first, he had to be taken to the hospital for the bullet wound to his leg. Disco's man had entered from the back of the courtroom and crept up behind him, wanting to disarm the man. When he felt Sweeney was about to shoot the detective, he withdrew his firearm and shot Sweeney in the leg, throwing off his aim.

Sweeney's weapon had fired, which added an attempted murder charge to his growing list of crimes—not to mention the attempted murder charge for shooting Alex—but Ricigliano wasn't hit. Her career was looking better and better. She solved numerous murders with one takedown.

Since Disco and his men needed anonymity and, for the record, weren't in the courthouse that night, they walked away, leaving Sarah in Ricigliano's care. They left behind all their equipment, which offered Ricigliano an explanation for how she had gained access to the building.

Her story for the bullet hole in Sweeney's leg was he shot at her, and when he turned to run, she shot him in the leg.

Since her gun was stolen recently and hadn't shown up by that night, she was using an old, unregistered weapon—which Disco's man left with her—for self-defense.

Last Sarah heard, no one was pressuring Ricigliano about her coming upon an unregistered weapon with a serial number filed off. The important issue was all the crimes she had solved and how she had saved Sarah's life and got Daniel, Benjamin, Alex, and Parkman out of the holding cells.

Aaron had been released, and all charges against him had been dropped. While in custody, they had allowed him to text a friend for a lawyer, and he'd sent the text to Sweeney as he told Sarah he would, which convinced Sweeney to come to the pool on Lakeshore Blvd., setting in motion the final hours of Sweeney's freedom. Investigators in Santa Rosa deemed Steve Cook's death an accident or an act of self-defense, depending on who Aaron talked to.

Arrest warrants on all of them had been canceled, and the authorities in Santa Rosa had officially apologized to the Roberts family. Flowers continued to arrive at Sarah's parents' house as a way of apology.

Apparently, her mother was taking it all in stride. When Sarah spoke with her on the phone, she said the police were just doing their jobs and thanked them for investigating things so aggressively.

Aaron flew home three days ago, and Sarah had sat him down. They talked, they cried, and they worked it all out.

Aaron would rather be with her and risking their lives than without her. He'd made a mistake in a fit of pain and anger after that brutal beating by Hamilton, and he wouldn't do it again.

He'd asked her to forgive him and allow him to regain his honor with her. Then she'd taken his hands in hers and stared him in the eye.

"Aaron, I need you to remain calm for what I'm about to tell you," she had said.

He nodded. "This is coming from Vivian?"

"Yes. But there's something else."

"Go ahead, hit me with it. I'm ready."

"It's bittersweet and emotional."

"Bittersweet? Okay." He adjusted himself to face her. "I'm ready. Bring it."

"Vivian said I have one more thing to deal with next month. She keeps calling it, *The Trap*."

"*The Trap?*"

Sarah nodded. "Something about walking into a trap. I have no idea what she means, but there's more."

"There is?"

"Vivian said something about having to get information approved."

"What?" He frowned.

"Like when she told me to steal Alistair McNeil's car, I was pissed at her. Sweeney had planted a device to blow it up, and I was driving it. Vivian said she knew I'd be okay."

Aaron shrugged. "Well, maybe that's better. Knowing Vivian isn't going off half-cocked sometimes makes me feel better. Now, what was that bittersweet comment about?"

"The reason I was pissed at her was because when I was in the hospital, I found out something about me."

"You did?" He edged closer, concern written all over his face. "What did you find out?"

Her eyes had welled up, and she couldn't hold the tears back. They were going to be parents. They were going to start a family.

"I'm pregnant," she whispered, staring into his eyes.

And Aaron had wept, too. He'd pushed himself into her arms, and the two of them stayed that way for well over an hour, discussing the future, planning for the baby, discussing names again, all the while the miscarriage in the backs of their heads.

Now, he sat beside her at the table. Alex was there, his side bandaged up. Other than a large scar, he would be a hundred percent again soon. He was already training and teaching again.

Benjamin had been so grateful to spend this one in a holding cell that he couldn't help himself when ribbing Alex for getting shot.

They'd had a conference call with Darwin in Italy, thanking him for sending Disco and his men. Without them, this wouldn't have come together, as everyone was so handicapped.

It was Detective Lynda Ricigliano who had called the meeting.

"She should be here any moment," Sarah said, checking the time on her phone.

"Any idea why she asked all of us to be here?" Aaron asked.

"None whatsoever."

Sarah's phone dinged. She glanced down.

"She's at the back door and asked to see Daniel."

"Me?" Daniel said. "Why me?"

Sarah shrugged. "No idea."

Daniel pushed back from the table. Before the text from Ricigliano, everyone had been discussing the baby. Even Parkman got teary-eyed.

No one wanted Sarah to deal with *The Trap* but understood Vivian wouldn't send her on any tasks that would endanger her baby. Besides, Sarah was only a few months pregnant. She wouldn't even start to show for another couple of months yet.

Everyone sat quietly, anticipating what Ricigliano had to tell them.

Less than a minute later, Daniel stuck his head in the door of the lunchroom.

"They're at the front. One second." Then he was gone again.

"And you have no idea what this is about?" Parkman asked.

Sarah shook her head. "Everything's over. The cases are basically wrapped up. I mean, investigators are still sifting through shit, but we're in the clear. So I don't think it's serious."

"Guys?" Daniel called from somewhere at the front of the dojo.

Everyone exchanged nervous glances.

"What the fuck is this?" Parkman asked.

Sarah got up using Aaron's shoulder for support. "Yeah, I don't like this one bit."

Aaron moved to the door first, then Alex, followed by Parkman and Benjamin. Sarah was the last one out as they all moved to the main wide open space of the dojo.

"Surprise," a woman yelled from behind them.

The group jumped and spun around, with Alex dropping into a stance and Aaron doing the same. They relaxed and stood to their full height when they saw who it was.

Ricigliano strode up to them with a rectangular box in her arms, followed by what looked like dozens of police officers, most in uniform.

"Sarah and the rest of you all," Ricigliano said. "We wanted to surprise you all with a cake and drinks. Rodney, bring the wine and beer." Ricigliano set the cake down on a side table.

"What's all this for?" Sarah asked. "This is not what I was expecting at all."

Officers piled in, forming a circle around their group. It had to be making some of them nervous as, usually, this many police officers only meant trouble. It was so unsettling that they were all smiling.

"After everything you've all been through over the years, not to mention what you all endured through lack of information, we thought we'd come and apologize to you in person. Not one single officer here wants to arrest the wrong people, but we move forward with the information we have at the time. For that, we're sorry to all of you. In fact, by holding Daniel and Benjamin, we put your lives at risk. So, please accept our apologies, and thanks for everything you guys do." They cheered and clapped. Sarah watched the faces of Alex and Parkman and saw them visibly relaxing. Aaron and Benjamin relaxed, too. Even Daniel was accepting pats on the back.

"Also," Ricigliano shouted over the din. "We wanted to be the first ones outside your group to congratulate you two on the new baby."

The cheer rose louder still.

Everyone drank, chatted, and ate cake. It was the warmest feeling Sarah had ever had while surrounded by so many members of the policing community. She got to meet Ricigliano's partner and Daniel and Benjamin's arresting officers. Even a few detectives in suits were around when she had the run-in with Waller back when she was dealing with the Rapture.

After one or two drinks, everyone calmed down even

further as more cops arrived. Sarah ate cake but avoided the alcohol. A baby was coming, after all.

At one point, Ricigliano pulled her aside.

"Sarah, guess what?"

"Just tell me. I'll never guess."

"They found my gun."

"What? Really?"

Ricigliano nodded. "Someone turned it in anonymously."

"Wow, that's great to hear."

"I still don't know why you took it, but none of that matters anymore."

Sarah pondered the shooting in the courtroom. How Disco's man had shot Sweeney to stop him from killing Ricigliano, and then Disco gave her the weapon to claim she shot Sweeney while he was running away. That story wouldn't have held up if she were carrying her own weapon.

It was a further reminder that Vivian, or whoever was approving the messages, knew exactly what was coming and when and how to keep Sarah safe.

And her baby safe.

"You're right, Detective. None of that matters now."

She smiled and moved to stand by her man.

He held her hand, offered her a warm smile, and kissed her cheek.

All was well in their world again.

At least until she had to deal with *The Trap*.

That was really bothering her.

Bothering her way too much.

Afterword

DEAR READER,

The Delivery was a fun book to write. I did this one a little differently. While writing, I kept notes on my start times, finish times, daily word count, and total word count. Then, at the end of each day, I wrote down my thoughts about where I was in the novel, how I felt about the plot's direction, and what I thought might work going forward.

This was the first time I'd done this. I usually have a notebook for research and notes throughout the writing process, small reminders about character traits, their full names, and things I might want to add at a later date, but I've never kept notes on progress.

This eye-opening thought process revealed how surprised I got when things happened in the novel. For example, when

I started writing, I had no idea who Jason Grant was and why Edward Sweeney would go after him. I didn't know Dale would die until Ed returned to the car, then returned to Jason's garage and found him dead.

This trend went on and on until I learned why Aaron was missing. I knew they would end up back together, but that was it. When I wrote about him missing, I had no idea where he was at the time. Then I thought it would be romantic if he dropped everything and raced after Sarah.

It continues like this until the end scene in the courtroom. It wasn't until I wrote it that I learned Jess and Lisa were Steve Cook's family and not Edward's and that Ed killed them out of a jealous rage, then killed Rueben to cover up his murder and offer a confession for his brother to accept. Edward Sweeney was a seriously sick man, and now I hope he gets the treatment he needs—or not.

I used the name Disco for the lead mercenary Darwin sent because Disco was my nickname in high school. That's a long story and one that isn't needed here, but I was called Disco for so long throughout my high school years that there were people who didn't even know my real name. To this day, I still have friends who call me Disco.

I'd like to thank two readers for allowing me to use their names in this novel.

Thank you to Vicki Herald from Ohio, the red-haired doctor (although she's a nurse in real life) who helped Sarah out after the car accident.

And thank you to Lynda Ricigliano for allowing me to make her a detective in this book.

I hope you're all doing well and enjoying Sarah's life. So

much is happening in book twenty-four, *The Trap*. Then, *The Ultimatum*, book twenty-five, is crazy, too.

As always, thank you for reading, and see you all on Facebook. If you hit the "Follow" button on my author profile on Bookbub, you'll receive updates on book releases.

Get caught reading,

Jonas Saul

About Jonas Saul

Jonas Saul is the bestselling author of the Sarah Roberts Series—more than two million sold!—and has written and published over sixty thrillers. After acquiring an agent, he signed several deals in Los Angeles, with MadRiver Pictures optioning his Sarah Roberts Series— over forty books!—(currently in development).

Jonas has often outranked Stephen King and Dean

Koontz on Amazon over the past decade. He's regularly invited to be a guest speaker, teacher, or workshop presenter at international writing conferences and film festivals worldwide. He hosts an annual writer's retreat in Greece, where he currently lives. He focuses his teaching on how to get tension and emotion in every scene, on every page, how he made it as a creator/writer, the path to success in this business, and the pitfalls to avoid. He also hosts a reading retreat in Greece with guest authors, yoga retreats, and hiking retreats. Visit the Imagine Greece Retreats website at www.imaginegreeceretreats.com, or email him directly to discuss an opportunity to join one of the retreats at jonas@imaginegreeceretreats.com.

Jonas is also a professional freelance editor. He works for several publishers and does private editing for clients, with many testimonials on his website at www.imaginepress.org, which details each author's response to Jonas's editing skills. Email Jonas directly for an editing quote at editor@imaginepress.org.

To book Jonas for a speaking engagement at a writer's conference/festival, to have him on your jury at a film festival, or even to say hello, email Jonas directly at jonassaul@icloud.com.

For updates on releases, hit the "Follow" button on Amazon or Bookbub, and join Jonas on Facebook, where he's most active.

Contact Jonas Saul
Linktree: Find me here
Email: jonassaul@icloud.com